The F
C

Clive S. Johnson

Daisy Bank

ISBN: 1545510474
ISBN-13: 978-1545510476

ALSO BY CLIVE S. JOHNSON

Beyond Ever Blue Skies

Solem

The Dica Series:

Leiyatel's Embrace (Book 1)
Of Weft and Weave (Book 2)
Last True World (Book 3)
Cold Angel Days (Book 4)
An Artist's Eye (Book 5)
Starmaker Stella (Book 6)

CONTENTS

I dedicate this novel to my partner and editor, Maureen Medley, for her assiduous attention to detail and vast knowledge of history, without which this work would never have been possible.

1 FIRST TWO PHANTASMS

A long hot summer of drought, parched grass and stifling nights; it was 1976, the year Colin had met Kate, their first intoxicating year of young love.

They'd bumped into each other that February as he'd staggered, dressed in borrowed pyjamas and a little worse for wear, across a beer-swilled dance floor. It had been his first year at the University of Salford, her final at prestigious Manchester. Had it not been for the student charity event of the Pyjama Dance, they'd likely never have crossed paths.

But now, eight years later and sitting in the spare back bedroom of their first home together, Colin stared at the screen of his new micro-computer and remembered back to that memorable night.

Kate had eventually invited him back to her flat in her university's student accommodation block. It happened to be within easy walking distance of the drunken debauchery into which the event had steadily descended, as apparently it always did.

When they'd entered the flat's common room,

they'd been met by the boisterous banter of Kate's flatmates, into which welcoming company Colin had quickly been accepted.

They'd eventually found themselves the last in that room when everyone else had gone to bed. He should have arranged to meet her again and then left, gone back to his own halls of residence, but this had been the nineteen-seventies and the night somehow magical, one neither had wanted to end. The offer of staying over had come quite naturally, for by then the bud of friendship between them had already blossomed.

In Kate's small room, sitting side by side on her narrow, unyielding bed, their coffees on a cluttered bedside cabinet, they'd talked on and on into the early hours of the morning about all manner of things. Things that before long revealed the lost halves each had seemingly found in the other.

The patient blink of the micro's cursor brought Colin back to the present, reminded him he'd yet to come up with a title for the story he'd at last decided to get down on paper. But as yet, nothing had sprung to mind.

He looked out into the short back yard of their terraced house, down at the suffusion of white pyracantha flowers that hid most of its redbrick wall. Along its top ran dark, almost black coping stones, their colour prompting him to look down at his hand. Even at the memory, his pulse quickened at seeing another man's skin.

"I wonder," and he took down his dictionary from its shelf and laid it on the desk, beside the micro. "Noun," he read, "*Archaic.* a person with dark skin [C15: see BLACK, MOOR]". His fingers soon flitted across the keyboard, swiftly entering "My Blackamoor

Other" before he smartly stabbed the return key a couple of times.

"There," he told himself. "At least I've a working title."

When he sat back to think, he couldn't remember having properly noticed the mysterious object that first night in Kate's room. Other things had been more engaging at the time. The longest drought in living memory had reached its height by the time he'd been drawn to have his first close look at the thing. He'd been sitting on the edge of Kate's bed whilst she'd gone to make them some coffee, his hair tied back in a ponytail to keep his neck cool as he wilted in the night's oppressive heat.

Standing on her bedside cabinet, it had been nothing more then than a hollow joss stick holder, bristling with spent slivers of wood like a small singed hedgehog with alopecia. About the size of a large apple, and crafted from a dark, weighty metal of some sort, it had stood on three clawed feet, its body peppered with holes.

Peering at their random pattern, he'd lit another joss stick without thinking, but it had been as he was jamming it into one of those holes that the first phantasm had taken him.

Confused then stunned, Colin found the dimly lit room had somehow given way to a bright, sunlit day. Even more disconcerting, his long, slender, almost translucently white-skinned hand had become large and dark-skinned. It clutched a broad wooden rail, below which swept a slow-swelling sea.

It hadn't been so much this startlingly unexpected vision, for no doubt a few spliffs had been shared by then, but the immediacy of the conjured surroundings he still so vividly remembered. A warm, stiff, southerly breeze had tugged at the fabric of some loose garment he wore, flapping it about his partially bare legs, and beneath his soft boots rolled a hot, wooden, tar-stained deck. The air of that breeze had carried with it hints of spices, of sun-baked sands and dried salted fish, of latrine-fed alleys and the sweat of honest toil mixed with dishonest treachery. All things alien to his nineteen-seventies, northern-English mind, despite that unusual year's parched Manchester summer.

A fleeting hallucination, he'd tried to tell himself. Probably just a bad score of dope. But it had happened again, a few days later when inserting yet another lit joss stick into the holder. That now familiar warm air had taken to it a gruff, Spanish-sounding voice.

"Jusuf al-Haddad?" it had called, unnerving Colin the more.

He'd hardly taken in the view of the sea before it spun away and a man appeared above him, looking down from over a dark wooden railing.

"Will you come up here onto the quarterdeck and meet my first mate, Rodrigo Fernandez?" the figure boomed, carrying an easy and clearly habitual authority. The man's deeply tanned face remained immobile, as the rail beneath his hand, the mast at his back and its attendant rigging and sails all leisurely rolled from side to side against the cloud-marred blue of the sky beyond.

Colin was startled when his head nodded, then his foot seemed to jar down wide to one side at Jusuf's first step. The queasiness swilling within his gut he was sure was also Jusuf's. Then the almost sheer steps up to the deck above didn't help, not with the sea's oily swell so close beside and below. By the time the uphill walk across that upper deck had become a downhill stagger, Colin's initial shock had tentatively given way to a perverse curiosity. He finally stood, unsteadily, looking down on the two shorter, now grinning men, hoping they'd make some sense of what was happening.

"It helps if you keep your eyes on the horizon," said the man Colin somehow knew was the merchantman's captain, who then turned to the man at his side. "Rodrigo, here, is prepared to offer you stowage in his own locker for your…" but he only waved his hand dismissively to one side. He drew in closer, his voice lower.

"We can't have you tripping over your big land-lubber feet and smashing it—not before time, anyway. Now, can we? Your master ain't paying me enough for that."

Colin sensed Jusuf's reluctance within himself as he staggered back a step, but the captain's expression made it clear it had not been a request but a command. Then a loud rattle and clatter jolted Colin from the memory and he found himself blinking at the room's central heating radiator that hung on the wall beneath the bedroom window.

Unsettled by the still vivid memory, even after all these years, Colin forced his thoughts to more prosaic matters: the heating system needed bleeding. He needed to buy a radiator key. Damn, he thought, but why don't I ever remember when I'm near the hardware shop?

Turning back to the micro's screen, he stared at the white cursor, still patiently blinking two lines below what he now recognised had been a well-chosen title. He blew out a long breath. "Well, that's how it started, but how do I put it all into words? Into a story that'll make some sense of it all, as Kate reckons it will."

As he leant back in his chair, he clasped his hands behind his head and grimaced blindly up at the ceiling. "Had it lasted only as long as that sweltering summer?" Colin asked himself. "Just three short months of doubting my own sanity."

Then he groaned, "It's one thing putting together technical reports for work, but this looks like it's going to be a whole different kettle of fish." He opened one eye and peered at the waiting screen, willing the right words to appear as if by magic beneath those three stark title words.

But it had been a good eight years since that summer, since Jusuf had last said anything within his hearing. And Jusuf had proved to be a far more eloquent speaker than Colin ever could, and surely that was what his story needed. An eloquence to make some sense of the mystery it clearly held, and in which Colin was sure Kate's joss stick holder somehow played a crucial part.

2 A LOVER'S GIFT

Although Colin had made mention of the weird experience at the time, he'd downplayed it, reluctant to reveal just how real it had felt. He'd been perhaps a little wary of Kate thinking him unhinged in some way, but he needn't have worried. Even had their love not grown as strong as it had by then, Kate possessed depths he'd yet to appreciate.

Come the late July of that heatwave summer, Kate had finished her finals and moved back in with her parents in a suburb of Manchester. Colin had also, not long after, returned to his own parents, to their home on the outskirts of Halifax in West Yorkshire, his first year exams at last over with.

Although a good forty miles apart for most of that summer break, they'd often talked at length on the telephone. Kate eventually travelled over to stay with him for a couple of weeks before starting her search for a job.

She'd been enthusiastically welcomed by Colin's parents, fussed over and made to feel at home, then

Colin had shown her to her room. He'd carried her travel case up and placed it on the bed, but when she clicked it open, there on top lay a plastic bag-wrapped object the size of a large apple.

"I had to clean it up before Mum saw it," Kate said, taking the object out. "Not sure what she would have thought of me using it as a joss stick holder."

"But I thought it was *meant* to be one," Colin said as he eyed it a little warily. "And why've you brought it with you?"

She put it on the broad sill of the window, beyond which the merciless sun highlighted the parched-yellow patches in the garden's lawn. Then she gave him a half smile.

"Do you want to know where it came from?"

He only tilted his head inquisitively.

Her smile grew, softening her features, and Colin's heart melted, as it always did at the way it gave her a faery-look.

"I got the impression," she said, clearly distracted by the longing look he gave her, "that you'd…you'd found it interesting somehow, especially after that odd experience you told me about. Remember? When you'd been carried aboard some ship or other."

Colin ran his fingers over the holder, its metal already warmed by the heat of the sun coming in at the open window. It reminded him of that hot wooden rail he'd felt beneath his strangely dark-skinned hand.

"But then I also noticed," she said, taking his real hand in hers, "that not long after that you always left *me* to light the joss sticks." He still didn't say anything. She drew closer and looked up into his eyes, that evocative scent of hers filling his senses.

He kissed her, tentatively along her lips and onto her cheek, up across her brow and then down to the tip of her nose. He gave it a gentle nip and then leant back, his head again on one side.

"All right," he finally said. "You tell me about it and I'll tell you what more happened that I didn't tell you about back then."

She looked vindicated for a moment before saying, "You know I said my mum's side of the family came from Plymouth, well, this used to belong to mum's Aunt Bella."

Kate sat on the bed, folding her long, slender legs beneath her. Colin perched his backside on the edge of the windowsill, the holder beside him, and pushed his long blond hair back behind his ears.

"When I was very young," she told him, "about five or six, Gran used to take me down on the train to stay with her at the start of the summer holidays. Before mum and dad finished work and could get down themselves. Each year they rented a place on Whitsand Bay; one of the chalets there."

"I thought you said your mum and dad owned one."

"They do now, but not back then. And it was actually Grandad who bought it. But before that, me and Gran would stay at Bella's for a couple of weeks before joining them for the rest of the summer."

She glanced at the holder, a darkness entering her eyes. "Bella's flat was in Stonehouse, beside the naval yards in Devonport. It was a bit of a frightening place, really, to me at that age, anyway. I think her and her sisters traded in antiques and bric-à-brac and whatnot, so the flat was always dark and forbidding, stuffed full of old furniture and ornaments. And I was tiny at that age, like a pixie," and she gave him that grin again.

Colin couldn't help but grin himself, his eyes no doubt glinting the more. He then realised his hand had found its own way onto the joss stick holder, resting on its weighty warmth.

"When Bella died some years later," Kate went on to say, "Gran went down for the funeral. When she got back, she gave that to me."

He lifted his hand and stared down at the lustre brought out by its recent cleaning.

"I can't say I remember much about it, to be honest, but Gran insisted I'd taken a liking to it and so wondered if I might want it as a memento of those stays. I can't imagine why I would have taken to it, though," and Kate laughed. "It's hardly attractive. But then, who knows; maybe there *was* something about it that gave me a bit of comfort in Bella's scary flat."

"So it's not a joss stick holder, then?"

"I don't think people went in for burning joss sticks back then, Colin, so I doubt it. And anyway, it probably goes back way before their time."

"I still don't see why you've brought it with you, though."

"I've had it since I was eleven, so I suppose it's grown to be a part of me…well, a part of my past, anyway. And I thought…" She searched his eyes for a moment, a glint coming to her own. "I thought I'd like to give it to you as a keepsake…so you've a piece of me when we're not together. Remind you of all those nights in my flat…"

She grinned again.

At first, he'd no idea what to say, other than "Thank you", but then, despite his reservations, that it was her special gift to him finally sank in. "Yeah, that's great, Kate. Thanks," and a broad smile spread across his face as he dreamily added, "A piece of you I can always treasure."

He ran his hand over it, trying to guard his new joy against the unsettling associations that came with the object. Ones he knew he'd now promised to divulge fully to Kate. And the later ones, of course, the two he'd failed to mention at all, the last of which had certainly made him suspicious of lighting any more joss sticks. But then his mother called up the stairs that lunch was ready, and with it came a short reprieve.

3 JUSUF'S PRESENT

Words hadn't somehow magically appeared on the micro's screen, although the central heating had long since settled down. Maybe, Colin thought, if I just try remembering how I told it to Kate and simply typed it in that way, and so he played out that first day of her stay in his mind's eye.

A school friend of his had phoned after lunch, suggesting a motorbike ride out into the Yorkshire Dales for the afternoon. It had been an opportunity to show Kate some of his favourite places, so it was the evening before they were alone. The house had been theirs, for Colin's parents had gone out, so Kate had made them supper. Afterwards, in his bedroom and with one of his quieter King Crimson albums playing, she finally said, "So, you were going to tell me about Jusuf al-Haddad."

Colin froze at her casual use of the name. Although he'd mentioned it to her before, having it spoken aloud by someone else made it seem all the more real. He went and stood by the open window and stared out at the dark-blue dusk slowly descending over the sultry city in the valley below. For a moment or two he gathered his thoughts, until Kate came and sat beside him on the sill.

"Standing before the captain and his first mate," he quietly told her, "wasn't where it ended, Kate." Strings of streetlights had begun to weave across the darkening city before he steeled himself to say, "After that I had another…er…phantasm, as you called them. Two more, in fact."

"You never said."

At last, he turned to look her in the eye. "It was so…unsettling. So much so I didn't really want to accept it myself. By telling you I thought…well, thought it would make it all too real to ignore," but her brow only knotted. "Does that make any sense?" to which she slowly nodded.

He took a deep breath. "The first carried on from where the last one I told you about left off—well, almost."

He recounted his experience of having been thrown straight into an overwhelming sense of suspicion, or perhaps more accurately an intense fear of betrayal. Jusuf had clearly not trusted the captain or his mate, maybe trusted no one. Colin could almost smell it on the air they breathed. Whatever the man had unwillingly entrusted to the mate's locker, its separation from him had clearly preyed heavily on his mind.

Having witnessed Rodrigo lock the chest, Jusuf had come out from the gloom beneath the quarterdeck and leant against the larboard rail. As the captain had advised, he stared out at the horizon, his queasiness indeed soon lessening.

Formed of pale greens and sandy browns and

yellows, the higher land bordering the coast along the southern horizon steadily dipped away to east and west. Towards its eastern end a far off peak peeped up against the canopy of a cloudless blue sky much further inland.

As Jusuf's gaze moved on further eastwards, to where only pale blue sea kissed the sky, he quietly asked himself, "Will I ever get to see you again, Ceuta? Will I once more be able to feast my eyes on the heights of Monte Anyera that guards your back?" He spat into the sea before glancing askance at the dark space beneath the quarterdeck.

His queasiness returned, so he spun his gaze across the galleon towards the north. There lay only a thin hint of land between sea and sky, and a shiver ran through him.

"Accursed Christians," Jusuf whispered to himself, so those few crew nearby wouldn't hear. "It won't be long before we take our country back from you…and more; Allah preserve me. But this time as easily as taking a child from its mother's milk."

He stared at the sea-bound horizon to the west, at its mantle of darker clouds. "May the charity of Bab el-Zakat grant me its good fortune. May it take me safely beyond its gate, past Tarifa and out onto the Western Sea. Then, Allah willing, north to strike at the heart of the thieving infidels."

This time when he peered at the shaded space beneath the quarterdeck, he narrowed his eyes at the two dark shapes of the Portuguese men on whom it all now hinged. Silently, he prayed their greed would ultimately ensure him a safe escape, if he lived to tell the tale—Allah grant him a long life. He turned back to the sea and spat once more into its lazy swell.

Kate's "Tarifa?" startled Colin, and his memory of that stain of spittle slipping steadily astern instantly dissolved. "Isn't that somewhere in Spain?"

Colin blinked at her for a moment. "Hang on; I've an atlas somewhere."

After a bit of a search he found his old, worn, cloth-bound school copy, its index quickly guiding him to the right page.

"Yep," he said, before tracing his finger down and along the grid references, finally stabbing it on the southernmost tip of the country. "Here we are, right above the Strait of Gibraltar. Ah, and there's Ceuta, on the North African coast."

"The Moroccan coast."

"No, it doesn't say that here. Says that corner's Spanish. I never knew Spain had territories in Africa. Like us with Gibraltar, I suppose."

"You said they were heading north, which'd take them up the west coast of Portugal. Do you know where they were going after that?"

Colin didn't say, for he remembered the captain coming up beside Jusuf and pointing out the darkening clouds to the west, the man then growling about the weather.

"Unusual time of year for storms," he went on to say. "We may have to put in at Faro if it turns nasty. If not, and we get ahead of it, then at least we'll have a fair wind behind us. But for now, all we can do is wait and see."

Colin silently stared at his memory of those clouds, the image staying with him even after Kate had asked, "So what happened next?"

"Nothing."

"Nothing?"

"Not in that phantasm."

"They seem a bit short," and Kate sounded disappointed.

"I wish I could say the same about the last one."

"You… You've gone a bit ashen, Colin. You all right?"

At first he only nodded, unsure how to go on. "Want some coffee?"

Her eyes narrowed. "Er, yes, I'd love some. But then…you will tell me what happened next, won't you?"

"I'll go and make the coffee, but then I think I need to skin-up and pop out into the garden before mum and dad get back. You interested?"

Kate nodded, concern clouding her beautiful face.

Beneath the kitchen's stark fluorescent light, Colin's memories faded a little. As he filled the kettle, Kate asked if he'd any idea when it had all happened.

"It feels like the here-and-now when I'm there," he told her as he lit the gas ring under the kettle. "Probably because I'm experiencing it through Jusuf, which I don't think I was right at the beginning. That's when I thought the captain had sounded Spanish, not Portuguese. To Jusuf it's all current, you see, his present, and so mine."

Colin opened the back door, a squall of night insects drawn in to the light. "I tell you what: if you finish making the coffee, I'll get a couple of deckchairs out. It must be cooler in the garden." He stared at the key for the shed, hanging on its hook by the backdoor, lost in thought until the kettle began to boil.

"Then I'll tell you what happened next," he barely whispered, before taking down the key and going out to the shed.

4 THE DEVIL'S OWN BREATH

The garden proved no cooler than the house. Sitting out in the dark in a deckchair, though, felt distinctly odd to Colin. But enough light came from the living room window to see the impatient expectation in Kate's eyes. How to start? he wondered.

"I don't know how it happened," he finally said, playing for time, "but for all the hours I spent away, the joss stick I still held when I came back had hardly burnt down. It was weird." He distractedly noticed how dusty the lawn smelt, how hard packed it felt beneath his trainers.

Kate's unblinking stare, as she passed him the spliff, reminded him of his promise. He took a deep toke and held it, its burn at his throat slowly easing before he blew out a long smoky breath that lingered sweetly about them in the still, late evening air. Kate's continued close scrutiny of his eyes finally forced him to grasp the nettle, and so at last he slowly and hesitantly unfolded his tale.

They were on the high stern deck, Jusuf and

Rodrigo, the first mate, that large hand of Jusuf's once more gripping the rail, which could hardly be seen in the noonday's unnatural gloom. The bitter taste in his mouth said he'd just been sick, and probably not for the first time. Then Colin realised what filled Jusuf's vision: the heave of a huge wave swelling towards them from the storm's raven darkness astern. The water's slate-grey mass ineluctably loomed above them as the deck tipped steadily for'ard, at which Jusuf gripped the rail with both hands this time.

"We should've put in at Faro," Rodrigo said more to himself than Jusuf. "There's the Devil in this storm; I can feel it," and the man crossed himself as the galleon rose up the face of the wave. "Even if we'd made Lisboa, as we'd hoped to, there'd have been no chance we could have put in there, not in this sea. All we can do for now is ride it out and pray it doesn't drive us ashore."

Too awed to beseech Allah, Jusuf only stared at the expanse of mountainous sea briefly revealed from their teetering vantage point atop the crest of the wave. Vainly, he searched for a stomach-settling horizon, but then the galleon lurched and lowered its stern. They descended once more into a deep, dark trough, another great wave looming out of the gloom beyond it.

As Jusuf heaved over the stern rail, his puke's untroubled arc made him wonder at the still air. Surely a storm brought with it great wind? he groggily reasoned. In between straining on his seemingly empty stomach, he asked this of the first mate.

"It will come," the man said as he looked up at the furled sailcloth above their heads. "Satan's breath," he hissed and again crossed himself. "And soon. Before we could safely lower the spars." He slowly shook his head as he bit at his lip, as though cursing the strength of the imminent storm.

Jusuf turned to stare for'ard as the deck once more rose beneath them. His gaze swept down its steepening slope, across the hidden main deck and to the galleon's fo'c'sle. Beyond it swept a dark hill of water, drawing his gaze to its high crest, hugely rolling away ahead. Its black and serrated outline heaved against the overcast sky before them.

Then the cloth of Jusuf's head-covering fluttered briefly, where it fell loose about his neck. Tucking it into his tunic, he quickly realised what it meant and whipped around to look astern once more. There he saw whitecaps luminous against the storm's darkness, a salty spray now speckling his face.

A sudden gust blew him back, his hands slipping from the rail as the ropes and rigging around him urgently complained, and the timbers of the ship creaked and groaned beneath his feet. He steadied himself, but when large raindrops spattered against his face and chest, Rodrigo took him by the arm, urging him back down to the main deck below.

When he stepped onto it, he turned and saw that most of the crew were huddled beneath the fo'c'sle deck. The whites of their eyes peppered its shadowed darkness as they resignedly stared out at the overtaking storm. Rodrigo splashed through the seawater currently sluicing from the deck, and led Jusuf beneath the quarterdeck.

The dim shapes of the captain and helmsman stood stooped at the tiller's opening, the captain firmly grasping the lashed beam of the tiller itself as he peered out at the chasing waves.

"Captain," Rodrigo called to announce their presence, but the man only gave them a brief look. "If you squat here," Rodrigo told Jusuf as the wind rose to a growl, "you'll be out of the worst of it, but near enough to puke over the rail."

Jusuf settled his bulk in as best he could, leaning his broad back into the crook between the chart desk and the wall. From his sheltered position he stared up past the black shapes of the masts at the northern sky. The receding strip of low grey cloud now appeared framed between the fo'c'sle rail and the press of the storm's dark mantle. It was the only light to see by until the sodden deck and masts reflected the flash of a bright, cold blue glare. Into the darker gloom of the lightning's wake rumbled a distant roll of thunder, lifting the hairs on Jusuf's neck.

The rain-laden wind had begun to blow in more insistently through the tiller opening. It forced the captain to retreat into the near-darkness swaddling his first mate and their handsomely-paid-for passenger. He said nothing, only stepped forward into what little light remained and stood as tall as the quarterdeck above him allowed, his presence there amongst them his only reassurance to his crew.

The Nao Providência—the name by which Jusuf knew their carrack—soon became engulfed by the storm proper. Spray and torrential rain quickly drenched the rigging as the sea heaved in through the bulwark scuppers. Water repeatedly raced across the deck as the growing wind whistled through the shrouds and howled past the yards and spars. Within it all, the ever-present groan and creak of the ship's timbers grew unnervingly louder, complaining at the storm's rising anger. And all the while, Jusuf braced himself against the elements and his own mortal fear.

"Allah preserve me," he mumbled, time and time again, the sound lost in the rising fury being unleashed about him.

When the wall at his back pushed him forward, he braced his feet against the deck, noticing that the masts had angled themselves against what little could now be seen of the sky. Rodrigo and the helmsman sprang into action in the dark behind Jusuf, unlashing the tiller's ropes before the two men groaned in their effort against it. Slowly, the masts righted, then Jusuf heard the tiller being secured once more.

When Rodrigo returned to stand near him, Jusuf asked what had happened. The first mate had to shout above the storm for Jusuf to hear, explaining they'd to keep the Nao Providência astern of the waves, so they'd not be swamped and sunk. The man crossed himself again, his eyes turning heavenward as another surge of seawater raced across the deck behind him. This time it washed up over the step and in below the quarterdeck, chasing Jusuf back into the darkness. He tripped and fell, banging his head.

For a moment he stared at the stars flashing before his vision, then the sound of the rapidly rising wind almost deafened him. The ship shuddered and sharp reports rang out. Then, somehow, he knew he was alone.

A flash of lightning lit up the scene out on deck: wide-eyed but determined men splashing through swilling water, lengths of rigging swinging loose about them. On the tail of the lightning's crack of thunder came another flash, this time revealing a long white crack in the mainmast, splintered wood jaggedly projecting from a point some way above head height.

Darkness returned, a howling darkness rent by

whistles and juddering groans. Then the wind blew yet harder still and another ear-splitting crack seemed to come up through the very planks of the deck. After a succession of snaps and the twanging of ropes an almighty crash rent the air. Then the thud of timber against timber and the agonised screams of men joined the wailing of the wind, and the Nao Providência once more listed astarboard.

Caught by the fear of being left alone, Jusuf staggered out on deck, immediately swept off his feet. Sent clattering against the bulwark, seawater pressed him there until it drained away enough for him to drag himself to his feet.

When a series of close flashes came, they revealed a mainmast lying at a shallow angle above the deck, its splintered end matching that of its nearby stump. The fallen mast had struck the starboard bulwark, smashing its way almost through to the planks just a few yards from where Jusuf stood. Beneath it, though, lay Rodrigo's body, awash with seawater.

Then all went black once more as the deck listed more steeply, throwing Jusuf this time against its rail. The impact bent him backwards, his shoulders perilously close to the grasp of the waves now forcing their way in through the scuppers beneath him. With his back painfully arched, his foot slipped, lifting off the deck as his head grew heavier at his head-covering's drenching. He rocked for a horrifying moment, one that seemed to last a lifetime, before timber groaned against timber and a man screamed out in agony.

The rising of the rail at last lifted Jusuf clear of the water, as another flash lit the tempest and he pushed himself back on deck and staggered upright. Yet another flash revealed the mast had slid further overboard, that part still above Rodrigo angled higher as the deck began to level. Again, a flash, and Rodrigo's prone body and ashen face became plain to see. But also revealed was the once more steadily descending mast, lowering towards his chest as the ship again began to list.

In the brief moment before darkness rushed in, the two men stared in horror at each other.

Within short order, though, a yellow light sent shadows lurching across the deck, then a lamp appeared, a seaman holding it aloft above the pinned first mate. More of the crew gathered around as the deck listed further and the mast relentlessly angled down against Rodrigo's chest.

The man's horror-filled eyes flashed before Jusuf. With no further thought, he pushed his way through the huddle of seamen and bent to the mast, wrapping it in his stoutly muscled arms. Bracing his legs against the deck, he summoned all his might and strained to lift the unyielding weight. Others joined in, heaving and groaning and cursing until the bulwark itself moaned its own relief as the mast raised an inch or two from the half-drowned Rodrigo.

Jusuf's blood sang in his ears at the effort, but through its pulsating red stain across his vision, he saw Rodrigo's body dragged from beneath their burden. With a great groan of relief, Jusuf called out "Clear!" before his muscles drained of their last strength, and the mast crashed down heavily onto the deck as the men fell clear.

The sea rushed in about Jusuf's knees, and he staggered away up the more steeply sloping deck, until he tripped and fell. Exhausted, he slumped down against a panting seaman, who promptly slapped him on his back. Yet more hands did the same, declaring the gratitude they were all plainly too exhausted to voice above the still howling storm.

But others were active now, busy about the dangerously listing deck and its encroaching sea. The lamplight illuminated two men and their handsaw, precariously perched on the bulwark rail, either side of the fallen mast. They set to, furiously sawing back and forth, the sounds of ropes and rigging being hacked free accompanying the blade's relentlessly rhythmic rasp.

Before long a sharp crack rang out and the severed end of the mast thudded to the deck, which immediately rose, dragging itself from the water. Two of the crew quickly got to work, manhandling the baulk of timber, quickly joined by those who'd sawn it free. Between them, they cast it overboard, no doubt to join the rest of the mast's far more perilous weight at last safely adrift upon the storm-tossed sea.

And that storm raged on, unabated. It blew and howled and tossed the Nao Providência mercilessly for the hours to come, time Jusuf spent beside a pain-wracked Rodrigo as he slipped in and out of consciousness. They'd carried him to the captain's quarters, stripped him as carefully as they could and then wrapped him in what dry blankets came to hand.

He'd not looked good, not good at all, but his care had distracted Jusuf from his own fears. And when the storm at long last began to abate, life miraculously still coursed through Rodrigo's veins.

Jusuf had gone out onto the quarterdeck at first light, relieved of his vigil at Rodrigo's side by one of the crew: a young lad clearly least needed for the repairs already in hand. About the now mercifully steadier deck and rigging, men were busy at work, hammering and hacking and sawing away. But the Nao Providência looked a sorry state.

Of the mainmast only its stump remained, and many of the remaining spars hung limply from their mast, unfurled sailcloth caught in amongst the ropes, torn and tattered. The captain stood amongst a handful of seamen beneath the foremast, its lowered spar the subject of a heated discussion. He noticed Jusuf and barked a couple of commands at his men, then nodded towards him before making his way over.

As the captain climbed onto the quarterdeck, he growled at Jusuf, "Well, my large, black *biscoito gorgulho*, you'll certainly not be in Santander anytime soon." He finally stood before Jusuf and drew in a long, deep breath as he tipped his head back, so he could look down his nose, regret clearly tainting his scowl. "I doubt we'll make much more than a few knots with what we can recover from this mess."

Jusuf's voice rumbled, low and menacing: "My master impressed upon you the need for a *safe* passage, *kạbtn syd*, above that of haste." The captain stepped back a pace, a glance down at the deck below as his hand slipped inside his jerkin.

Jusuf felt for his own blade, but the captain's still empty hand slowly slid out once more into the open. A grin cracked his face. "You've done my first mate a good service, though," he said. "As you've made no mention of him, I assume *Senhor* Rodrigo Fernandez still lives."

"He does, though he's in great pain from his broken ribs."

"Shame. I could do with him right now. Still, he's

made of stern stuff. I'm sure it won't be long before he's at least able to—" The captain stared past Jusuf, his eyes rapidly widening, then he turned to the main deck and shouted for a watch to go aloft. "*Diga-me que está o quarteirão de bombordo, senhor.*"

One of the seamen broke away from his task and quickly shinned up a foremast shroud to the topcastle. He wasn't long in hailing down "Um navio inglês, capitão! Inglês!"

"Shit," hissed the captain through bared teeth. "That's all we need, an *Englisher.* Blast this calmer sea; where's the swell when it's needed? There's no way she'll miss seeing us," and he pushed past Jusuf to stare out across the rolling sea. Jusuf followed his gaze, and there, off the larboard quarter, saw a distant ship under full sail.

"*Devemos preparar o canhão, Capitão?*" came up from the main deck, but the captain only shook his head, resignation seeming to flood his features. Slowly, he turned to face Jusuf, his jaw firmly set.

"However fast we make repairs, we've no chance of running ahead. And it'll only make matters worse if we try to fight them off with the cannon. So, my unlucky *gorgulho*, I fear you certainly won't be seeing Santander very soon…if at all." He turned back to stare at the *navio inglês*, now clearly bearing down on their becalmed and defenceless vessel.

Jusuf's heart sank, but then his mind turned to the first mate's locker, and to what he'd seen about Rodrigo's neck. His thoughts quickly filled with the one thing he knew had to be back about his person. With the captain's own thoughts held elsewhere, Jusuf quietly slipped back in to relieve the young lad of his vigil at Rodrigo's side.

5 CIRCUMSTANTIAL EVIDENCE

The printer chattered back and forth, its listing paper juddering out a line at a time. It carried Colin's story onto a fanfold pile behind. He himself had been leaning back in his chair, trying to calm his nerves at the memories his story had brought back. Kate then called up the stairs that dinner was nearly ready.

"Right down," he called back, but waited until the listing had finished, then flicked the edge of the perforation and tore the sheets free.

In the dining room, he tossed the short stack onto the table as he rushed past and into the kitchen. There, he quickly grabbed together cutlery, a butter dish and their salt and pepper mills. He was still setting the table when Kate swept in, putting his plate down at his place.

"That looks good, as always," Colin enthused, and pulled his chair up beneath him and sat down.

"Well, we had some cheese that needed using up," Kate said as she came back in with her own. "But we don't need the butter," she added, nodding at the dish as Colin tucked into his cheese and potato casserole.

"Eh? Oh, right. Habit."

Kate sat down at her place, across the corner of the table, but then looked over at the short stack of paper on the other side. "Is that your story?"

"Yeah, as best I can manage."

"I'll read through it after we've eaten, then; although *The Young Ones* are on at nine."

Colin checked his watch, about an hour to go, and they both fell silent as they began to eat. But then Kate lifted her eyes to look at him.

"Well," she softly said, "do you think it's helped any?" She gazed hopefully across at him as she slowly chewed her next mouthful.

He kept on eating as he thought about it, finally opting for "Bit early to tell".

"Oh, I nearly forgot," Kate then said, "dad phoned me at work today. Said they'd be coming back for the first two full weeks in August. He's got some school commitment or other and his cousin's fiftieth, so we can go down then."

"Ah, right, that'll be good. I'll book the leave tomorrow, then. It'll be interesting to see the place, after all I've heard about it."

"Hmm, well, don't expect too much. An outside loo isn't much fun, nor the running cold-and-cold water, but that corner of Cornwall's so beautiful; nice and quiet, and with plenty of good walks."

At the end of the meal, Colin cleared the table after them, washed up, then made some coffee. He finally plonked himself down in his chair in the front room, the television programme before *The Young Ones* already drawing to a close. He nipped back into the dining room and retrieved his story, putting it on the floor beside his chair for later.

Rick, Vyvyan, Mike, and Alexei Sayle's manic rampage across the screen kept them riveted for the next half-hour: a satirical lampooning of the snobbery inherent in the BBC's own *University Challenge* programme. As the final timpani drumbeat of the closing credits faded away, Colin and Kate were left exhausted by laughter, invigorated by the show's raw mayhem.

Jumping to his feet, Colin suggested another coffee, to which Kate said she'd love one. "And if you pass me your story, I'll read through it whilst you're out there," she offered.

The thought took some of the edge off the programme's clinging buzz, so it was with a little less pizazz that he passed her the sheets, turned off the television and went out to the kitchen. By the time he got back with the coffees she was reading down the last sheet.

"You've remembered it well," she said when she'd finished. "I know at the time, and when we discussed it over the weekend, that you said it'd been really vivid, but there's stuff in here I don't remember you telling me about at all."

"I've not made any of it up."

"No, I'm not suggesting you have, but, well, like this bit of spoken Portuguese. Now, where is it," and she scanned back through the sheets. "You've never mentioned having studied it before."

"Portuguese? No, I haven't. Just a bit of Spanish at school, but only for a year. But that's one of the things that's come to bug me more and more. I mean, I've no idea if it's genuine Portuguese, but I know it's certainly not Spanish."

"In which case, maybe that's your proof, if only we

knew someone who spoke the language. We could then find out if it *was* authentic. Mind you, there's the name of the ship; that might be more useful; the... Now, where was it?"

"The Nao Providência."

"That's it. If there really was a merchant ship with that name, then that'd be even stronger evidence. Something to stand up to your... What was it you wanted? Scientific rigour?"

"I don't want to prove it *happened*, Kate; I want to prove it *couldn't* have. And anyway, how the hell are we supposed to check that? I wouldn't know where to start, nor for that matter what period in history we're talking about, which might help."

"I thought you said a scientific approach was one that maintained an 'Open mind'?"

"Stop changing the subject."

"Well, there certainly doesn't seem to be anything here that tells us when it hap...when it *might* have happened. For instance: cannons. Ships have carried them since about the thirteenth century to well into the nineteenth. I know that from my own research at the Rylands."

Colin breathed in deeply and let out a long breath. "If only Jusuf had come across a clearly dated newspaper, eh?"

"Hmm, well, what about the hill you say's behind Ceuta, the—"

"Monte Anyera. But I'm not sure that'd prove anything. I spent a lot of my childhood poring over maps; you know, copying them out and stuff. So, if I were to be proven right on that count, it'd still only be circumstantial: possibly a submerged memory, or whatever they call them."

Colin then remembered something else he'd had back in his childhood: the family encyclopaedia, the one on the shelves in their middle bedroom. "Hang on a minute," he said and rushed upstairs.

"Here we are," he told her when he got back down. "Everyman's, volume three, 'BUL' to 'COA'," and he sat with it open on his lap, flicking through its pages. Presently, he looked up—deflated.

"The nearest mention of any hill associated with Ceuta is: 'It consists of an old town right on the tongue of the peninsula, and a new town running up the hill at the back'."

"No name?"

"Nope."

"Well, at least it's a bit of supporting—"

"Hang on. It's only a short entry, but the last bit says: 'It was conquered by King John I. of Portugal in 1415, but passed into the hands of Spain in 1580'."

"So?"

"Jusuf's on a Portuguese ship, Kate, not a Spanish one."

"Yeah, but there would have been loads of different nationalities trading through there. Even during wartime trade rarely got affected."

"But a ship an Arab like Jusuf, one from Ceuta, would have trusted? And when he was carrying something clearly valuable in some way? No, it wouldn't have been a foreign one, I'm sure of that. They wouldn't have risked it."

Kate seemed distant for a moment, then quickly turned back a few sheets, her finger tracing down the lines. "Here we are, early on, when Jusuf looked north from the ship at the Spanish coast, when he whispered 'Accursed Christians' and then said, 'It won't be long before we take our country back from you'."

Colin hadn't the foggiest idea where she was going with this.

"Don't you see? For an Arab to consider Spain a stolen country, stolen from them, must put it not that long after the Reconquista, sometime around the end of the, er, fifteenth century, I think."

"Right. You mean when the Moors were turfed out of Spain? In which case, that'd narrow it down to sometime from just before the turn of the sixteenth century to no later than fifteen-eighty."

They were both quiet for a while, until Colin took a slurp of his coffee.

"Mine's gone cold," he said. "Want a fresh one?"

"It's getting late for me, Colin. Work again in the morning, don't forget."

"All right, but before you go up, can we just go through what we've got so far?"

Kate reached into a cupboard beside the chimneybreast and found a highlighter and a pen, then went through Colin's story again. Eventually, she summarised, "We have a big, strong Arab called Jusuf al-Haddad travelling on a Portuguese ship called the Nao Providência, sometime around the sixteenth century. And this Arab is taking something important to Santander—north coast of Spain if I remember rightly—seemingly with an eye to recovering more than the Moors lost when they were kicked off the Iberian Peninsula. Then they hit a storm that severely damaged the ship before they could reach Lisbon. Oh, and an English ship's bearing down on them, which is a bit of a bum place to leave it, if you ask me, Colin."

"It's all supposition, though; nothing concrete. Nothing much we'd be able to check, not without doing loads of research and legwork, and even then… And where would we start?"

"Well, I doubt even the Central Library's got a book listing all the Portuguese merchantmen from that time. I know the John Rylands library won't have, so there's no point me checking that at work." Kate sighed and got up, clearly finally on her way to bed, but then paused, staring down at him.

"We need to know more of Jusuf's story, Colin, if you still want to prove whether or not it could really have happened. But that'd mean you being prepared to go back there again."

Colin gazed up at her for a moment, then drew a deep breath. "I don't mind telling you, Kate: it scared me shitless, it really did. So yes, the thought of going through anything like it again does put the willies up me. But I know I can't just let it go. It'll only fester if I do, I know it will. So I really ought to settle it once and for all, if it's at all possible." He looked despondently at the sheets of paper still on the arm of Kate's chair.

"Only you can decide, Colin. It's up to you. And anyway, where *is* the joss stick holder? I don't remember seeing it since we moved in."

"Still in one of the unpacked boxes in the loft."

"Okay, but be that as it may, I'm afraid bed's calling me. I'll have to go up, Colin, I'm beginning to drop. There's always tomorrow to talk more about it."

She put the pens away in the cupboard, but then mentioned, "There are still some joss sticks in here, by the way," and she brought them out to show him: an old cellophane pack of patchouli.

After Kate had said goodnight and gone up to get ready for bed, Colin went to make himself a fresh mug of coffee. Standing in the kitchen as he waited for the kettle to boil, he absently looked through the utility room doorway. Part of the stepladder he'd need to get up into the loft caught his eye.

A cold shiver ran down his back, but then he told himself, "Well, there's a few other things I could do with unpacking from that box, I suppose." He glanced once more at the stepladder as the kettle came to the boil, its whistle shrill and urgent. As he filled his mug, he could still hear Kate in the bathroom, cleaning her teeth.

Before he knew it, he was carrying the stepladder carefully up the steep stairs, past the bathroom and along the landing. He clattered it down beneath the loft's small hatch.

"What you doing?" Kate called out.

"Just nipping into the loft. Won't be long," by which time he had his head through the hatch and was reaching for the box.

"You're a bit in the way there, Colin," Kate called up from below him as he squeezed the box between his chest and the edge of the opening, the ladder plaintively creaking. "You're not going to try again tonight, are you?"

"No," he could only mumble against the lid of the box as it somehow became jammed.

"Good, because I'd prefer to be there this time when you do."

"Don't worry," and the ladder swayed as the box jerked free at the sound of tearing cardboard. "I'm just bringing it down whilst I think on," Colin assured her as he propped his head against the ceiling to steady himself. "Just want to check I did actually pack the thing."

Kate moved back as he came down the ladder and put the box on the floor to one side, quickly going back up to close the hatch before finally climbing down and folding the stepladder against the wall. At last, Kate could slip past.

"Well, don't be up late. I'll be nice and warm when you come up. And tomorrow, don't forget those first two weeks in August, will you? Starting on the sixth."

"I won't," then she was in the bedroom, its door closing behind her. Colin looked down at the box, the joss stick holder just visible through the half-opened flaps. Another shiver ran up his spine.

Soon sitting in the quiet of the front room, Colin stared for some time at the pack of joss sticks and the holder he'd carefully placed to one side on the broad arm of his chair. Then a distinct and familiar clatter came from the utility room, and Grimalkin, their Russian Blue cat, wandered in. He jumped straight onto Colin's lap.

"Hello, lad. What've you been up to, then?" but the cat only pressed his purring neck against Colin's stroking hand. Then he padded briefly, before circling a few times and contentedly curling up.

"Doesn't look like I'll be going straight to bed, not with you in my lap, now does it?" and he ran his hand along the cat's rounded back, its purr full and deep.

And that was all it took: the soft reassurance of a contented cat. Without really thinking, Colin took out his lighter and removed one of the joss sticks from the cellophane wrapper.

The nostalgic scent of patchouli filled the air about them, a thin thread of pale-blue smoke lazily drifting from the stick in his hand. The smoke snaked its way above Grimalkin and through the holes in the holder, leaving a ghostly trail his hand somehow seemed to follow of its own volition.

6 TAKEN NORTH

Grimalkin twisted his head around and stared up at the joss stick as it passed over him, his Chartreuse-coloured eyes following its determined path as Colin slipped it into the holder. Then they both stared at it.

The cat lost interest way before Colin, moaning contentedly as he stretched out. He twisted his upper body and raised his bent front paws endearingly above his chest, seeming to grin up at Colin.

Sound eventually slipped from Colin's open mouth, a simple "Eh?" as a raised cheek lifted one side of his lips. He snatched the joss stick out and peered at it, narrowing his eyes. Once more, he carefully inserted it into the holder, and once more both man and cat stared at it, expectantly.

"Bugger," Colin barely breathed.

He lit another joss stick, but it proved no more efficacious than the first.

"What's wrong with it, eh, lad?" and he sat back, his body noticeably relaxing. He took out and lit a cigarette, filling his lungs with its even more settling smoke.

It was with thoughts of times and places, of heatwaves and more youthful outlooks, each and all now consigned to an inaccessible past, that Colin eventually joined a fast-asleep Kate in bed. He lay there for some time, getting warm and wondering whether the phantasms had really happened at all, progressively doubting his own recollections.

"They must all just have been hallucinations," he for some reason reluctantly concluded, as he snuggled up against Kate's warmth and finally fell asleep himself.

The alarm startled Colin awake at seven-fifteen, the lightless curtains hinting at a clearly overcast morning. He was already up and cleaning his teeth before he remembered the previous night's failure. He paused and stared at his reflection in the bathroom mirror.

"I wonder if the joss sticks were too old," he mused through his foam-filled mouth. "Maybe I should nip out at lunchtime and buy some fresh ones."

Soon finished and dressed, he rushed downstairs and into the dining room, finding a cup of tea standing on the table.

"Your drink's there," Kate called from the kitchen.

"Thanks," and he slurped some of the scalding brew before taking it with him into the kitchen. "Morning," and he kissed Kate's neck as she bit into a slice of toast.

"Good morning. So…what happened last night, then?" but he only stared at her. "I could smell the joss sticks when I came down, Colin."

"Oh."

"The ones I then noticed sticking out of the holder on the shelf in the front room."

"Right."

"So, despite not waiting until I could be with you, what more did you learn?" and Colin recoiled from the admonishing look in her eyes.

"Er...nothing. It... It didn't work, not that I'd actually been meaning to. It was just Grimalkin; he sort of—"

"Twisted your arm, did he?"

Colin drank some more of his tea, burning the roof of his mouth, then checked his watch. "Bugger; the time! Discuss it tonight, eh?" and he rushed off to find his wallet and keys.

He finally popped back into the kitchen as he was putting on his coat. "Must dash," and he glanced out of the window. "Looks shitty out there. You have a good day, Kate; I'll see you tonight."

He was then out of the front door, swiftly through the light rain and fumbling with the driver's door lock before finally slipping into the dry of his car.

When he arrived at work, wet coats already hung from the backs of chairs and from coat stands tucked in between the desks in the long, wide, open-plan first-floor office. He finally dropped his own coat onto the back of his chair and flicked on his terminal before taking his mug to the brew-station. The only person there was Miguel. Now a colleague, they'd both been friends since university, Miguel still living the student lifestyle of cheap flats, plenty of ale and a good supply of dope. He was pouring boiling water into his purple-stained mug, the pungent smell of Vimto reaching Colin's nostrils.

"Hi," Miguel said, in his laidback Burnley accent.

"Morning, Miguel," and they passed the usual pleasantries, but then Miguel glanced around, covertly, making sure no one was near before letting out a long telltale "Er" followed by his trademark "What's-it" as he leaned in closer.

"You're not in need of, what's-it, any gear, are you?" he quietly said. "It's just—"

"I tell you what, Miguel: I could do with a fag before I get stuck in. You coming down?" and Colin led the way to the ground floor and out through a turnstile into a covered walkway, the rain pattering depressingly on its metal roof. They rested their mugs on the glazed wall's handrail and leant against it.

"Er, it's Electric Pete," Miguel said into the chill, damp air. "He's off on another one of his trips out of the country, so, er, what's-it, I've arranged to score from Jimmy Wrigley."

"Jimmy Wrigley? Bloody 'ell, Miguel, I'm amazed he's still around. Thought he'd have been in an institution of some sort by now."

"No. He's in Higher Broughton, in a flat on Great Cheetham Street. Near the park. It's just that, well, er, what's-it…getting to his place by bus is a real bummer. I just wondered if you needed owt, you know, and fancied—"

"I don't do much these days, Miguel, but…seeing you need a lift, I don't mind running you up there. When were you planning on going?" and Miguel told him he'd arranged it for after work.

As the day wore on into late afternoon, Colin forgot all about it, engrossed as he'd become in the design he was working on at an out-of-the-way workstation—until Miguel appeared at his side. "Ah, you're here," he said, the sky through the window behind him a yet darker shade of grey.

Colin looked at his watch. "Oh, sorry, Miguel. Didn't realise the time. Won't be long. I'll just finish off here and come by your desk on my way out."

When they left the building, Colin reckoned the rain had got even heavier, the light gloomier than was usual for a late afternoon in early May. He drove them down onto Ashton Old Road, where they joined the usual rush-hour traffic crawling into the city centre.

"So, what's around at the moment?" Colin asked when they soon came to a standstill.

"Er, well, I think the, what's-it, the Sheep-Shit's finished, but Jimmy reckoned he could get some good Lebanese Red. I'll see what's doing when we get there. You still not interested?"

The traffic moved forward a short way but again stopped, the traffic lights ahead back to red.

"Probably not. Got the bank loan for this leeching my 'Disposable income'," and Colin tapped the steering wheel.

"Well, what's-it, there's always cheap Moroccan around. It's not what it used to be, but it still gives a good enough hit."

"Moroccan, eh?" Colin said, more to himself, something at the back of his mind beginning to stir, edging out thoughts of old joss sticks. Then a horn blared out behind, and he realised the traffic in front had moved off. Raising his hand in apology, he slammed into first and they were off again.

By the time they got north of the city centre and into Higher Broughton the sky had gone a yet darker shade of grey. The backstreet where Miguel directed Colin to park glistened like oil in the car's headlights. Miraculously, they found a space and Colin pulled in.

"I hope we're not that far from Jimmy's," he said. "I don't want to get piss-wet-through."

"Ah, it's only water, you mardy Yorkshireman,"

and Miguel laughed in that avuncular belittling way he had as he got out of the car.

He led Colin to a Victorian terrace of large, once-moneyed properties and up a short flight of stone steps to a front door, pressing one of its many doorbells. Then they both stepped back down and stood in the litter-strewn front garden, staring up through the rain at the first floor windows.

A curtain twitched and a face briefly appeared. Presently, a dim light came through the grime of an arched window above the front door, which then swung open.

"Hiya, Miguel," came from the forty-watt-bulb-outlined silhouette of a short and skinny figure, the voice that of a seemingly unchanged Jimmy Wrigley. Then he vanished into the darkness as the hall light went out.

"Hang on a sec'," he said, before a moment later the light came back on, Jimmy now standing with his hand pressed against a timer switch. "Go on up, then, ar'kids" and Colin followed Miguel to the first floor landing.

A bright, warming glow escaped around a partially open door, putting the landing light to such shame it went out as Jimmy got only half way up the stairs.

"Fuck," he gasped, clearly missing his footing, then bowled past them and into the flat. "Hey, Cheryl," Colin heard him say as they followed him in. "Move up, flower. Make room."

Jimmy turned, his eyes widening at his first proper sight of Colin. "Hey, Magic! What's up, mate? Long-time, and all that."

He wove his way between a huge colour television against one wall and an equally gaudily-coloured three piece suite set against the other. In the middle of the sofa lounged a girl, feet outstretched, midriff on show, eyes fixed on the television's soundless picture.

"Come on, Cheryl, move up," Jimmy said to her, then directed "Sit down, ar'kids" at Colin and Miguel. "Crap day, innit? Drink, anyone? Go make us some brews, Cheryl, will you? Go on; be a love," but the girl remained almost comatose, seemingly lip-reading what kept her glued to the screen.

As Colin and Miguel sat either side of her, Jimmy pulled a large square pouffe from beside the sofa. He whipped off its cushioned top, revealing an Aladdin's cave of plastics bags, Tupperware boxes, Clingfilm-wrapped blocks of dope, and a large set of scales.

"Def' no Sheep Shit around," he told Miguel. "Sorry, mate, but this Red's fucking ace; you'll like it; just in; have a try," and he quickly skinned up, passing the spliff to Miguel after drawing it to a raging inferno with his own single but protracted toke.

Miguel seemed impressed, enough to ask after the price as he passed it across an unflinching Cheryl to Colin. Colin took a good toke himself then almost choked at hearing Jimmy's response: forty-two a quarter! Shit, he thought, but prices are definitely keeping pace with inflation. Miguel ended up asking for a half, and Colin felt thankful he'd largely given up.

"So, you after some, as well, Magic?" Jimmy asked as he cut and weighed Miguel's.

Colin had intended saying "No" but ended up asking if he'd any Moroccan, holding his next toke and his breath after Jimmy said he had. Twenty-five seemed a reasonable price in comparison, but Jimmy warned it wasn't the best.

Colin, though, wasn't that bothered, for something else now drove his decision, or to be more precise, the thought of another but stronger Moroccan—one Arab called Jusuf.

7 THE FURTHERANCE OF SCIENCE

The windows of Colin's car immediately steamed up when they leapt in from their dash through the bouncing rain. Miguel wiped his face and pushed his dripping hair behind his ears before letting out a long "Yuck" of disgust.

"Fucking 'ell," he exclaimed, followed by a long sighing whistle. "Jeez," he blew in exasperation. "Where did that come from?"

"Ah, you're just being a nesh Lancastrian, Miguel," Colin told him, grinning as he wiped his glasses.

Once he'd started the car and set the heater to "Demist" Colin waited for the windscreen to clear. The rain became even heavier, drumming more insistently on the roof, the backstreet deserted.

"Hey, but that Red's pretty good stuff," Miguel presently said, staring out through the rain-laced windscreen, as though seeing Valhalla.

Colin bent to check the quarter of Moroccan in his sock—its secretion there an old habit born of hippy paranoia.

Miguel then turned to Colin, his head tilted to one side, his brow knotted. "Magic?" he said.

"Eh? Oh, Wrigley's name for me. Yeah, well, it's funny now," and Colin remembered the old car he'd had at university. "I once went to score from him when he lived up Bury Old Road, but he didn't have anything in. Said he could get some, though, if I had wheels and could take him; some place the other side of Manchester; turned out to be Sale. I spent the whole drive freaked out we'd get stopped, especially as he kept rolling spliffs all the way. So I drove as carefully as I'd done on my Driving Test."

The windscreen had by now cleared enough, so Colin pulled out of their parking space and set off, unknowingly slowly and cautiously towards Miguel's flat in Seedley.

"When we got to Sale," Colin went on to say, "Wrigley turned to me, wonder in those crazed eyes of his, and said, 'Wow, you're a really good driver; dead smooth'. Then he took a last toke, threw the roach out of the window and told me it had been like 'Flying 'ere on a *magic carpet*, ar'kid'."

Miguel laughed. "Sounds like Jimmy Wrigley."

"Yeah, well, I didn't know him that well back then. The bummer was: his contact in Sale didn't have anything, either. Complete waste of time," to which Miguel fell into a fit of giggles, but it could just as equally well have been the Lebanese Red.

Having dropped Miguel off, Colin drove down through Weaste and Eccles, finally out of Salford altogether and into the leafy suburbs of Manchester. The rain never eased the once. When he got home, Kate had clearly only just got in from work. The lights were all on, her sodden umbrella standing open in the utility room, a pool of water beneath it.

"Hiya," he called upstairs, her reply coming from the bathroom. "Want a drink?" he asked and she shouted down that she could kill for one. Colin went to put the kettle on.

"You're back late. Traffic?" Kate said, rubbing her hair with a towel as she came into the kitchen.

"You look like you got drenched."

"The earlier bus hadn't come, so the shelter was full to bursting. Had to wait out in the rain for half an hour before one finally turned up."

He passed Kate her tea.

"So," she then asked, "did you book those first two weeks in August?"

"Oh. Damn. Forgot."

"Correct me if I'm wrong, but didn't your company recently spend a shedload of money putting you all through a Time Manager course, with all its daft paraphernalia, just so you wouldn't forget things?"

"Yeah, but I forgot to put it in my Time Manager, didn't I. I'll make sure tomorrow, though. Don't worry," but Kate didn't look convinced. "Oh, and I've had an idea about the joss stick holder."

"Oh yeah?"

Colin took the quarter of Moroccan out from down his sock and put it on the worktop, relating his visit to Jimmy Wrigley's.

"Jimmy Wrigley? Bloody 'ell, Colin, I'm amazed he's still around. Thought he'd have been in an institution of some sort by now."

Colin stared at her, open-mouthed.

"What?"

"That's exactly what I said to Miguel. Weird. But no, he seemed a lot more normal than I remembered him.

But then, when Miguel suggested I could get some Moroccan, it dawned on me what else there'd been in common each time—I'd always been a bit stoned."

"Hmm, sounds like a good excuse, to me."

"It's a legitimate scientific procedure, Kate, I'll have you know. There are always sacrifices to be made for the furtherance of science."

"If you say so."

"And funnily enough, it was always Moroccan; at least I think it was. Bit of an odd coincidence that, don't you think?"

That evening, sitting warmly before the gas fire in the front room, Colin once again stared at the joss stick holder and the pack of sticks. In one hand he held a passably well-rolled spliff, and in the other a lighter.

"Last time was a few months back, on my birthday," he absently reminded Kate, before lighting up and taking a long first toke. He held it for a while then took another, soon feeling dizzy. When he offered it to Kate, she shook her head.

"Best stay straight, Colin, as your observer."

"Right," he wheezed, coughing out smoke before having a drink of his coffee. "I'll finish this spliff off then give it a go. Then we'll see, eh?"

"Well, one way or the other."

Finally stubbing the roach out in his ashtray, Colin steeled himself to light a joss stick, its trail of smoke once again snaking towards the holder. He glanced at Kate who carefully watched his every move.

"Here we go, then," and holding his breath, Colin slowly slid the joss stick into one of the holder's holes.

8 IN THE LAND OF THE GALLANTS

The steady approach of the Nao Providência to a quay on the larboard side met Colin's startled gaze, from where he stared out from the quarterdeck. Sun-bleached, whitewashed buildings hemmed in the narrow harbour front, yet more rising a short way up the steep hillside beyond, all higgledy-piggledy and close-pressed. A square tower topped their reach, its lofty outline stark against an azure sky.

Seagulls swept overhead in turning arcs, their raucous calls pointing the rhythmic chant of a team of men turning the galleon's capstan. From this ran two ropes, each to a block slung fore and aft, their taut lengths to the quayside shortening all the while.

Before long the vessel nudged up tight against the harbour wall, practiced hands catching hawsers thrown to them by those on deck. Others jumped aboard, amongst them the fortunately resilient Rodrigo, although he crossed somewhat stiffly. With difficulty, he climbed the ladder to the quarterdeck, then grinned as he approached Jusuf.

"Good morning, *meu gorgulho*," and the man winced, clearly still in some pain, his tunic tied tightly about him. "How are you?"

"I'm well enough, Rodrigo. I trust the *Ingleses* have been tending your injuries whilst you've been aboard their ship?"

"Little they could do; little anyone can. At least I was allowed some deck-room on which to lie flat," and Jusuf couldn't help but respect the man's fortitude.

"Where are we, Rodrigo?" Jusuf then quietly asked. "We're clearly not in Santander. Even I could tell we'd kept northerly."

"So, I take it none of the *Ingleses* speaks Berber, then? Or has your size and dark skin kept them at arm's length?"

"I'm a passenger, Rodrigo, so they've kept me apart from your men, and no, my gaoler couldn't understand a word I said, nor me him. So, come on, what is this place?"

Rodrigo stared at the harbour, his expression souring. "Foy, Jusuf. This, apparently, is Foy, in the far west of *Inglaterra*, a place that's long put the fear of God into all those who ply the Western Sea and its approaches. Somewhere I never thought I'd see."

"Foy?"

"Where we're about to go ashore." He leant in but angled his face up, lifting his mouth nearer Jusuf's ear. "During this kingdom's long war with *França*, it was the lair of the fearsome 'Foy Gallants'."

"Gallants?"

"Privateers, Jusuf: pirates bearing a king's wartime warrant. But even if this *had* been Santander, I'm afraid it would no longer have served your purpose." He stepped away, wincing before warily clutching his chest. He sighed and looked up at Jusuf.

"All ship's lockers have been seized, my poor weevil, mine included—and, of course, what it contains of yours. Just a little extra we didn't expect them to add to their plundering of our hold. But at least the crew," and he attempted a grin, "in addition to our one passenger, of course, are being put ashore unharmed, which is why I'm here."

An unintelligible voice called from the quayside. Rodrigo turned to nod its way.

"Come on, Jusuf, we're being ordered off. Get your things together and I'll show you our lodgings."

Jusuf slipped back into the captain's cabin and quickly packed his shoulder bag. When they got down onto the main deck, men were already carrying things ashore. Jusuf spotted the first mate's locker, Rodrigo giving way to the two men carrying it. The chest went ahead, heaved over the rail and dropped to the quayside.

Rodrigo cringed. "Only our dear Lord knows where your special gift for *Castilla y León* will end up. So let's pray they discard it as a worthless trinket, eh? And carefully so, for all our sakes—even those of these damned *Ingleses*."

The pervasive smell of fish grew stronger as Jusuf stepped onto the hot quayside, the firm ground beneath his feet a welcome relief. Rodrigo led him through the harbour's mounting activity, between growing piles of the Nao Providência's goods, and on towards a cobbled alley. From out of it, between a stout stone property and a three storeyed, whitewashed building, came a donkey-drawn cart and its driver. Jusuf and Rodrigo stood aside as it clip-clopped and rumbled past, on its way into the bustle they were leaving behind.

The alley led to a narrow road, a gate in the wall on the far side giving entry into a yard around a large buttressed building, above which rose the tower Jusuf had seen from the quarterdeck. He stopped and stared up. From each surmounting corner rose a tall, thin and pointed spire, as though there to prick the very sky above. A Christian church, Jusuf guessed, although cruder and less finished than those in Ceuta, and with only the one tower. Then Rodrigo called his name.

Jusuf turned to find him standing in the doorway of a building that angled away from a corner of the church's yard. Slipping past him from within came the sound of voices, the occasional call and the sporadic bouts of raucous laughter.

But only now did Jusuf notice the stares he got from those who slowed as they passed, or who lingered together in supposed discourse nearby. Many were gaily attired in bright colours, others in drab workaday clothes, but the cut and sharpness of each suggested a place of some no mean wealth. When Jusuf nodded at two aged women, on his way to join Rodrigo, they dipped their heads in acknowledgement as they drew near, but each held her gaze upon his face. Then, as they passed him by, one reached out and briefly touched his arm before they both hurried on without a backward glance, heads held close in keen discourse.

The gloom inside the building made it hard for Jusuf to see much at first: a low beamed ceiling, a solid dark-wood counter along one long wall, a stout and surly-looking man behind it, tables and stools crammed in across the room's narrow width, and alcoves revealed in the meagre light of their small open-shuttered windows. A dozen or so silent men either stood at the counter or lounged on stools, their arms propped on the counter or tables. Flagons and earthenware drinking vessels stood at their elbows, a large dog at one man's feet, sprawled out before a hearth's damped-down fire.

Jusuf manoeuvred his bulk through the eerily silent room, the glint of eyes following his progress. Carefully, in Rodrigo's wake, he stepped over the dog and finally arrived at the furthest alcove, at whose table sat the Nao Providência's captain.

The man indicated the empty benches around him and Jusuf sat on the one opposite, Rodrigo settling beside him. Then the captain regarded Jusuf closely for a moment before raising his hand in the direction of the man behind the counter, calling across in a language Jusuf couldn't understand. Two large pots of a scum-topped liquid were brought to their table, joining the already half empty one set before the captain.

Rodrigo raised his to his lips, plunging them beneath the scum before drinking, long and seemingly with pleasure. He put the pot down and wiped his mouth before nodding at Jusuf to follow suit.

Although not sure, Jusuf dipped his own lips all the same, drawing in a strangely flat and almost metallic tasting clear liquid from beneath the scum. It had a tang to it, a gentle fizz against his tongue, and a not unpleasant freshening of his throat as he swallowed it down.

He looked across at the captain, about to speak when the man imperceptibly shook his head. Only when a hubbub had returned to the room did the captain then momentarily roll his eyes to one side before staring back at Jusuf.

"Has my first mate told you the bad tidings about your...your burden, Jusuf al-Haddad?"

"He has," Jusuf quietly said as he nodded.

"And that it's now likely lost to you for all time?" and again Jusuf nodded. "I must say: you don't look down-spirited."

"If it be the will of Allah, then so be it; Allah the wise, Allah the merciful, before your might I bow down."

"Well, be that as it may, but I suppose you and your master can always try again another day, if and when you eventually get back to Ceuta. But I'm afraid it'll not be for some time if you rely on me and my ship. *Capitão* Treffry has only preserved our lives because our two nations are not at war. He knows his act has been one of piracy, not that of a privateer. But not content with making a pretty *reis* or two from the Nao Providência's lading, he will also hold my ship to his own profit for as long as he can."

"Hold your ship?" Jusuf said.

"I will have to travel to *Londres*, there to search out King Manuel's representative to the English king's court. If I can afford the gift-in-gratitude payment, he may be inclined to represent me in my petition to have the Nao Providência returned."

"But how long will that take?"

"A fair bit of time just to get to *Londres*. No one here will afford me passage, at whatever fee, and I'm sure word will quickly get well ahead of me along the south coast ports. So, I'll be forced to go by land. That's two hundred and seventy leagues, or so I've been told. A week perhaps, maybe more. But that'll be nothing compared with how slowly my petition's likely to grind. Then, of course, there'll be the long wait to take possession once I'm back."

For a while the captain only stared at Jusuf, but then he drew breath and warned him, "I'd be surprised if I was back here before the end of the summer. So, my advice to you would be to seek out your own passage back to Ceuta."

Jusuf swallowed hard, then looked between the two men. "In which case," he slowly said, "I think I should make you aware of something: my burden hasn't been lost."

"What?" the two men said a little too loudly, the room once more briefly falling silent.

"I'm sorry, Rodrigo," Jusuf said, turning to him, "but whilst I was tending your injury, I noticed the key about your neck." Rodrigo's hand shot there, clearly reassured. "Whilst you slept, I borrowed it and slipped down to your locker when all eyes were on the nearing *navio inglês*." He pointedly lifted the bag at his side a few inches off the bench before settling it carefully back down again.

The captain slowly began laughing, a glint in his eyes as they narrowed at Jusuf, but then, clearly aware he was drawing attention, he abruptly stopped.

"So, as the likelihood you'll find passage to Santander on a ship you can trust to wait for you whilst you do the deed, one prepared to set sail as soon as the tide allows once you're back on board, with no delays for unloading and taking on new goods… Well," and he barked a single laugh, "as such a prospect strikes me as somewhat remote, then I have to say, it seems you'll be biding your time here with us in Cornwall, Jusuf al-Haddad. And probably until next spring at the earliest.

"So, *meu gorgulho*, I'd strongly suggest you pray to your good god Allah that I do indeed finally recover my ship. But in the meantime, you need to keep the contents of that bag of yours safe…very safe indeed."

9 ROOM AT THE INN

They remained drinking in silence for a while, until the captain called for more. The man behind the counter brought over a large jug and topped up their pots.

When he'd gone, Jusuf told the captain, "I have something of a problem, though: the allowance I was given isn't big enough for such a long wait. What I have will maybe last a couple of months, depending on how costly things are here, but certainly not the best part of a year."

The captain gave Jusuf a wry grin. "*Capitão* Treffry has made arrangements at his own expense for the two of you, at least for the time it takes Rodrigo to regain his strength. That's if you don't mind being on hand as his nursemaid, Jusuf."

Jusuf nodded, oddly at ease with the thought.

"The man clearly has much sway in Foy," the captain then told them. "He made a point of telling me his father had been one of the Gallants. One of those who'd survived the English king's suppression of their continued pirating after the long war with

França had ended. Something he kept telling me about every chance he got," and the captain rolled his eyes.

"He'd clearly hoped we were a French ship when he first spied us, seeing *Inglaterra's* now part of this League of Venice alliance that's against them. But men of Cornwall are ever pirates, Jusuf, clearly unable to resist easy prey. So, I suspect his largesse is in some part a paltry recompense. But once you're fit enough, Rodrigo, you'll both then have to find some work to pay your own ways."

Rodrigo nodded, saying he'd have to dust off the old shipwright's skills he'd learnt as a youngster, the not overly impressive ones he'd finally put aside in favour of going to sea. Jusuf, though, only sought to confirm that the captain still intended leaving for *Londres* the following day.

"Indeed. I'll take six of the crew for protection; the most my own funds will allow. The rest will have to scratch their own keep, from what money they have and work they can find. Mind you, I think many will be looking for something well before the week's out, judging by how many I've seen already sniffing around the whorehouse."

"Well," Rodrigo smiled, "it is the first chance they've had in weeks. In truth, were my ribs in much better fettle…"

The captain grinned, but then his face dropped and he turned a concerned eye towards Jusuf's bag. "I'd suggest you don't leave it too long before finding somewhere safe to hide your burden, Jusuf. Somewhere undisturbed, where nobody will come upon it by chance until you need it again, eh?"

"Unlike one of your ship's lockers?" Jusuf couldn't resist saying, to which the captain's expression darkened, although he kept his own counsel.

Jusuf had begun to acquire quite a taste for his unusual drink, but then learned from the others that it was an English small ale, much to his consternation. It took them quite a while to reassure him it wasn't real beer, that even English children supped it in preference to the unsafe water.

"Look upon it as a kind of watered-down potage," Rodrigo said, slamming his empty pot down on the table. "A way of avoiding being plagued by a constant bellyache, eh? Then maybe you'll drink it down and I can finally show you where we'll be sleeping."

Lifting it to his lips, Jusuf surreptitiously sniffed at his drink, at least content it didn't smell like beer. He finally put his trust in Rodrigo and swiftly drank it down to the dregs.

"Good. Now, come on," and they both nodded at the captain as they got up, the man returning a dismissive wave of his hand.

They stepped back over the still sleeping dog and on between the tables to the inn's entrance, from which climbed a narrow flight of stairs. Rodrigo went ahead, the treads creaking under Jusuf's weight as he followed him up. At the top they turned onto a dimly lit corridor that appeared to run the length of the building. Along both sides stood barely discernible doors, the only light seeping in through a small window opening at the far end. Rodrigo took them to the very last room at the rear and stepped inside.

When Jusuf went in behind him, he found a room not much bigger than the short but wide pallet it held, his head brushing the low ceiling.

"Wall or this side?" Rodrigo said. "Your choice, seeing you were the Nao Providência's paying passenger."

Placing a large hand on the shabby coverlet, Jusuf pressed down hard. His hand pushed straight through the meagre straw to the boards. "Best take the wall. Don't want to end up crushing you against it if I turn over in my sleep."

He squeezed past Rodrigo and inspected the already open window shutters, then the mullion gaps, deciding they were too small for all but a child to get through. Poking his head out, he peered down into a small yard below, seeing stacked barrels and a woodpile over in one corner.

"I wouldn't leave anything in here," Rodrigo noted. "The door only locks from the inside," and he rattled its latch back and forth to demonstrate.

Jusuf again stared out of the window, beyond the yard and its high rear wall, over what looked like a labyrinth of further small yards. They laced the gap between their own building and the rear of a row of unalike properties, all steeply climbing away from the waterfront. Some abutted their neighbours, but others offered narrow alleys between, although Jusuf could see no easy way through from them.

"It will have to do," he finally said, wiping off the muck from the windowsill his hands had picked up. "I'll just have to keep everything close by me," and he swung his bag from his shoulder and onto the pallet's coverlet.

"In which case," Rodrigo said, "I'll get back down to the captain. Do you want another pot of ale?" Jusuf gave him a smile and nodded, then the man was gone.

Rummaging in his bag, Jusuf drew out a cotton-wrapped block of *kief* about the size of his hand, all tied tight with twine. He carefully undid the knot and peeled back a flap of the fine cloth. It revealed a dense, dark-brown resin that soon filled the room with its sweet but flat aroma.

"I'd better make it last," he told himself as he folded back the edge of the pallet and placed the block on one of the boards below. He slipped his knife out, laying its blade at a carefully judged angle across an already cut corner, then pressed down hard to remove enough for the rest of the day.

He was still chewing a piece when he threaded his way through the now emptier ground floor room and joined the two men at their table. A fresh pot of small ale stood before his place, but he left it untouched after sitting down, his mouth still working the bitter-tasting *kief*.

The captain leaned over his drink, peering absently at its scummy surface before looking across at Jusuf through his straggly eyebrows. "You'd do well to acquaint yourself with the local tongue, you know, Jusuf al-Haddad. You'd fare far better by it." He then lifted his gaze fully to Rodrigo. "Ensiná-lo a língua inglesa, eh?"

"Sim, Capitão," Rodrigo responded and swung a smile at Jusuf. "I'll make you fluent enough to order ale and woo abed the fairest of maidens…which is about as much as I know," and he grinned as he raised his pot in salute before taking a swig.

Jusuf finally swallowed what was left of the *kief* still in his mouth and did the same, his first grin in a long time finally cracking his features.

"And, Rodrigo," the captain went on to say, "when you're recovered enough to be able to enjoy ploughing those fair maidens, you'd best take yourselves off inland to find work. Jusuf is hardly a seaman, what'll be most needed hereabouts. I should imagine a fine blacksmith, though—as I'm assured our *haddad*, here, most certainly is—would find his skills eagerly snapped up in some nearby hamlet or town."

As the captain gulped down another mouthful of ale, Jusuf asked him, "But how will we know when you've returned?"

"Simple," and the captain wiped the scum from his lips with the back of his hand. "Come the end of July, get word of your whereabouts back here to this inn, so I'll know where to find you when I do return. I can't imagine I'll be back before then. And if you move on, do the same again from wherever you cast up. Impress upon the crew to do likewise, Rodrigo, if they too come to stray too far from Foy."

Rodrigo nodded, then the captain stood and stretched. "Well, there's much I still need to do before I can get off tomorrow. I'll take my leave of you." He downed the last of his ale and made his way towards the street outside.

"So," Rodrigo said as the captain's figure passed their window opening, "after you've finished your ale, what do you say we start your first *inglês* lesson? We can take a wander around our new berth. See what it offers in the way of words and phrases you'll need, whilst at the same time finding our feet. After all, we've nothing else to do until my ribs are mended."

But Jusuf thought back to the captain's warning, then felt at the bag beside him. His fingers searched out the outline of that one thing that now demanded its own task, a task that needed doing sooner rather than later: the finding of a hidey-hole, one that would remain undiscovered by all but himself for probably the next year at least.

10 NO TIME TO LOSE

"So it hasn't worked?"

Jusuf realised he was staring blankly at a young woman, a beautiful young woman; a slowly more perplexed young woman in strange clothing. At Kate.

"It bloody well has," Colin almost gasped.

"But it's…it's only been—"

"Quick. Get some paper and a pen. You've got to get this down, whilst it's still fresh in my mind." He gawped at Kate's inactivity. "Come on. Quick."

"All right, all right," she scolded as she jerked upright. "No need to snap," but she reached into the cupboard beside her, finally pulling out a pad and a pencil. Then she frowned and stared at him. "But… But it's only been moments. You're still holding the joss stick." He stared down at his hand, the stick's stem between his finger and thumb.

"I know it can't have been real," he slowly said, letting go the joss stick, "it's not possible, but it damn well felt like it. Although…" and he looked around the front room, absorbing its immediacy, "I definitely do feel straight now, and I know I was stoned before."

Over the next hour or so, Colin related what had happened, his urgency steadily tempered by Kate's insistence he slow down and her repeated checks on details. Every so often she'd mutter "Interesting" or "That helps", sometimes "We'd need to check on that". At last, when Colin could remember no more, Kate sat back and stared at her pages of notes.

"I just don't see," she carefully measured, "how so much could have happened in such a short time," and she shook the wad of sheets at him as she stared into his eyes. When he didn't reply, she scanned through the pages, all the while imperceptibly shaking her head.

"Well," she eventually said, "you've either done a lot of homework and are having me on, or there's something to all this. I mean, you said Jusuf was in 'Foy', and that thing about the 'Foy Gallants', but if you'd only ever read about it somewhere, you'd have pronounced it 'Fowey', the way it's now spelt."

"So you know the place?"

"It's about twenty miles down the coast from mum and dad's place in Whitsand Bay. We used to go there occasionally when I was a kid, but I've not been back in years. I remember it had a nice church, though. Norman, I think, but knocked about quite a bit since; much of it these days from later periods."

"But it would have been there in Jusuf's time?"

"Oh yes, which reminds me," and Kate looked back through her notes. "What do you know about the League of Venice?"

"Nothing; never heard of it before."

"I'm sure England joined just at the end of the fifteenth century, and you said the captain told Jusuf and Rodrigo, and I quote: 'Seeing England's now part of it'. That makes it sound like it had only recently happened. Hang on," and she went upstairs, returning with one of her weighty history text books.

"There you go," and she placed the volume on his lap, her finger indicating the sentence: "The Kingdom of England joined in 1496". "And," she said, flipping a ream of pages over to where she'd kept a mark, "that ties in with King Manuel the first of Portugal's reign being between fourteen-ninety-five and fifteen-twenty-one."

"Hey, you're good at this, aren't you, chuck?"

"History *was* my degree subject, Colin, though all this isn't from any of the periods I studied, nor the ones I deal with at work."

"So you reckon we're in the backend of the fourteen-nineties?"

She gave him a Gallic shrug, then asked if he wanted a coffee.

"I could murder one."

He followed her into the kitchen, leaning against a work unit as she filled the kettle. After a while he quietly said, "So, seeing you're so on-the-ball, what do you reckon Jusuf's 'Burden' is?"

She stared at him for a moment. "That I haven't got a clue about, but it sounds a bit dangerous."

"And fragile."

"But small enough to fit unnoticed into his shoulder bag. You sure you didn't see it whilst camped in Jusuf's mind? You know, like when he was packing his bag before going off the ship."

She spooned coffee and sugar into two mugs.

"Camped in his mind? It was more than that, Kate; I *was* him, in his own thoughts…my thoughts…our thoughts, seeing the world as *we* saw it."

"Then why don't you know what it was?"

"I dunno. Maybe he just didn't visualise it whilst I was 'Camped in his mind', because he certainly didn't put anything out of the ordinary in his bag; just a few items of clothing and his *sebsi.* Whatever it was, it must've already been in there."

"His what?" and Kate passed him his coffee.

"Ta," and he took a careful sip. "It's a pipe, for smoking dope: small, narrow clay bowl, long wooden stem."

"Moroccan dope, no doubt."

"Yeah, and I think I might have been right about that. It does look like there's some sort of dope connection between us, through your joss stick holder."

"You called *his* dope '*Kief*.'"

"Yeah, but it looked, smelt and tasted like Moroccan. Good gear, though. Better than the stuff I got from Jimmy Wrigley."

"So what do you know about *kief*?"

"Nothing at all. I'd never heard the term before, but it looked like the sort of stuff we used to get in the seventies. Decent gear, not cut with any old crap. I remember getting some from—"

"Colin?"

"Eh? What?"

"You said Jusuf said he'd have to use his sparingly, once he realised he was going to be stuck in Cornwall."

"Yeah. So?"

"Well, if they are connected—yours and his smoking of dope—then that probably means there's going to be a limit to how long the joss stick holder's going to work. Think about it: do you reckon he's likely to be able to just nip out and visit his own fifteenth century Cornish Jimmy Wrigley?"

"Ah, I'm with you. Obviously not."

"So there'll come a time when he runs out."

"After which I'll probably not be able to travel back there again."

"Precisely."

"Shit."

"Apposite."

"Eh? Oh, unintended."

"So, you up to doing it again?"

"What? Tonight?"

"No, I didn't mean now. It's getting late, anyway. Tomorrow maybe?"

"Well, I suppose so. At least this last phantasm wasn't as scary, and what can happen now they're in Cornwall?"

"Hmm, well…anything, really. It is Cornwall, after all: a world unto itself. It was considered a different country back then…still is today by many, especially the Cornish themselves. And anyway, time for bed, me thinks, once I've drunk this," and she gave him one of her best pixie-looks before wandering off, back into the front room with her coffee.

11 TO LOSTWITHIEL

As it turned out, it wasn't until the end of the week, until the Friday, that they could try the joss stick holder again. This time, Kate sat ready with pen and pad in hand.

Colin took his time over rolling a spliff, then, as he lit it, suggested another coffee. Deep down, his gut swilled with dread, but then again, his thoughts seemed to fizz with their own intrigue. His head finally won out and he took a last gulp of coffee, then a final toke on his spliff before stubbing it out.

"Jusuf definitely got the better score," he couldn't help but nervously giggle as he slipped a joss stick from the wrapper and once more lit his Zippo. A thin, curling thread of blue-grey smoke again coiled towards the holder, seemingly drawn there. Colin flicked a glance at Kate, then slid the stick's thin sliver of bamboo into the first hole it came to.

Kate must have grabbed his hand, but Rodrigo's worried face met Colin's confused gaze.

"Shit, Jusuf!" the man hissed. "Do you want to end up in the water?"

"But I…"

Rodrigo pulled him fully into the small boat from the harbour steps where he'd been standing. Jusuf's stomach lurched in sympathy with the sway his extra weight gave it. As he stumbled and grabbed at the boom, which only moved away from his grasp, he saw pain flash across Rodrigo's expression, quickly veiled.

"Come on," Rodrigo said when Jusuf had at last steadied himself, "sit down before you capsize us," and he shuffled to one side of the bench to make room.

Facing them at the stern sat a gnarled old man, his weather-beaten hand on the tiller, his distrustful eyes firmly fixed on Jusuf, who unsteadily sat down beside Rodrigo. Jusuf kept telling himself it was only a river trip, but unnerving memories of the storm still flashed before his mind's eye.

"And keep your head low, clear of the boom, unless you want to lose it," Rodrigo then said, before nodding at the man at the stern as Jusuf carefully settled his shoulder bag down beside himself. Shivering at the cold air coming in off the water, he drew his new coat closer about him and watched the ferryman let slip a line.

The boat's impatiently straining sails pushed it out into the flow of the estuary's inbound tide, where it rolled onto a larboard keel as the boom whipped across their smartly dipped heads. Jusuf looked beyond their ferryman and watched Foy's overcast harbour slip steadily faster astern as the sails caught the stronger wind out of its lee.

Rodrigo stared up at the grey clouds racing across the louring sky above Foy and said to the man—in his best English, "Good sou'west-by-south for our course this morning, Ferryman."

"Aar, so it be," the man seemed to say from the back of his throat, before taking his gaze from Jusuf and off upstream. He pressed more firmly against the tiller and let slip some of the mainsheet. The bow slowly nosed around towards the northeast, more upstream, until the boom again swung across Jusuf and Rodrigo's head. The wind now in the sails quickly pushed the boat over onto a starboard keel and the bow sank lower in the water as it turned to point inland. They were brought abeam of the estuary's western shore, not far off the larboard side.

Foy's dwindling northern reach slipped dully by, its whitewashed buildings seeming ashen in the grey light. But then Rodrigo pointed out the Nao Providência, sitting high and dry in its boatyard berth, where Foy's last few properties dotted the shoreline.

"Looks like they're well on with refitting her," Rodrigo said, somewhat bitterly. Jusuf stared at the reminder of that terrifying storm, at how forlorn the Nao Providência looked, seemingly afloat upon the morning's dank Cornish air. He turned away and looked across at the more distant opposite bank.

There lay a wooded shoreline, beyond which gently rose a patchwork of long, thin fields dotted with toiling figures. A narrow combe soon directed the fields' hemming trees into a sharp curve away from the estuary, giving way to a small cove. A landing ramp dipped down into the water's edge, from a lane bordered by buildings that snaked their way up the climb of the narrow valley.

Jusuf steeled himself to gather what little English he'd so far learnt, and finally pointed it out as he said to the ferryman: "What be…er, be that…piece?" to which the old man only looked baffled.

"What is the name of that place?" Rodrigo clarified.

The ferryman ran his gaze across the water. "Ah, well, 'im be Bodinnick, as fer we'm be goin' 'cross be ferry," to which even Rodrigo furrowed his brow. But by now the cove had fallen astern, the estuary narrowing more to a river as its course curved towards a bend ahead.

"You know, Rodrigo," Jusuf quietly said, "I don't think I'll ever find an ear for this infuriating language."

"Be fair to yourself, Jusuf; we're not in the best part of *Inglaterra* to learn it. As I've already said, it's not the mother tongue for most in Cornwall, especially the further west you go. Although most in Foy speak *inglês* well enough, it being a trading port and what have you. But that won't be the case the further inland we go, I'm afraid. Once we've disembarked and passed through Lostwithiel, I expect we'll likely both be equally adrift."

"How can we expect to get by in Bodmyn if neither of us understands a word they're saying? I'm beginning to wonder if Captain Treffry's idea was at all wise, or whether he was just looking to cut his expenditure on both our accounts. After all, he's already had to pay out nearly four weeks for our board and lodgings."

"I must admit, he did seem a bit evasive when he suggested it, and there's definitely been an air of something going on these past couple of weeks: lots of toing and froing, all manner of gatherings and heated arguments. I just wish I'd been able to understand some of it, but I think their *Kernowek* tongue will always defeat me."

The ferryman drew in the mainsheet and they tacked toward larboard as they approached a sharper bend in the river, one that took them westwards. The boom swung back over Jusuf and Rodrigo as water splashed in, wetting Jusuf and bringing a curse from under his breath.

Another bend shortly took them north again, between low wooded rises. A small hamlet, one they agreed the old man had called Golant, presently slipped by on the western bank, more slowly now they'd lost the freshness of the coastal wind. But on they steadily pushed, chivvied by the urgency of the high tide's pressing midday turn, as the river narrowed yet further still.

Eventually, their passage now no more than upon a broad river, and after tacking through a series of sharp meanders, they sailed on between a lower spread of woods and occasional patchwork fields. Dotted about them were more figures, and here and there low, tree-shrouded buildings, but little else. Before long knots of buildings appeared, some looking like storehouses, others workshops, and small cottages like those in Foy.

Then more properties came into sight, jostled yet closer still, one to another, often shoulder-to-shoulder. Finally there were workmanlike frontages along both banks ahead. Stacked in front of them were barrels and boxes, and what looked like rolls of cloth. Thronged in amongst it all, men and wagons, and donkeys, horses, carts and boys all laboured back and forth, to and from lines of boats moored along each quay.

Their ferryman found a gap close by some steps and brought their boat with a thump against the western quay. Rodrigo grabbed at a wooden pile, to heave them to. He grimaced as he turned to take a line from the ferryman, then jumped across to the steps. There, he stumbled and swore before running the line through a loop in the wall beside him.

Once secured and the boat held fast, Jusuf shouldered his bag and clambered across onto the steps himself. Rodrigo continued to look pained as he drew his purse from his pouch and squeezed past Jusuf, pressing their fare into the ferryman's hand. With a "Thank 'e" the man touched his cap, bit each coin and signalled Rodrigo to let go the line. Then he pushed himself off and lowered the mainsail, as his boat drifted out into the current and slowly slid off downstream, back towards Foy.

"We should have left it a couple of weeks more at least," Jusuf said as he halted Rodrigo's climb up to the quayside. The man seemed to look through Jusuf for a moment, then his shoulders sagged and he dropped his gaze to the steps at his feet.

"Stop worrying like an old hen, Jusuf," he finally said, lifting his gaze. "My ribs are already less painful, and *Capitão* Treffry was right: another blacksmith could well step in before you. And from the sound of it, *Senhora* Trewin would snap up the first to turn up on her doorstep."

"Even a blackamoor?"

"If she truly is in straitened times, then yes, even a blackamoor as big and as ugly as you, Jusuf." A grin cracked his strained features as he slapped Jusuf on the arm. Jusuf, though, just hoped he was right.

As they stepped up onto the quayside, he noticed an arc of blue sky away to the southwest. The air felt chill to Jusuf, but the lightening sky lifted his spirits as they stood and surveyed the bustle of commerce before them.

It reminded Jusuf somewhat of the quayside not far from his smithy in Ceuta, where his favourite *taberna* would look out onto a similar but undoubtedly hotter scene. He imagined himself drinking a refreshing cup of *chá de menta*, whilst watching out for Safira taking her family's washing down to the washhouse.

Then he noticed Rodrigo no longer stood beside him, finally spotting him with a group of men further down the quayside. They looked as though they too had recently disembarked, trunks and satchels piled around them. Rodrigo, though, appeared deferential, often nodding, his shoulders rounded.

It took a moment for Jusuf to recognise the cloak worn by the man he was talking to. Although no doubt sullied from the man's travels, Jusuf knew the undyed woollen cloak of a Cistercian monk when he saw one, the hem of a dark habit hanging below.

The monk was nodding, pointing out others of his party, to whom Rodrigo once more nodded. Then he looked around, finally setting eyes on Jusuf. A quick word with the monk, and he threaded his way back through the activity between them until he came alongside and took Jusuf's arm.

"I'm sorry, Jusuf, I thought you were behind me. Come and meet Dom Francisco Lopes. He's a monk from *Mosteiro de Santa Maria de Alcobaça*, not far from Lisboa. His party are going to visit the Canons Regular of the Lateran at their Priory of Saint Mary in Bodmyn, and he's graciously consented to allow us to walk with them. It'll be safer, and save us having to ask our way, and no doubt getting lost."

As they negotiated their way along the quayside, towards the monk and his travelling companions, doubt struck Jusuf. "But I'm not a Christian," he whispered, pulling Rodrigo to a halt. "They won't want—"

"I've already explained. You've no need to worry. Come on. Dom Francisco seems a kindly brother."

"Explained what?" but Rodrigo was too busy avoiding those busily about them as he encouraged Jusuf on.

As they approached the monk, he fixed Jusuf in his kindly gaze, finally greeting him with, "*Ah, o Bom Samaritano.*" His blossoming smile gave Jusuf a warm welcome. The Dom took Jusuf's large hand in his own, and lightly patted it. He then leant in closer and, in passably good Arabic, offered, "May God favour you through the one you call Allah."

"In his name may I…" Jusuf habitually began, but then swallowed and held his tongue.

"God works in mysterious ways, Jusuf al-Haddad. It beholds us all to look for His ways in those of others." Then he drew in another monk, one draped in a black cloak worn over a black habit. Dom Francisco spoke to him in English, too rapidly for Jusuf to follow, but he understood the returned suspicion in the man's eyes, and the brief, hollow smile he offered Jusuf.

After a rapid exchange between the two monks and Rodrigo, in both English and Portuguese, Dom Francisco explained in Arabic, "I have much to discuss with my *fratrem in Deo* Brother Thomas, Jusuf al-Haddad, but perhaps time will allow us a word or two later." He again smiled up at Jusuf before joining Brother Thomas at the head of their party as it made preparations for leaving.

Jusuf whispered to Rodrigo, "What did you tell him?"

"Only the truth," Rodrigo said, a genuine warmth in the smile he then gave Jusuf.

12 THE LAST TO KNOW

"What I don't understand," Rodrigo said to Jusuf, as they waited for the travelling party's baggage to be loaded onto a handcart, "is why this quay's so large." He looked about it, then down into the river flowing between its quaysides.

"Well, I suppose it must be because they do a lot of trade," Jusuf offered, not sure what Rodrigo was getting at.

"But nothing bigger than a small boat can get in here. Just look at the draught it's got," and he pointed down into the clear water.

Jusuf saw the glint of small fish darting here and there against the dark grey-brown sludge at the bottom, the water clearly no more than waist deep. He looked again at the long and broad quaysides, then at the large two-storey buildings facing onto them. Finally, he shrugged.

"Maybe you ought to ask."

A young, black-robed monk stood nearby, directing two lads in the loading of the handcart.

Rodrigo drew him into discourse, a smile slowly growing on the monk's face as he pointed towards the North. When they'd finished, Rodrigo seemed surprised as he came back to Jusuf and stared down into the water again.

"Tin mining," he said. "The brother told me that until about a hundred years ago this was known as 'The Port of Fawi', one of the busiest along the south coast. It was from here that most of the tin was carried out, and what made Lostwithiel Cornwall's capital. He said seagoing vessels could ply their way to and from here, up and down the river on the high tide."

"But it's high tide now, and the river's not that deep."

"It isn't now, Jusuf, no, but it used to be a lot deeper." He barked a short laugh. "It seems that what raised Lostwithiel's fortunes also diminished them: the tin, Jusuf, the tin."

When Jusuf only stared blankly at him, Rodrigo explained: "I've learnt that tin's mined by washing the loose spoil off into a nearby stream. What they never put a thought to, though, was what happens to the spoil after that. Well, it eventually gets carried down into the rivers, of course...like this one." Rodrigo pointed into the water. "And that's what that is: hundreds of years of silt, washed down from off the moors north of here."

Jusuf stared at Rodrigo. "Sounds a bit like digging your own grave! And, well, strikes me there's a lesson somewhere in that tale. It's weird, though. I never realised this was the part of *Inglaterra* where all the tin I use comes from," but then movement stirred about them.

The baggage had finally been loaded, the monks already stepping out along the quayside, the two lads drawing the handcart falling in behind. Rodrigo and

Jusuf followed at the rear as the quayside led them all out into a narrow street that ran between low, grey rubble-stone houses. Jusuf only got a brief look, however, before the party ahead turned off. They dipped into a low arched passage beneath the upper storey of one of the first properties.

Beyond it and down a narrow alley, they came to the crossing of a wider street. Here, they turned north onto its busier way, its throng of townsfolk readily stepping aside. But Jusuf's gaze was drawn above the bobbing heads of the monks, up beyond the roofs of the tight-pressed buildings further down the long curving street, and he drew in a sharp breath.

A spire, like the point of an upthrust spear, seemed to float in the air above the town, reaching high into the fleeting grey sky. It appeared to beckon them on until briefly obscured as they came between two facing gable walls at the end of the street.

But as they walked out into another but busier and broader one, Jusuf had to stop and stare. Before him, reaching up from within its sacred patch of open ground and high above everything else around, rose a huge and mighty Christian church.

Rodrigo's calls eventually nudged Jusuf's wonder aside, bringing his gaze lower, to where his companion now stood before an arched gate in a low wall on the other side of the street, urging him over.

When Jusuf joined him, Rodrigo suggested Jusuf wait with the cart and its two attendants, whilst he caught up with the monks, at whom he then pointed. They were entering the church by a long porch, jutting out from its south aisle.

"These lads have just told me," Rodrigo said, nodding towards the cart's attendants, "that Dom

Francisco and his travelling companion had to come upriver shortly after putting in at Foy, to catch the tide. So this is their first chance to give thanks to God for their safe passage. And you know, I think I'd like to give thanks to God myself, Jusuf, for having put us on the same path as the brothers. At least now we're not likely to get lost."

Jusuf smiled and nodded, then watched Rodrigo hurry along the path to the church. As he disappeared inside, Jusuf felt eyes upon him. He turned to find himself held in the cold stares of the two young lads. A chill ran up his back, his wary eyes searching out the look on the faces of those passing by.

He felt a little easier, a little less alone, when he found nothing more than curiosity. The older ones even returned him the odd nod.

Jusuf breathed in deeply before walking a little way into a lane that ran beside the west wall of the churchyard. He stopped and gazed along it, beyond where it passed beneath the spire and on towards yet more town properties. He then sat down on a raised tuft of grass, apart from the cart, and leant back against the wall, his shoulder bag safely between his legs.

The warmth of a suddenly freed sun struck his face, lifting both his gaze and his spirits. The morning's curtain of grey cloud had finally been swept aside by the hot and high sun's beam, casting Jusuf's shadow dark against the bright dirt of the lane at his dusty feet. And sitting there, warming his bones, he again breathed in deeply, and this time waited.

"You nodding off?" Rodrigo's voice eventually challenged.

Jusuf opened an eye and peered up at him as Rodrigo leant down, nearer Jusuf's ear.

"I wouldn't, not if you want to hang on to that bag of yours—and what's inside," and they both looked down at it, the shoulder strap fortunately still looped around Jusuf's leg.

"Maybe," Jusuf said, "your thanks to your God have placed a blessing upon it," and he grinned up at his companion's narrowing eyes. Then he looked around, realising they were alone. "Where's your monks…and the cart?"

"The brothers have gone on by a door on the north side. They waved the cart on to them, but for some reason you didn't seem to notice," and Rodrigo grinned knowingly as he offered Jusuf his hand.

"I wouldn't want to bring you any more pain, Rodrigo," and Jusuf pushed himself to his feet unaided, hoisting the bag carefully onto his shoulder.

When they got to the end of the lane, the monks were well ahead. Jusuf could see them further down the wider street they'd turned into, already beyond the end of the churchyard's northern wall and between the press of yet more huddled houses. Jusuf reckoned they were heading back in the direction of the river.

Indeed, a long stone bridge, stretching out over the river beyond the last of the buildings, eventually did come into sight as they caught up with the monks. The cart rumbled on whilst the brothers turned in through a low and wide doorway into an inn.

Rodrigo and Jusuf followed, Jusuf having to bob under the door lintel before he straightened and cracked his head against a ceiling beam. He cursed under his breath, a musty smell then assailing his nose whilst he stood still behind Rodrigo, his eyes slowly adjusting to the gloom.

He could hear a solicitous voice at the head of

their halted party, rising above the hushed mumblings of the clearly packed inn. Somewhere, a small dog yelped, then a remote peal of laughter cut through the clammy air before Rodrigo's dark shape moved on. Jusuf lowered his head and cautiously followed.

Two rooms, dimly lit by daylight, passed either side, giving a brief glimpse into their close press of drinkers, some straining to see the new arrivals, others hunched over their food. At the end of a barely lit passage, they turned into a bright and airy room at thc rear of the inn.

Its window shutters were all thrown back, sunlight slanting in through the openings along the southern wall, adding a golden glow to a long table and its benches. An enclosed cobbled yard could be seen through the openings in the eastern wall, voices and the recognisable clatter of a kitchen drifting in on the now warm, early afternoon air. It reminded Jusuf just how hungry he'd become.

"Should we be here?" he whispered to Rodrigo as he noticed the handcart being drawn into the yard outside.

"Dom Francisco insisted we join them in their late breaking of their fast," Rodrigo whispered back. "I get the feeling he's making some kind of point to his Canon hosts."

"What makes you say that?"

"Because he assured me the cost wouldn't come out of our own purses."

"In which case, I'll wager the Canons are paying."

"I'd say, by the look on Brother Thomas's face, you're probably right, Jusuf."

As they waited to be the last to sit down at the table, Jusuf asked Rodrigo if he knew how far they'd yet to walk for Bodmyn. Rodrigo told him he'd heard Brother Thomas tell Dom Francisco that it was five and a half miles.

"I hope we're not long eating, then," Jusuf said. "We've still to find Mistress Trewin once we get there, which somehow I don't think we ought to be doing in the dark."

They ended up sitting facing one another across the table, at the end nearest the door. Dom Francisco and Brother Thomas sat by the embers of the fire at the other, the remaining few monks in between. A succession of serving girls, their rose-red faces brightly scrubbed clean, came in with bowls of broth and baskets of bread, carefully placed before each man. Then they brought in beer, and a tankard of small ale for Jusuf.

Once the girls had left, Brother Thomas brought his hands together, all but Jusuf immediately bowing their heads. Slow to realise, he was about to do the same when he noticed Dom Francisco place his hand on Brother Thomas's arm to stay him.

He said something in English, to which Brother Thomas's mouth shrank to a thin line across his now pale face as he held the Dom in his unblinking gaze.

In a whisper, Rodrigo told Jusuf what Dom Francisco had said, translating it as: "Perhaps we may allow our heathen guest's own Allah be included in our gratitude for this fine repast before us," which surprised and shocked Jusuf.

An ominous silence remained in the air, until Brother Thomas lightly coughed before briefly dipping his head in acquiescence. Jusuf caught enough of his dry response to know he'd passed the saying of grace on to Dom Francisco himself. The man smiled as he tilted his own head in acceptance. Then he turned to the table and made the sign of the cross before him.

"Bless this, O Lord," Rodrigo again translated, "and thou, *Allahumma*, who art His own servant, and these, Thy gifts, which we are *all* about to receive from Thy bounty, and by it save us *all* from the punishment of everlasting hellfire. Through Christ, our Lord. Amen."

All those present softly, albeit somewhat hesitantly, chorused "Amen", all except Jusuf. He dared a look at Dom Francisco. The smile he found in the man's eyes seemed so freely given that Jusuf found himself raising his head into the continuing silence and loudly speaking the word "Amen", clear for all to hear.

Amidst the room's still persisting silence, Dom Francisco quietly took up his spoon and began eating, a veil of innocence obscuring his features.

For some time the room filled only with the subdued sounds of their fast being broken before discourse again arose, clearly mere pleasantries and largely between the two senior brothers. Jusuf strained to understand any of it, catching only the odd word or two here and there. But eventually, Rodrigo leant forward, distracting Jusuf from his broth.

"They've just been talking about some unrest," he whispered, "and strangely enough in English, not their common Latin tongue. Something about a…a rebellion."

"A rebellion? Where?"

"*Here.*"

"What? In Cornwall? But—"

Rodrigo quietly shushed him, clearly again cocking his ear.

"Brother Thomas has been telling Dom Francisco that an army of some five thousand Cornishmen set out from Bodmyn only last week." He paused again, his eyes widening the more as he listened.

"He says they're marching on *Londres*, to petition the *inglês* sovereign, King Henry. Something about *Escócia* and some unjust taxes."

Jusuf's mouth dropped open, then his own eyes widened. "*Londres*? But that's where the captain should be by now."

"Indeed, and it's clearly why there's been all the toing and froing in Foy, why there was so much heated discussion." He sat back, slowly shaking his head. "The land's been alive with rebellion, Jusuf. Rebellion, do you hear, ever since we landed here," then he seemed to become aware of his rising voice. "But by the Gods," he strained to whisper, "we poor damned *foreigners* seem to be the last two to know anything at all about it!"

13 A BODMYN SMITHY

"It more than likely explains *Senhora* Trewin's urgent need of a blacksmith," Jusuf said to Rodrigo as they climbed what they'd been told was the road up Bodmyn Hill, although it had turned into more of a track not long after leaving Lostwithiel.

"I'm sorry we didn't get a quiet word with Dom Francisco, seeing the Canon brothers seem so wary of talking to me about what's going on. But you're probably right, *Senhora* Trewin's husband will almost certainly have gone off with the Cornish force. After all, armies always have need of blacksmiths."

The hill wasn't steep, but the sharp and loosened black stones of the road's potholed and rutted surface steadily bruised Jusuf's feet through his soft-soled boots. It didn't help that somehow he seemed intent on standing on those stones dislodged by the wheels of the handcart ahead of them.

They'd also seen nothing of the countryside, not over the unbroken high hedgebanks that seemed to hem in all highways in what they'd so far seen of

Cornwall. Here, though, unlike around Foy, old and twisted trees, growing from the tops of the banks, kept them yet more removed. These trees also sheltered the road, denying Jusuf the direct warmth of the sun he'd so enjoyed on their way out of Lostwithiel.

Ahead of their party, where the road seemed to level and become straighter, Jusuf noticed a stationary wagon and its team of donkeys facing towards them. Dust rose into the air beyond it, and Jusuf could see what looked like men labouring there. The handcart came to a halt as the monks squeezed past the wagon, between its sizeable bulk and the brambled and tormentil-covered hedgebanks.

As Jusuf and Rodrigo also reached the rear of the wagon, they found men raking out a new road surface. A labourer in the back of the wagon stopped shovelling ballast out when he saw that Brother Thomas had halted to talk with one of them. He leant against his shovel but then narrowed his eyes at Jusuf and watched him gingerly walk on along the edge of the loose stones and earth.

Brother Thomas shouted something back to the handcart attendants, then fell into further discussion with a man who seemed to be in charge. In the meantime, Dom Francisco casually wandered over to Jusuf and Rodrigo as everyone else stood around and waited.

"It seems our baggage," the Dom told them in Arabic, "is proving a bit of a problem. From what I can gather, if they move the wagon down to where the road's wide enough for the handcart to come past, the wagon will then have to carry on by a long roundabout way to get back here. This should prove to be interesting, for the work seems to have the authority of Brother Thomas's own priory behind it.

So, I suspect we could be here for a little while yet." He grinned as he looked past Jusuf at the two men, clearly both digging in their heels when Jusuf also turned to look.

After a while, Dom Francisco asked, "Have you got somewhere to stay in Bodmyn, Jusuf al-Haddad? An inn perhaps, or maybe with this young wife of the blacksmith you're visiting, the one *Senhor* Fernandez, here, told me about, down at the quay." Jusuf wondered what the man could possibly be thinking now.

Rodrigo assured him they had the name of two good inns, but that they were hoping to search out *Senhora* Trewin first. That was if they got there before dark, he pointedly added. He then looked askance at Brother Thomas and his prospective combatant, each now pointing a finger at the other.

Dom Francisco softly called out "Brother Hammett," and the young monk from whom Rodrigo had learnt so much about the mining of tin stepped across, crunching on the newly spread ballast.

"Dom Francisco?"

As the two men fell into discourse with Rodrigo, Jusuf again cursed his slow-wittedness with the English tongue, although he heard *Senhora* Trewin's name and the English word "Smithy" a few times.

Finally, Rodrigo turned back to Jusuf and told him that Brother Hammett was to show them to *Senhora* Trewin's when, or as he then corrected himself to say "If", they ever got to Bodmyn. This time they both turned to stare at Brother Thomas's even redder face, somehow reflected in the supervisor's own.

Dom Francisco stepped over to join the two men, a benign smile hiding the sparkle in his eyes as he spoke with them both. Brother Thomas presently fell silent, staring into the Dom's placid eyes, then he nodded, the once, and withdrew.

Once Dom Francisco and Brother Thomas had returned to the head of their reassembling party, Jusuf said to Rodrigo "Come on, then, what did he say?"

"That he and his companion could do without their baggage, until it might catch up with them. So the handcart can wait for the wagon to work its way down to where they're able to pass one another."

One of the brothers remained behind with the cart when the rest of their party carried on up the hill. The clatter of the cart's descent was soon consumed by the sound of road ballast once again being shovelled from the wagon.

Jusuf had expected a descent shortly after the road became level, but it carried on flat for some time, again winding its way between obscuring hedgebanks. When it did eventually show signs of dropping, it was only gradual, but gave occasional glimpses towards the northeast of a distant, higher ground, somewhere bare of trees.

Bodmyn, though, lay in the North, the road's last couple of miles hardly taking them much lower. So they had no sight of the town, not until they drew near its first few properties along the road as their party slipped into a shallow valley. But here the hedgebanks finally gave out, laying open an untilled rise of heathland to one side but a lower expanse of grass and trees to the other. Within this, Jusuf glimpsed large, stout stone buildings laced by tall windows, a tower rising from amidst them all. A way beyond this rose a tall spire, like some great ladder vanishing towards the heavens.

His view quickly fell behind the first huddle of

buildings lining the road, then behind more, until the familiar jostle of properties reminded Jusuf of Lostwithiel. The town didn't seem quite as busy, though, perhaps less mercantile. Then they rounded a bend onto a wide but quiet descending street, rows of houses clumped along both sides.

At its end lay a broad junction of four ways, on the other side of which rose a fair-sized church, from which the spire Jusuf had seen earlier rose high above the surrounding roofs. Now, though, the clear view revealed just how inordinately high it really was, far more so than the already impressive loft of Lostwithiel's own church spire.

"Our church of Saint Petroc," Brother Hammett told them, even Jusuf recognising some clearly unchristian pride in his voice. "And where we three must part company with my brothers if I'm to take you to the Trewin smithy." This latter somehow came more intelligibly to Jusuf's ears.

As the other brothers carried on down the road that ran past the south side of the church, Brother Hammett led them up a short but steep cobbled rise beside its west front. At the top, they turned onto a gentle incline between small and haphazardly placed houses, mostly single storeyed, many set apart from their neighbours.

At times broad, and at others tightly squeezed between gable ends, the busier street ran straight in its aim towards the west. Eventually, though, Brother Hammett brought them to a halt before a low and seemingly jumbled building on its northern side. It immediately said "Smithy" to Jusuf. At its centre stood a ridged barn, an attached low cottage to one side, a smaller square building to the other—a forge,

Jusuf realised from its chimney stack.

"Is Mistress Trewin expecting your visit?" the brother asked them, to which Rodrigo shook his head. "In which case, perhaps I ought to raise her for you," and he stared at Jusuf for a moment before pursing his lips and nodding to himself.

He stepped from the dirt of the street onto an area of quarry-stone flags set before the barn's large door, then rapped smartly on a wicket one set within it. A voice called from somewhere within, a young woman's voice. Then the sound of boots on a stone floor escaped through the gaps between the door's plain planks.

"Who be it, there?" Jusuf managed to understand, along with Brother Hammett's reply of his own name. A bolt could be heard being thrust back, then the door cracked open a touch and an eye peered out at the brother. It soon looked past him, directly at Jusuf as it grew wide in alarm.

Brother Hammett said something more in English, or it could have been *Kernowek*, and the eye's gaze returned to him, albeit briefly. Finally, it settled back on Jusuf.

"A blacksmith?" he understood her to ask. "A Blackamoor blacksmith? He'm be no Turkoman, be he?" which he didn't quite follow.

This time Rodrigo spoke to her, and at some length, until he mentioned *Capitão* Treffry. He had to clarify it to "Captain Treffry" before the alarm finally drained from the woman's eye and her voice lightened.

That eye then dipped, clearly carried upon a nod, and the door creaked open. Then Colin gasped a sharp intake of breath at the sight of Kate, standing there, as plain as day in the open doorway.

14 GATEWAY TO CORNWALL

"At least let me write it down," Kate said to Colin as she leant forward in her armchair, pen poised above the pad on her knee.

"I've told you the important bit, Kate. There's no point in going over the rest of it."

"But I'd—"

"Don't you see? It's the conclusive proof I've been looking for. The lie to my own deception. I mean, how else could you be there *and* here. It just doesn't make sense otherwise."

"Well, it could be that—"

"When I saw you there, I knew it had to be some kind of illusion, something conjured up from my…from my subconscious. An hallucination, nothing more. A waking dream. Or… like you called it yourself, back when it first happened: a *phantasm*."

Colin sighed as he leant his head back against the sofa and stared up at the ceiling. "And anyway, I've fooled myself enough to feel like I've walked miles today. My feet ache. The power of self-deception, eh?" He lowered his gaze to Kate and she opened her mouth, as if to speak.

"Can we just leave it?" he quietly implored. She hesitated, but then nodded.

"Do you want a drink?" she finally asked.

"No. Thanks. I think I could do with just going up to bed. Thank God it's Friday. I feel like I need a week's rest, never mind just a weekend."

Once they were both in bed and the lights out, the curtains dully lit by a nearby streetlamp, Colin found the image of Kate standing in the smithy doorway plaguing his mind. He realised just how jarring it had been: to be convinced of one reality one minute, only to have another smash in on it the next. He could tell from Kate's breathing that she wasn't asleep, too still beside him, clearly thinking. Then she propped herself up on one elbow. He could feel her eyes upon him, searching out his features.

"Colin?"

"Hmm?"

"I'd like to know what happened before you saw me? Just to stop me wondering. You can do that for me, can't you?"

A sliver of orange light lay at a slant across the ceiling, coming in through where the curtains didn't quite meet. It wavered slightly as the night air wafted in through the partially open window, nudging the curtains.

"What? Now?"

"It's not too late, and we don't have to be up early in the morning."

Colin knew it couldn't be avoided. He didn't want to hurt Kate's feelings. So he pushed himself further up the bed, pulling his pillow higher behind his head, and quietly took a long breath.

"I'm sorry," he eventually said, hardly above a whisper. "It was just such a shock. You were the last person I expected to see. But it wasn't just that you were there, Kate. I felt that shock of recognition actually course through Jusuf himself."

She laid her hand on his chest, her fingers lightly running through the sparse few hairs it boasted. "I don't quite follow," she said. "Jusuf's recognition?"

"It's not easy to explain, but if Jusuf really did once exist, and I was experiencing his life through him, then why would he have been so startled at the sight of you? Because he was. Me, yes, certainly, but he would never have seen you before, wouldn't have known you from Adam."

When Kate said nothing, Colin searched out the glint of her eyes in the darkness. "That's what I meant by 'Proof'," he finally told her. "Jusuf's clear recognition of you could only really have been my own. Therefore, Jusuf could only ever have been me, all along; me just fooling myself; 'Q', 'E', 'D'."

Kate laid back down and cuddled up beside him, her arm across his chest, her hand this time stroking his arm. "So," she whispered, "tell me about your…your *dream*, then," and he did, knowing full well she'd remember it all, every last detail. Just as he would himself, yet easier this time, now content it really had been nothing more than a weird dope trip.

In the morning, before they went out to do the weekly shop, Colin nipped into the front room and put the joss sticks and the holder at the back of the cupboard beside the fireplace, along with the small box of dope. And there they stayed, well out of sight and so out of mind, as the summer rolled on to a rather cold and wet first few days of August.

"You can never tell," Kate said as they were packing in their bedroom, the evening before their overnight drive down to Cornwall to avoid the traffic. "It tends to have its own weather down there, right on the coast. We always used to take the forecasts with a pinch of salt. I remember us quite often coming up from a sweltering day on the beach only to find it had been pissing it down just inland."

Kate dropped another bag at his feet. "Don't worry. I've only one last big one, then it's just bits and bats...honest." Her pixie grin shone from beneath her new pageboy haircut. "Oh, and I found this." She handed him his dope box, its lid's psychedelic 3D pattern shimmering in the evening light.

He rattled it.

"There's still some left. Thought you might fancy a spliff or two in the evenings. There's bugger all else to do there once it's gone dark, apart from going to the pub or staying in to read."

"*Nothing* else?" and Colin slipped a sly grin onto his face, getting another one of Kate's pixie looks in return as she added, "Well, there is stargazing when it's clear."

He managed to get their little Fiat coupe packed whilst it was still light, everything squeezed in with military precision. Its small boot soon filled up, the two excuses for rear seats likewise quickly overflowing with bags and boxes and overlaid with bedding. "Self-catering," he muttered to himself when he checked and found he could no longer see anything through the rear-view mirror.

Come one o'clock in the morning, he fired up the car's sportily rasping engine and drove them away from their now dark and secured house, through the quiet neighbourhood streets and out onto the motorway. Before long, a completely empty M6 stretched ahead of them, through the almost dark Cheshire countryside. The car gabbled away to itself as Colin gave it its head, streaking towards the dark blue hem of the southern summer sky.

The exciting prospect of discovering a wholly new place kept Colin company when Kate eventually fell asleep, somewhere not far north of Birmingham. He glanced at the tripometer: seventy-six miles, and did a quick subtraction from three hundred. Exactly, door to door, Kate had told him. Then he worked his way through his tapes of "New Order", "Prefab Sprout" and a few other New Wave bands.

Apart from a single distant set of taillights, glimpsed somewhere around Glastonbury, Colin never saw another vehicle until Exeter, where the motorway finally handed over to a dual carriageway. They'd not stopped once, the tank still a quarter full as they climbed a steep but fast incline towards a noticeably lightening sky.

"Telegraph Hill," Kate surprised Colin by saying, and she stretched as best she could in the car's close confines. "It used to be a slow climb up here when it was the old road, stuck behind caravans and coaches. When I think back: the journey down was a full day's drive then, early morning start, late night finish, picnics on the way. A real adventure."

The dual carriageway's rollercoaster run, with its dips and brows and sweeping bends—and the odd sharp one to keep him awake—finally saw the low-fuel light come on. Its glow seemed to accentuate the darkness beyond the car's headlights.

"Er, Kate? Every garage we've passed so far has been closed, not that I've seen that many."

"Everywhere down here shuts at ten."

"Eh?"

"I told you it was a different world."

"Shit," and Colin eased off the throttle.

When they eventually got to a long gentle descent towards a distant glow of sodium light against the brightening dawn sky, the low-fuel light had begun to flash. A sign for an exit slip appeared up ahead: "Plymouth, 1 mile". Then he remembered they were now in a "Different world".

"Kate?"

"Yes?"

"Does that ten o'clock closing time apply to Plymouth?"

The road into the city not only ran past a couple more closed petrol stations but also a long stretch of water, what Colin assumed was a first hint of the coastline awaiting them. The river Plym, Kate told him, although to Colin it looked too broad for a river.

It wasn't until she'd directed him through the deserted streets of the city, past the Barbican and out towards the ferry for Cornwall, that an open garage finally appeared. Relief flooded through Colin as he pulled up on its forecourt. When he got out to fill up, though, the sweet, rounded warmth of the heavier dawn air surprised him. It conjured boyhood memories of Mediterranean holidays with his parents.

After he'd filled up, paid, found out there was no toilet, and was driving them off, Kate told him they were now in Stonehouse. "You remember?" she said, "where mum's Aunt Bella's flat used to be. Where the…the joss stick holder came from."

"Oh, right," Colin said as he wound his window down to let in some more of that strong impression of being abroad.

Before long they were into Devonport, the signs for the ferry taking them off down a short, steep hill into a large and deserted tarmacked area. Marked out into about half a dozen long lanes, a traffic light gantry ran across the far end. The one marked with a number "1" showed a green light. Beyond it and through a gateway, an illuminated sign declared "Ferry This Way", complete with a helpful arrow. Beside this stood what looked like a Berlin Wall watchtower.

"Just go straight through under the green light and follow that yellow arrow," Kate told him, and he grinned and asked at what point they'd have to show their passports.

They came straight onto the top of a wide and empty concrete ramp that slipped straight down into the lapping water's edge of a broad river or estuary. As Kate clarified it was the River Tamar, Colin stopped the car and stared out at their first open view since sunrise.

Bathed in a pearlescent light, the river seemed a cleaner blue and silver than Colin ever remembered seeing from within these his own shores. Its body of water appeared more immediate, as though flowing through his seemingly lighter heart. The sky looked closer, its few clouds a brighter white, slipping more fluidly through the sharper edge of its salt-laden breath.

"And that's Torpoint on the other side," Kate added, nodding across the water at a jumbled mound of buildings on the far side, most tinted pink by the rising sun. Colin at last pulled his thoughts from the arms of this strangely seductive view's promise.

"So…so where's the ferry?"

"It's there," and she pointed.

"Where? I can't see one."

"Can you see that building next to—"

"Hey! Just a minute. Something's moving over there," and Colin peered more intently. "You don't mean that shed, there, do you?" and he too pointed. Kate burst out laughing, then choked it back when she stared at his confused face, until she couldn't help but laugh again.

"What?" but she only shook her head as she tried to get her breath back.

After maybe four or five minutes, a large blue and white pontoon affair with tall, narrow superstructures down each side—one topped by yet another suggestion of a watchtower—neared the concrete ramp. When the ferry at last nudged against it, a man in Hi-Viz wandered out on deck. He swung back two gates that ran across the nearest end, opening the way from its four short lanes of floating road for the half-dozen cars aboard. Meanwhile, its wide, uplifted ramp-of-a-nose had steadily lowered, clattering against the concrete slope. The man waved the cars off, and their little Fiat on.

"Off you go, then," Kate said. "Our gateway to Cornwall awaits us. Oh, and we don't have to pay going *in*, only on the way out," and she grinned, knowingly.

"Great," Colin said, feeling he was beginning to get a sense of what Kate really meant when she talked about this remote corner of their country. Intrigue, but then mixed with a little trepidation, stirred in his soul as he slipped the car into first gear and revved its eager little engine. As he drove them down to board the ferry, though, he anxiously asked, "They do have a loo on this thing, don't they?"

15 DONKEY LANE

A loud and pervasive clatter and clank reverberated around Colin as he got back in the car, relief at last plastered across his face. By now a couple of other vehicles had also driven aboard, clearly more than enough for the ferry to make its next crossing.

"Better?" Kate asked.

"Much," and Colin realised they were rocking in time to the tune of what he took to be the ferry clawing itself across the river by its chains—an oddly pleasant feeling. Then, in the wing mirror, came confirmation: the shore slowly slipping away behind.

"What time is it, Colin? I haven't got my watch on."

He checked the dash clock. "Er, nearly quarter to six."

Kate's brows were furrowed when she turned to look at him. "We did set off at one, didn't we?"

"Yeah, bang on. Not a bad time, eh? Just over four and a half hours."

"Christ, Colin, Dad never did it in less than six. You must've been motoring."

"No, just steady. It was the empty roads that did it;

honest, Officer," but then he couldn't help but remember the full day it had taken Jusuf and Rodrigo just to get from Fowey to Bodmin, a mere tenth of the distance they'd just completed. Then he realised he'd not thought of them for quite a while.

It wasn't long before they were climbing through Torpoint, past another couple of closed petrol stations then out onto a fast, tree lined main road, heading west. Before long, they'd turned off, south between rolling fields and to what Kate said was the start of the coast road. And then there it was, before them: a glittering grey expanse of ocean.

"Oh, I always love this first sight of the sea," Kate enthused. "I really feel my holiday's begun when I see that view. And what's more, it looks like it's going to be a nice day, as well."

Eventually, as they forged on along the high clifftop road, Colin spotted a speckle of pastel-coloured properties littering a blunt and rounded headland not that much further along.

"Nearly there," Kate said, staring that same way, her face lit with anticipation.

They weren't long swapping the coast road for a tarmacked track, then the grass of a field that shushed beneath the car, before finally coming to a halt in front of a rickety and overgrown picket fence. Low down behind it stood a small green hut, roofed in lichen-embossed corrugated-iron. A light-grey stone wall ran past behind, bramble-choked and timeless.

The "Chalet" looked very old, though warm and welcoming, in a rustic kind of way. The side facing them had a single small window midway along and a door at one end. Beside the door hung a sun-bleached sign, identifying the attached abode as "Downfield".

"Dad said he'd leave the key under the shed," Kate said, opening her door.

"The shed has a shed?" Colin marvelled, then noticed it amongst a patch of nettles in the corner of the plot, its furthest end up against the wall. It had two doors. "Don't tell me: that's also the loo."

"Far door," and she slammed the car's own before heading through where a gate had once stood.

Eventually, rubbing at a nettle sting, Colin at last unlocked the chalet's door, pushing it open against a cagoule-swathed row of coat hooks and the escape of its imprisoned warmth.

Inside, he found a close embrace of mellow light, filtering in through the pale-yellow fabric of daintily rose-printed curtains. Beneath them stood a narrow folding table, an upright chair to either side, a sofa-divan against one wall, an electric fire against another.

"All mod-cons," Colin said as Kate slid back the curtains, the improved light revealing an opening in the wall opposite and closed doors at either end of the room. Kate slipped through the opening, the sound of running water then disturbing the previously un-breathed air. Colin peered in after her at a galley kitchen that seemed somehow more suited to a narrowboat.

"Cosy," he this time said, and she pecked him on his lips.

"Soon feel like home," she assured him as she unplugged a kettle and swung it under the flow of the solitary tap.

"Ah, so we do have electricity. In which case, I'll go unpack."

Where everything went, he wasn't sure. A chest of drawers in one miniature bunkbed-filled bedroom, the surplus on the bunks themselves, and some in a narrow wardrobe in the other slightly larger but double-bed-filled bedroom. Eventually, though, they both sat with their black teas on the sofa and enjoyed the balm of the chalet's perfect peace and quiet—and its simple charm, Colin finally had to admit.

"Are you okay after your drive?" Kate asked. "Do you want me to make up the bed, so you can have a few hours' kip?"

"No, I'll be fine on the sofa, thanks. Just need to stretch out for a couple of hours, then get out to stretch my legs. Somewhere that'll have Rizlas, if possible."

"Well, we do need a few other things, like fresh milk, unless you're happy with black tea and coffee until Monday. So we could go down into Millbrook after you've had a rest."

And so, later that morning, Kate showed Colin the way to the nearest large village. They went a little way along the coast road at first, then inland. "The short way," she'd said, "through the back lanes."

The first, apparently, was Donkey Lane, not only a steep descent but barely wider than the Fiat, the poor car's flanks coming in for a bit of a whipping from the roadside growth. But then Colin's concerns for his car's paintwork gave way to a disturbing familiarity: the high brambled and tormentil-covered hedgebanks, the overarching shade of bordering trees, the morning's growing close-heat, the tang of salt and seaweed and dry dusty fields hanging so intimately in the bright but mellow air.

The slide of locked tyres on gravelly tarmac and the squeal of brake discs quickly brought absolute stillness to Colin's world. Dimly aware of a yelp of surprise and the engine's now burbling tick-over, he could only sit and stare out through the windscreen, at the descent of the winding lane before him.

Then came the pap of a horn, and he realised Kate had been saying "What's wrong, Colin, are you all right?" before he noticed a car faced them. It had been up close but currently juddered slowly back down the hill in reverse. A more urgent blare of its horn finally dragged him firmly back to the here-and-now.

"Oh. Shit. Er, hang on. Didn't we just come past a passing place?" and he stared a little wildly into Kate's eyes.

"Yeah…yes, yes we did, just before the last bend," and Colin saw confusion marring her face.

He swivelled around, peered through the rear window and slammed the car into reverse, revving hard as he sent the Fiat whining back up the hill and niftily into a space before a field gate. After a distant grinding of gears and the over-revving of a small engine, the other car eventually wheezed past, its driver staring daggers at them both.

"Are you sure you're all right to drive, Colin?" Kate asked, clearly worried. Colin, though, couldn't get his words past his memory of Brother Thomas's reddened face, that time the man had stood toe-to-toe with the road leveller.

"We can't stay here, Colin. We're in a passing place."

He nodded, unable to face her, but managed to find his voice. "I'm all right. It was just…just a bit of a sort of flashback. You know, to…to that business with Jusuf." He tried to swallow, his mouth too dry, the feel of Kate's gaze scrutinising his face, but he still couldn't bring himself to look at her. "Is… Is Millbrook far?"

"No. Not far at all," she said, a little warily.

"Okay, then. Let's get there, get what we need, then find a pub. I reckon I could do with a drink…and…and a bit of a think."

Although probably no more than a mile, the rest of the way to Millbrook took them down even more disconcertingly familiar lanes. It wasn't the places themselves as such but more their claustrophobic evocations of somewhere he'd convinced himself he'd never been. And he didn't dare admit, not even to himself, how relieved he felt when they at last emerged into the narrow but bright streets of the village and found somewhere to park.

They walked back, past what looked like a nineteen-fifties film-set garage—complete with pump attendant and car repair business—through a narrow alley and out into a barely wider street of shops. There, Colin spotted a pub, already open despite it only being a little after eleven, and a Spar, towards which Kate carried on.

He called after her, and she stopped and turned. "I need to stretch my legs. Would you mind getting me twenty Silk Cut Purple and some green Rizla?"

"Okay," she said, a little uncertainly. "I'll meet you in there, then, when I'm done," and she pointed at the pub opposite's open door. Colin nodded and turned to note the name above its door: appropriately enough, the Devon & Cornwall. Kate had already vanished into the shop when Colin came to look around at the village, wondering where to wander first.

A bit of peace and quiet seemed best, so he slipped down the side of the shop, away from the main street. But then he stopped and stared at the close-facing properties lining the narrow street before him. At its end lay a junction, no doubt offering yet more keenly overlooking windows. Then he realised what it was about this place that unnerved him, other than a strange feeling he'd been somewhere like it before: it felt uncomfortably like being in someone else's living room.

Retracing his steps, he soon nipped in through the Devon & Cornwall's door, nearly falling over its bar. Beneath low ceiling beams, a small lounge opened out on one side, a taproom on the other, a table of local old ladies all sitting around their stouts, shopping bags at their feet, gabbing away unintelligibly. The lounge side stood temptingly empty.

"Morning," a Cockney voice greeted him, and on the other side of the bar the landlord's practiced smile awaited Colin's order.

"Good morning. Er," and Colin looked from one pump to the next. "A pint of Tribute and a gin and tonic, please."

"Ice and lemon?"

"If you would."

"Down on holiday?" the man asked as he drew Colin's pint, but as he was answering, Kate came in with a carrier bag full of shopping.

They presently sat at a window table in the lounge side, Colin's upper lip cooling beneath its borrowed beer-head moustache. He wiped the back of his hand across his mouth and sighed as Kate sipped her drink.

"Oh, that's good," he said and twisted to look out of the window at the deep shadows slanting across the brightly sunlit street. When the rather mundane view held his gaze overly long, Kate put her drink down carefully on its beer mat and rested her hand on his.

"So, Colin," she quietly said, "what was all that about back at Donkey Lane? You went as white as a sheet, never mind slamming the brakes on for no good reason."

Finally, he looked at her, but found his lips refusing to part company, clamped to a thin line.

"You scared the shit out of me, do you know that?"

He nodded, then dropped his gaze to his pint. "It was weird, Kate. I can't explain it. That view down the lane… Well, it was like…like déjà vu, but really strong. You know, more than just a feeling." When he finally raised his gaze to her eyes, he found none of the disbelief he'd expected.

"When we've drunk up," she said, "let's go back to the chalet the long way, on the newer, wider roads—and I've something to show you."

However much he knitted his brows and stared at her, she'd say no more. So they quietly drank up in the cool shade of the pub, before returning to the stifling heat of their car, baking under a now scorching midday Cornish sun.

16 PROOF POSITIVE

They drove out of Millbrook and around the south shore of a lake dotted with small boats. Its twisting shoreline took them past a few Victorian villas set within large and well-tended gardens, then beneath a wooded hill and finally onto a climb between steep-sided fields. An open stretch of road along the ridgetop above gave a wonderfully panoramic view back down to the village, and across open water beyond, to Torpoint and its ferry over to Devonport.

Colin felt they'd already been here for ages, as though the very lie of the land had somehow found its way into his blood. Then they were down onto the edge of what looked to him like a fishing village. The tortuous road that skirted above it gave glimpses down into its small bay and onto its higgledy-piggledy press of cottages.

It was all quickly behind them, and they were soon climbing a deep verdant valley and on to a sharp bend. Beyond it an expanse of ocean filled a startlingly broad and bright horizon, the high sun beaming down from within a cloudless blue sky, its gaze sprinkling the seemingly endless watery spread with ripples of diamonds. As Colin swung them onto a clifftop road and the curve of a long sweeping bay appeared before them, he gasped.

"Wow! What a view," and he slowed to take it in.

"Whitsand Bay," Kate told him, "and this is the other end of the coast road. And there, can you see?" and she pointed. "Dodman Point in the distance. Sometimes you can see The Lizard beyond it, but it's a bit too hazy for that now."

Only later, when Colin was opening the chalet's door, did he remember Kate's promise, but his reminder to her only brought the offer of tea first, and with milk this time. Whilst Kate clattered around in the galley, he sat beside the table, opened the window and looked out at the gulls wheeling above.

When she eventually placed their mugs of tea on the table, Kate wandered off into the small bedroom, clearly rummaging about. Colin slurped at his scalding tea, listening to the gulls' raucous cries until Kate finally came and sat down opposite him, something hidden in her hand.

She sipped her own tea before saying: "Some time ago, I remembered mum once telling me about someone in her family from way back when. It struck me it might be relevant. So, before they came down here, I asked if she'd search out a photo I knew she had. I think the last time I saw this, before she gave it to me in June, must've been when I was fourteen," and she placed a small, rather battered sepia coloured photograph on the table between them, facing Colin.

He leant forward and peered at it. "Bloody 'ell, Kate, but that's you," and he carefully lifted it closer to his eyes, flicking them between the sharp image and Kate's own face. The name within the broad white base of its frame said "John Hawke". Although in a florid script, he realised it had been printed, alongside an address in Plymouth.

He turned the photograph over to find a large ornate crest overarched by "PATRONIZED BY H.R.H. THE DUKE OF EDINBURGH", it's rather appropriate motto beneath reading: "LIGHT AND TRUTH". Under this was again printed: "J. Hawke. 8, George Street, PLYMOUTH.". Other than some information at the very bottom about negatives always being kept and future copies possible, the only other mark was an ink written number scratched in an upper corner.

"I can't believe how alike you are," he again marvelled, then the look on Kate's face brought him up short. Before he could say anything, she reached across and touched the photograph, where it still rested in his hand.

"I thought of this again when we were on our way through Devonport this morning. You see, when Mum found it for me and read the back, she got all nostalgic. She knew where George Street was. We passed the end of it not long before turning off for the ferry." Kate stroked the photograph before withdrawing her hand.

"Her name was Eleanor, although mum couldn't remember her surname. She thought it might have been Menhenick but wasn't sure; there were so many in her family. We reckoned it was taken sometime in the eighteen-nineties."

She took a longer swig of her tea. "Mum laughed that they always knew I was hers because of that photo, that there hadn't been a mix up at the hospital, seeing I don't look much like either her or my dad."

Colin again looked out at the seagulls wheeling past the window, then quietly said, "But remarkably like Mistress Trewin, eh, Kate?"

"I'm obviously a throwback to Eleanor, so… So, yes, why not to Mistress Trewin before her."

"But…" Colin began, then swigged down the last of his own now almost cold tea. "But that would mean—"

"That your conclusive proof is not necessarily conclusive." She smiled at him. "*I* couldn't be both here and back then in Jusuf's time, no, but my family line could. And I reckon it *was*, certainly from the look on your face this morning on Donkey Lane, then later in Millbrook. This, Colin, is not really your first visit to Cornwall…now, is it?"

"It would seem not," he quietly allowed as she rummaged in her bag beside her. She straightened and placed a couple of packets of green Rizla cigarette papers on the table before him. He stared at them as he finally lowered Eleanor's photograph, placing it neatly beside the Rizlas.

"Pity we don't have the joss sticks and the holder, then, otherwise…" but Kate got up and went back into the small bedroom. When those two very items appeared beside the photograph and cigarette papers, Colin sighed before turning Kate a lopsided grin.

"Let's take a walk on the beach," she said, brightly, "seeing the tide's still on its way out," and she tossed a tide table booklet onto the table as well, beside the other items. "Then we can come back up and have an early tea before you go find out what Jusuf's been up to since your last visit. How's that sound?" and he nodded, resignedly, looking forward more to the beach than anything else.

Kate smiled as she regarded him, then she leant across and kissed him sweetly on his lips, her evocative scent mingling with the warm summer breeze drifting in so temptingly through the open window.

17 OF SERVICE TO THE PRIORY

"I be finished wi' them there tats o' the Tremethyk's," Mistress Trewin announced as she bustled in to the hot smithy barn from her cottage, a bundle of clothes under one arm. "They be more rags than dillas," and she humphed, as though the task had sullied her hands.

At first, Colin stared uncomprehendingly at her as he lowered the cooling metal he'd been working, resting it carefully on the anvil before hefting his hammer to a looser grip in his other hand. Their gazes met for a moment, Jusuf again seeing what Rodrigo had meant about Mistress Trewin's elvish looks. But he then turned back to his work, picking up the dull red iron again in his tongs. As he carried it over to the raised brick hearth at the centre of the dimly lit forge, he marshalled an answer, as best he could.

"Master Fernandez said he be back mid-morning," and he thrust the metal into the glowing charcoal, laid the tongs and his hammer aside and began pumping the forge's bellows. The charcoal quickly glowed white.

"They be on bench for when him's back," she said from behind him, but then she was at his side, emptyhanded, staring at his sweat-glistening arm as it rhythmically worked air into the forge's fire. She noticed him catching her stare and looked away, across at his heap of charcoal.

"Need more bringing in?" she asked, and he too glanced at the pile. He nodded, a smile escaping the hold he'd had on his features. She turned for the backdoor, but then stopped at the sound of hurried footsteps approaching from the front. An out of breath Rodrigo rushed in through the open wicket door.

He said something in English, too quickly for Jusuf to catch, but then, as Mistress Trewin's hands shot to her mouth, said in Arabic: "Some men from the Cornish army are back, Jusuf."

Mistress Trewin was halfway into her coat before Rodrigo managed to say, "They were only passing through, *Senhora*, on their way to the priory. You'd be too late to catch them up by now."

"What did they say?" she urged as she slowly slipped her arm from the sleeve of her coat and hung the garment back up.

"From what I could gather, the men were injured from the march, not from any battle. They couldn't keep up so turned back. But people were saying they'd parted company just before Reading, and that the Cornishmen had got all that way without being challenged."

"Where's Reading?" Jusuf asked, to be told it lay about forty miles west of London. "So why haven't they been met by the king's army?"

"There's talk in the Taverns," Rodrigo said, "that it's in the North, marching to meet a threat from the *escocês*."

Mistress Trewin clearly recognised the Portuguese name. "They'm Scottish be the curse of us all," she almost spat. "What care be they of ours? They be hundreds of miles away. So why should we 'ave a tax brought down on us to pay for a fight against 'em, eh?" Through her anger, though, welled a vulnerability, her fears for her husband written plainly across her face and in the wringing of her hands.

"It'd serve the king right," she more quietly said, "if our men break in on him and force him to see reason. We ain't no hung boar him can bleed dry."

Jusuf had managed to follow enough of her words, and seen more than enough of the hurt in her eyes, that he couldn't help but stand before her, fighting back an urge to offer comfort. Instead, he fixed resolve onto his face and told her, "I have hinges done for Brother Jowan, sacrist at the priory. If I go fit them today, maybe I might learn more of them returned men. Maybe news of your husband."

She went to grasp his arm, but her hand stopped short as she turned her liquid eyes up to meet his own. Jusuf knew how hard this must have been for her, this not knowing. The more so as their army's leader was her husband's own cousin, another young blacksmith but from way down towards the Lizard Point. An unfortunate kinship, Jusuf thought, for it would surely put her husband in the very thick of any battle.

And so Jusuf gathered his things together and hefted his leather bag onto his shoulder. The new hinges, the iron roves to secure them and his tools dully clattered from within. Rodrigo picked up Mistress Trewin's bundle of repaired clothes and led the way out.

"I'll just have a drink of water," Jusuf said and

wandered across the road to a small spring, where a narrow lane from the road led up a low hill opposite the smithy.

"Your English is good enough now to get you into the priory, Jusuf," Rodrigo said, standing at Jusuf's side as he knelt to scoop water into his hands. "Good enough to discuss the fitting of hinges to a chapterhouse door. So why do you need me with you?"

"It's a two-handed task, Rodrigo," he told him, the water trickling between his fingers, "and I'd prefer your help than one of the brothers, seeing your ribs are just about mended. But the other thing is that I might miss overhearing something important. Something about this rebellion. And your better ease with their language means you might be able to get talking with the monks about their new guests. My dearest hope is to bring back some peace of mind for Mistress Trewin. She's been very good to us since we arrived."

"She has that," Rodrigo half-grinned at Jusuf. "But then, you have kept her smithy going, and very well by all accounts. Which must be something of a miracle when I think back to the way you acted when you first laid eyes on the pretty lass." He cocked his head slightly and peered down at Jusuf.

At first, Jusuf only stared up at Rodrigo, trying to get his thoughts in order, but then they struck him as too fanciful. He took his drink then shook his head and was about to urge them on when Rodrigo clamped his hand firmly on Jusuf's shoulder.

"What was it, Jusuf? What made you so unsettled when she first opened her door to us?"

Jusuf stared at him for quite a while, feeling the man's grip still firm upon his shoulder, the grip of a—of a valued but now worried friend. As though he'd been holding his breath since that first sight of their mistress, Jusuf let out a long and heartfelt sigh. He stood and looked back over at the smithy, his voice studied when it eventually came.

"I'd seen her before, Rodrigo." He could almost feel his friend's puzzled look. "Not really in Foy, though, no; not there; nor anywhere else, come to that; but in…" His words—his own mother tongue of Arabic—finally failed him. He could only clutch at an insufficient "In a waking dream" before lowering his gaze to his feet.

Rodrigo said nothing, but dipped his head into Jusuf's line of sight, laying bare his confusion.

"You remember," Jusuf said, almost meeting Rodrigo's questioning eyes, "the day my feet first stepped onto Cornish soil, the day before the captain left Foy for *Londres*? When we were sitting in the Ship Inn, just after he'd walked out and passed by the window?" Rodrigo nodded. "As I turned back to look at you, she…Mistress Trewin appeared before me, as plain as the light of that day. As clear and as real as you had been, only sitting off to your side."

"A ghost?"

"No, not a ghost, Rodrigo. Too real and too solid, but…but dressed in strange attire, and lit by an unearthly light." He flicked his gaze at Rodrigo, unsure he should have said anything. But the man seemed more puzzled than worried.

"God works in mysterious ways, Jusuf…even through Allah," and he gently urged Jusuf on, down the street towards the Tremethyks and their need of repaired clothes. He said no more, although Jusuf could see the words he'd spoken still occupied his friend's thoughts.

Having delivered Rodrigo's bundle and carried on past Saint Petroc's church and the short way out of Bodmyn to the priory, they had little hindrance gaining entry through its gatehouse and into its precincts. Someone was found to escort them in search of Brother Jowan. They bumped into him in the cloisters, the sight of Jusuf instantly cheering the man's clearly clouded features.

"Ah, Master Jusuf. Just the man," he hailed, then tipped his head as he brought his hands together in greeting. He lifted a beaming face to Jusuf, then nodded at Rodrigo. "Your companion's worth as a smith, Master Fernandez, has not gone unnoticed." He peered at Jusuf's shoulder bag. "The chapterhouse door hinges, I hope?"

Jusuf nodded, clearly surprising Brother Jowan.

"Ah, so your ear is at last finding its feet amidst the jostle of our language, eh, Master Jusuf?"

Again, Jusuf nodded, carefully assuring him, "Ready for affixing, Brother Jowan."

"Good. Good. Very good. I'll go with you," and he dismissed the monk who'd escorted them. "I have another task for which I believe your fine blacksmith skills may very well prove to be of most excellent service."

At the other side of the cloister, the door to the chapterhouse remained chocked in place, seemingly as precisely as Jusuf had left it some few days before. As he carefully checked it was so, Brother Jowan told them how glad they'd all be once they could shut out the wind again.

"You wouldn't believe how draughty it can get along here," he said, swinging his arm to imitate strong gusts coming in from the cloister.

As Jusuf got to work, Brother Jowan seemed to

take great interest in what he was doing, as he chattered on about this and that. Nothing of it bore upon the uprising, though, not that Jusuf could tell, and Rodrigo looked just as wearied by it. Then the brother moved on to the nature of some further work he wished Jusuf to undertake.

He'd just begun to explain that one of their Truro diocesan churches had been deemed in dire need of repair—to its bell's headstock and frame—when the nearby ringing of a rather different bell interrupted him.

"Ah, noonday. We're called to dinner. I must leave you, but I'll likely be back before you finish," and he nodded to them both before walking off down the cloister.

The monastery precincts soon fell to an even more eerie silence, into which Jusuf's work on the door's new hinges presently resounded. When it came to striking home the roves, Jusuf cringed at the clash of iron upon iron, seeming loud enough to raise the dead. They'd got as far as finishing the upper hinge, Jusuf by then kneeling to position the lower strapwork, when a familiar voice startled them.

"I trust I find our Ceuta blacksmith in good health," and Jusuf looked up to see Dom Francisco beaming down at him. "And the good *Senhor* Fernandez," he then directed at Rodrigo when he stuck his head around the door from the other side.

"Good day, Dom Francisco," Rodrigo returned, but Jusuf saw a glint in the Dom's eyes as he removed a couple of roves from between his own lips, so he too could bid the monk a proper good day.

Then he surprised himself by blurting out, "Do you happen to know anything of the Cornishmen who've been brought to the infirmary here? Our

Mistress Trewin's husband is with their army."

Dom Francisco's face clouded a little as he eyed them both. Then he glanced around before quietly telling them that more recent news had already overtaken whatever tidings the men may have brought.

"The brothers," he said in a whisper, despite speaking in Arabic, "received a messenger only yesterday. It seems the Cornish army reached *Londres* on the sixteenth of this month, whereupon they camped themselves upon a hill without its walls."

"Reached *Londres*?" Rodrigo gasped. "And three days ago. So the king's army is indeed away in the North."

"*Was*," Dom Francisco corrected. "Led by a Lord Daubeney, it appears it returned in good time to a place called Blackheath. By then the Cornishmen he met there were fifteen thousand strong. Although Lord Daubeney was greatly outnumbered, the Cornish army… Well, I'm afraid to say it was evidently not at all well led, and hence easily overcome."

"Overcome," Jusuf said, his thoughts filling with the look he'd seen on Mistress Trewin's face that morning.

"They were quickly put to rout, but not until…" but the Dom's face then dropped, as did his voice, "until some thousand Cornishmen had been felled. Their leaders, the blacksmith Michael an Gof and, er…Lord Audley I think it was, were both captured. So, it would seem the Cornish rebellion has in the end been brought to naught."

"Well, at least our captain should be safe in *Londres* now," Rodrigo said, "but at what cost; a thousand dead!" and he looked at Jusuf. "And Mistress Trewin's cousin-in-law captured. That doesn't bode well for her poor young husband."

"Brother Thomas did make mention," Dom

Francisco said, "that you both fell to good fortune on the back of their smith's ill-choice. I will pray for her foolhardy husband's safe return. Something I'm sure the other brothers here would join me in doing, given the order is no longer in such an invidious position."

"Invidious?" Rodrigo said.

"Caught between a king's need to finance a war, a Cornish anger, and the diminishment of the priory's own income."

"Well, I suppose that explains why they've been so loath to talk about it with either of us."

Dom Francisco looked meaningfully at them, then quietly suggested, "Best keep that close between us three," before his face took on an air of innocence as he looked past them. "Brother Jowan, I do believe," he called in English. "And how fares you this fine afternoon?"

"Ah, Dom Fancisco," the brother returned as he drew near along the cloister. "I am well, thank you. I trust the same may be said of yourself?"

"It looks as though your spiteful draught will soon be banished," and the Dom gazed admiringly at the chapterhouse door. "I can see your new blacksmith possesses fine skills, but I have equally rare skills in a far more venerable work to attend." He bade them each a cheery farewell, then carried on along the cloister.

"Would you be free from tomorrow to visit the church I mentioned earlier?" Brother Jowan immediately asked Jusuf. "I have a cart setting out from here early in the morning, returning in three days' time. You'd be in purse by our agreed rate, of course, in addition to compensation for such short notice."

Jusuf could see no reason why not and so nodded.

"Good. The next chance would be some weeks hence, otherwise. I'll have a letter of introduction ready for you, instructing you be given food and lodgings, and all aid in surveying the bell's needs of its new fixing."

"Is the church far?"

"A day's journey, Master Jusuf. A return to the coast for you, although this time not far from the town of Plymouth. To Saint Germanus in the parish of Rame." He glanced at the chapterhouse door and smiled. "But for now, I'll leave you to finish off this important task," and he briefly dipped his head at them each in turn before leaving them to their work.

An hour or so later, and Jusuf swung the door smoothly and precisely into its stone frame. He then opened it and pushed and pulled until satisfied it was secure before finally allowing a smile to suffuse his face. He slanted a look at Rodrigo.

"Once we've made good here, I suppose we'd best get straight back to Mistress Trewin. I must say, though, I'm not looking forward to telling her what we've learnt of the fate of her husband's army."

He took out a small piece of what he lamented was his too quickly diminishing *kief* and scraped a small amount into his mouth with his teeth. Then he briefly closed his eyes as he sucked on it, savouring its reminder of far simpler childhood times in the Rif Mountains. But when he opened his eyes again, he found Rodrigo staring narrowly at him.

"What?" Jusuf exclaimed.

"You don't think your seeing the apparition of Mistress Trewin in the Ship Inn might be something to do with the *kief* you chew, do you?"

"My *kief*?" Jusuf laughed, but it set him to thinking, thoughts that led him by a roundabout way to an obscure and arcane Berber practice. It wasn't long before he began to wonder if this might not truly lend some sense to what had left him so perplexed ever since that strange vision. On a day he'd regarded as worrisome, when perhaps he should rightly have deemed it a rare and most wondrous day indeed.

18 SONGS OF OUR FOREBEARS

As the Priory's gatehouse door closed behind them, Jusuf stood in the bright sunshine and thought back to the few childhood memories he held of his grandfather. One that had always stuck in his mind had been of the old man's thin voice wavering as it tried to rise to the notes of some plaintive-sounding song.

Then he realised he was alone, Rodrigo standing in the road a little way off, hands on hips, staring back at Jusuf as he waited. Jusuf wandered on to join him, his feet somehow feeling leaden on the road's dry and dusty earth.

"You all right, Jusuf?" Rodrigo said. "You seem far away."

Jusuf stopped before his friend, but could only stare through him, his father's words this time tumbling through his mind.

"Jusuf? You're not seeing ghosts again, are you?" and Rodrigo turned to look behind him. "It's not Mistress Trewin, is it?"

When Jusuf said, "My father told me they were

songs of our forebears," Rodrigo turned back to face him, confusion filling his features.

"I think, Rodrigo, I could do with wetting my throat; do you know that? There's a tavern just down the road, opposite the church. Come on," and he hurried Rodrigo on as he hitched his lighter bag higher onto his shoulder.

The cramped "Salutation" proved both dark and sparsely occupied. They chose a bench around one of its small bay windows for the better light and squeezed in behind its table. Once they'd called their orders to the tavern keeper, and he'd brought them over, Jusuf paid the man before once more staring through Rodrigo.

"What in God's name's got into you, Jusuf?"

"*Kief*, you said '*Kief*'; my 'Waking dream', Mistress Trewin; my grandfather, may Allah preserve his soul; Allah the Great, in your name I bow down before you."

"I take it I should just wait until you make some sense," and Rodrigo lifted his ale and gulped down a few mouthfuls as he warily watched Jusuf out of the corner of his eye.

At first, Jusuf only took a sip of his own small ale, thought for a moment, then downed half the leather mug's charge in one. He smiled at Rodrigo, which only seemed to worry the man further.

"You know my Berber faith holds true to our forebears," Jusuf eventually said. "That we revere their wisdom and hold them in great veneration."

Rodrigo nodded as he placed his mug down.

"Well, there are some rare few of my people who can bring voice to those who have passed into Allah's divine embrace; Allah the bountiful, may he ever grace me with his wise words."

Rodrigo only lifted his brows, clearly waiting.

"I was fourteen when I left my village in the mountains, never to return. An uncle had encouraged me to better my smithying by going to Algiers—where he'd gone himself as a carter. I was to search out an apprenticehood there, where your Portuguese knowledge abounded. So, I left my village having reached an age when I still couldn't be told much about my grandfather's divine gift."

"Is this the 'Songs of Our Forebears' you mentioned?"

Jusuf nodded. "I saw him do it a few times, though, from some hiding place, or beyond the light of the fire where I could watch and listen without being seen. He would sit on the ground and light some *kief* in his *sebsi*, then settle down to a quiet chant as someone else played softly on a *taghanimt*—a blown pipe not unlike your shawm. His singing and the *taghanimt* made for a haunting sound, especially when the chant rose to a song and his old voice steadily became stronger and sweeter."

A couple of drovers came into the tavern and settled in the far corner, shouting their needs to the keeper. Rodrigo and Jusuf raised their mugs to them, but then Rodrigo asked, "So, what did you see from your hiding place?"

"Not see, Rodrigo; heard." Jusuf took another swig of his small ale. "After singing for some time, the song would stop and a story begin."

"A story?"

"Yes, a short tale that would draw in and enchant all those sitting around him, the many who came to listen. It would usually tell of some plight of a villager, a problem they couldn't see a way through, or maybe an opportunity: to gain a profit or a girl's hand. But they always ended with a surprise; a lesson, I suppose. Maybe a warning, of how not to live your life."

His mug proved empty when Jusuf once again lifted it to his lips, and so he called for another each.

"You're not putting off having to tell Mistress Trewin what we've learnt, are you?" Rodrigo asked, "for I don't really see what this has got to do with you seeing her ghost."

"No, I can't say *I* do, either, my…my friend. You see, they were stories spoken by our forebears, but through my grandfather. Tales from our dead kin to guide the living who followed on. But Mistress Trewin isn't dead, nor could she be a forebear of mine even if she were. So no, I can't yet quite see what it is myself that I feel deep down has some real bearing."

"So…why make mention of it now?"

"Because I was once caught watching, and chastised by my father as he dragged me from the room. When I said I'd just wanted to listen to the stories, he told me I'd have to wait until I became a man. 'Why?' I'd said, as you do when you're young. 'They're only tales, and I like tales'.

"His anger had then drained from his face as he put his arm around me, which was so unlike him. 'You cannot,' he quietly told me, 'for you are still too young to look from the eyes of those who have gone before us.' But it was when he stared back into the room that I then saw his own eyes sharpen, saw them become fixed on a place all those inside had purposely left clear. I now know he was seeing, Rodrigo, seeing as I had seen on that rare and wondrous day in Foy, sitting there in the Ship Inn."

An ear-splitting crack of what Jusuf took to be

thunder reverberated around them and Colin jerked his gaze up at the roof of the chalet, his heart beating ten-to-the-dozen.

"Shit!" he yelped, and looked wide-eyed at Kate.

"Seagulls," she said. "Stomping around on the metal roof," and she smiled. "You get used to it," but then she frowned down at the single joss stick, sticking out of the holder, before lifting her frown to Colin. "But the joss stick, it's… Did you…"

Colin slowly nodded, his heart rate finally settling back to normal. "When you get all this one down," he said, "I think you'll find we've a fair bit to chew over this time, Kate."

"Okay," she said, and noisily clicked the end of her biro. "Go on, then. Fire away."

19 AN INCOMING TIDE

By the time Kate had written down everything Colin could remember, midnight had passed and the soft sea air had brought them both teetering on the edge of sleep. Kate suggested they go down on the beach the next day. The weather forecast was good and the tide would be favourable. They could talk properly about Colin's latest phantasm there. And so they were soon in bed, quickly lulled to sleep by the shush of the distant but carrying sound of the surf, rolling in on the ocean's waves.

In the morning, they packed a rucksack for their day on the beach, the sun already beating down on the chalet, its roof crackling as the metal warmed and expanded. Before long they'd walked back down the narrow track to the coast road, then across to the start of a steeply descending path.

Spread out before them lay the ocean, its waters deeply blue beneath a seemingly endless dome of cloudless sky. The ascending sun slanted its golden light down from over a headland at the easternmost end of the bay, the land's sharp outline suggesting to Colin a female figure lying on her back. Her head, though, appeared disconcertingly tipped beneath the waves that crashed in about her tapering throat.

Kate stopped them and pointed unknowingly towards the maiden's flat stomach. "You see those fields along the top of the headland? Well, just before they start there's a spire sticking up to the right of some trees. You see it?"

"Trees? Ah, right. Got it."

"You know last night I said Saint Germanus was nearby, well, that's it, although people generally refer to it these days as Rame Parish Church. And that headland is Rame Head."

"Wow. I didn't realise you meant it was that close. I wonder if Jusuf got there in the end." Kate, though, had already pressed on, her head bobbing above the blanket of gorse that swathed the steep dip down beyond the clifftop.

He followed, but the beach then came into view, clearly a long way below. It brought him to another halt. "Bloody 'ell," he called after her. She stopped and turned. "These cliffs must be two hundred foot high," but she said nothing until he'd caught up.

"From the road to the beach, yes. It's much higher coming back up, though," and Kate grinned before carrying on down the path.

She eventually took him to an even steeper path, down into a small cove, then a short leap from rocks onto a stretch of smooth and empty beach, a single set of dog prints its only disfigurement. They found a suitable place against some rocks, laid out their towels and each stripped down to their swimming costumes.

Kate was clearly excited, falling to recounting the

many summers she'd spent on this very beach, of the adventures, hilarities and the quirkiness that came from being in this quiet corner of a forgotten land. For Colin, though, its foreignness overwhelmed much of what Kate was saying. The heat of the sun and the air, the colour of the sky and the sea, and the glare of the light off the fine-grained sandy beach all said he was abroad. Some secluded Mediterranean shore, it seemed, far from the England he knew so well.

It also remained otherworldly quiet: a dog walker slowly passing along the distant waterline, then later a couple with a child, but no one invaded their seemingly private cove.

"Is it always this quiet?" he eventually asked. "I mean, it's the height of the season."

"Main Beach will be a bit busier, but pretty much, although it'll be rammed further down, in Newquay and Penzance, places like that."

"I suppose it was more or less like this in Jusuf's time."

"Fourteen-ninety-seven."

"Eh? How do you know that?"

"After that last phantasm you had back in May, you said Jusuf and Rodrigo had overheard the brothers talking about a Cornish army setting out from Bodmin. You mentioned they'd said it was to do with *Escócia* and some unjust taxes. I looked it up at work. Although there were three rebellions around that time, it has to be the first Cornish Rebellion of fourteen-ninety-seven. When King Henry the seventh forced an Act through parliament in the January, to pave the way for raising taxes to fight the Scottish."

"But why didn't you say anything at the time? Ah…right. Okay. Yeah, well, I don't suppose I've been that receptive until yesterday's shock of finding it so familiar down here. Sorry."

She stood up and brushed sand from her slender and shapely legs. "I think I'll go for a swim. The tide's okay for another hour. Then a bit of sunbathing's definitely going to be on the cards. You joining me?"

"Swim? In the sea? In the sea off the coast of England?"

"Once you get used to it, it's great." His expression must have said it all. "Well, *I'm* going in. I'm going to enjoy just being a grockle for the day, because—"

"A what?"

"What the locals call tourists; and because…because the first thing we need to do tomorrow is go to Bodmin, which I'm pretty sure has a small museum, and it should be open on a Monday. After all, that's where Jusuf has spent most of his time so far, and we still don't have conclusive proof he ever existed."

"But—"

"Everything you've witnessed so far through him only goes to confirm the date; the Cornish army *was* defeated at Blackheath, and in the June of that year. But it's still only circumstantial, what you could have read somewhere without consciously remembering. We need to find something that pins Jusuf down as having been here then, which we can't do down here on the beach, but we might in Bodmin."

"All right. Agreed. But I'm still not going in the water."

"Well, when I get back, what we *will* have to do is go through that business of Mistress Trewin's ghost and Jusuf's 'Songs of our forebears'. Because you can bet your bottom dollar Bodmin museum's not going to have any answers to that one," and with that, she made a beeline for the sea.

As Colin watched her walk away, he realised what a clearer view Kate must have, her mind not clouded by the intimacy of feelings he clearly shared with Jusuf. For him, his worry over Mistress Trewin's fears for her husband obscured much else, along with another but rather less altruistic feeling. One his view of Kate's scantily clad backside, now walking away from him down the beach, brought into far greater relief.

By the time Kate returned and was drying herself off on her towel he'd got a couple of chapters into Tom Sharpe's *Wilt*.

"Any good?" she asked, looking down at his book.

"Yeah, great so far. Really funny. Has a ribald sense of humour, our Mr Sharpe."

"Thought you'd like it."

Colin marked his place and put the book back in the rucksack. "Good swim?"

"Invigorating."

"Hmm, that sounds like a euphemism to me."

"No, really. It was." Her skin, now coated in fine crystals of salt, glistened in the sun.

"This visit to Bodmin tomorrow: won't it kind of invalidate the reliability of any further observations I might have of Jusuf's time there?"

"If you can find your way about when we get there, however vaguely, I think we should be able to judge if you've seen it before through Jusuf's eyes. So I wouldn't worry. I also think you ought to leave going back to visit Jusuf until afterwards, seeing we've a clear record at the moment of what's happened so far. We don't want to have to assimilate a whole load of new stuff at the last minute. After all, we can always go back to Bodmin another day."

She spread her towel out on the sand, on which she then laid down, her eyes closed against the sun. "Oh, that's lovely; nice and hot. If you want more sunscreen, the bottle's in one of the side pockets."

"Okay."

When he didn't stir, she told him, "The sun's stronger than you think down here, Colin."

"Okay."

"Don't say I didn't warn you."

Colin propped himself up and stared at the sea for a while, at the sunlight glistening on the myriad strings of diamonds across its ceaselessly moving surface.

"It's funny, isn't it?" he said, "how the tide always seems to be coming in, even when it's going out."

"It's not far off turning."

"Yeah, but I mean the way the waves coming ashore make it look like it's forever coming in, that you don't notice the water of the spent waves slipping back out beneath them."

"I can't say I've ever really thought of it that way."

"Just an illusion, of course," but then something else struck him, something else that must also have been an illusion, if his visits to Jusuf were anything to go by.

"Like time," he said, emphatically. "It's just like time," and he stared down at Kate.

She opened an eye and stared up at him. "Time?"

"It always seems to be going forwards, but…but we know now it also goes backwards. Somehow, in some way, it folds back on itself." Kate had opened both eyes, both narrowed on Colin. "I've been doing what the surf's returning water does, slipping back unseen beneath the illusion of time's relentless onward march. And you know what, Kate? This must be how Jusuf sees it, too. But what *we* now know that he doesn't know is that the returning water isn't made opaque by the froth and foam of the breaking waves above it."

Kate had herself up on one elbow. "So?"

"So…that returning water is *clear*. Clear water you can see through, both ways if you only turn to look …backwards *and* forwards in time."

"Oh, I get it. When Jusuf saw me—saw the future—he just assumed I was someone from the past."

"Exactly. That's what's left him flummoxed."

"I'm not surprised; I'm having problems myself getting my own head around it…and we know more about what's going on than he does. But then, I don't suppose his seasickness would have lent itself to him sitting there, contemplating waves."

"The trouble is, Kate, this is all effect, not cause."

"Go on; surprise me."

"Well, it may be a good analogy for how it *works*, but not the 'Why'. I mean: why are Jusuf and I able to see through the clear water below the turbulence of time's onward crashing waves? And why now?"

"I dare say dope's got something to do with it. Maybe what allows you both to dip your heads beneath the waves without drowning."

"Eh? Oh, right. Yeah, you're probably right. Then there's your family line going right back to Mistress Trewin. A sort of fishing line, maybe?"

"I think you're pushing the analogy somewhat, but I can see how that might work; the thing that links our two different times. But it still doesn't answer the 'Why'."

Colin stared again at the ocean, at the waves rolling in to crash as a racing surf up the wide and even beach. "But other than that, what haven't we accounted for so far?" he asked her.

Kate's silence and stare eventually drew his gaze from the seagulls wheeling above a distant fishing boat. He stared back at her narrowing eyes.

"You've thought of something?" he asked.

"Where's Jusuf's burden?"

"His… Oh, yeah, I'd forgotten about that. Let me see: the last I remember was when he was dozing outside the church in Lostwithiel, waiting for Rodrigo and the monks. I'm sure that's what Rodrigo was referring to when he said 'You want to hang on to that bag of yours—and what's inside'. And it's unlikely he'd have found a suitable hiding place on the way, so it should be in Bodmin with him. Probably hidden in the smithy somewhere."

"In the smithy where one of my ancestors once lived, and through whose descendants the joss stick holder eventually ended up coming into my possession."

Colin's mouth didn't stay open long. "Shit," he barely breathed, and they both stared at each other.

"The joss stick holder!" they both said as one.

"It can't be, Colin. It can't."

"But I think it is, Kate; I think it bloody well is."

20 BODMIN

They both sat either side of the table, staring at the joss stick holder, where it innocently stood in the centre of the table top between them.

"It doesn't look very dangerous," Kate said.

"Nor fragile," Colin reckoned as he bent to stare through its plethora of holes into what little could be seen of its interior. "It can't be Jusuf's burden. It can't be. Remember how cautious the captain was, insisting it be kept in Rodrigo's locker. And how they wanted him to hide it away somewhere safe as soon as they landed here."

Kate looked across at him. "You know where everything is, Colin. Go make us both a cup of tea, will you? Then I'll think about getting our meal on a bit earlier. A day on the beach always gives me an appetite."

Colin got up and wandered into the galley. "It must have originally contained something, though," he called back, "something Jusuf was going to use after landing in Santander. But whatever it was, it's obviously long gone now. I mean, you can see it's empty."

"Well, I don't know about that; the holes are a bit too small to be sure."

"Yeah, but there's enough of them. I put the torch on the shelf above you; see if you can see inside any better with that."

The kettle boiled just as Kate called in that there was too much reflected glare for it to be of much help. "I suppose we'd better take good care of it from here on in," Colin said. "just in case. You never know, we might bc missing something."

"To think," Kate said, in a rather shocked voice, "I gave it a thorough clean before giving it to you, all those years ago."

"Well, it must've been through plenty of hands before then," he said as he put two mugs of tea on the table, well clear of the holder. He sat down before his own. "What was it Jusuf said? Right at the beginning. Something like: 'As easily as taking a babe from its mother's milk'."

"What?"

"On his way through the Strait of Gibraltar. You remember, when he was talking about taking their country back. When he said they were going to strike at the heart of the thieving infidels."

"Which we took to mean some sort of physical attack."

"Like the last component for a bomb. But maybe we were wrong, eh? What if it was… Well, I dunno. Something else, an information attack, say."

"A what?"

"Intelligence. Some dirt on the Spanish king, or something like that."

"But why worry about it getting broken?"

"Ah, well. There you have me."

"Because the captain made it sound like it posed a direct threat to their lives. I can't think of any information that could be that much of an immediate risk."

Neither of them could come up with anything more constructive during what was left of the afternoon, nor through their meal and into the evening. As on the previous night, they both retired early, exhausted by the sun, the fresh sea air and the steep climb back up from the beach to the chalet.

The following morning looked set to be fine when Colin stumbled through the nettles to the outside toilet, although a high bank of cloud marred the ocean's southwestern horizon. Otherwise the sky arched blue above him as he opened the dew-dampened door. It seemed a shame to be going inland and away from the beach on such a promising day. But then part of him really did want to see how much of Bodmin he might recognise.

Before long they were motoring back between rolling fields, the coast behind them, the main road for Bodmin ahead. The journey proved as straightforward as their road atlas had promised, but as they at last drove towards the town centre and into heavier traffic, Colin cleared his throat.

"You know," he said, rather reticently, "the sun down here really is pretty strong. The…the tops of my feet are really stinging."

Kate lofted her brows and drew in a long and quiet breath. "And probably as red-looking as your face and nose are now, especially your nose, Colin."

They'd agreed they'd follow the first signs they came across for parking, hoping to get on foot at the earliest. They wanted to minimise the chance of Colin getting a feel for the place before they could do a proper cold test on his recall. But as they came into the centre itself, Kate warned Colin to keep his eyes on the road and try not to look around.

"Why?" he said, glancing at her, but she just pointed two fingers at her eyes, then jabbed them forward at the slowing traffic ahead.

Not long after, she said, "Aha, just the thing: a sign for the town centre car park. Left at the next mini-roundabout," then she pointed out a tourist sign that showed the Town Museum was also that same way.

Colin found it hard not looking about, although it had the feel of the market towns he knew in Yorkshire, places like Skipton. Before long they'd left the roundabout behind and climbed a short rise, following the next sign at a set of traffic lights into a side street and to a Pay and Display at its end.

"I can't see any spaces," he said, crawling along the lines of parked cars.

"Let me out here, Colin. I spotted a Tourist Information Centre back at the lights. I'll go get us a town guide while you find one. Wait at the entrance once you have," and when he'd stopped the car, she got out.

On his third circuit, Colin noticed someone pulling out and was soon parked up and buying a ticket at the machine. The notice board behind it announced he was in "Bodmin Town Council's Priory Car Park". He froze, a ticket in his hand, as a flashback overwhelmed him.

Bright sunlight slanted dark shadows down the front of the priory's gatehouse, now before him at the end of a short dirt track. Its double gate was closed, a smaller wicket door wide open within it, a paved pathway beyond in yet deeper shade. Even its familiar smell pervaded his nose and mouth.

"I'm sorry, but are you finished?" a man's voice said, and the vision evaporated.

"Oh, sorry. Yes. Just reading the sign," and Colin stepped out of the way. But as he turned around in a circle, the lie of the land about him somehow didn't feel right, then he spotted Kate coming towards him, leaflets in hand.

"Found somewhere then?" she called.

"Yep. I'll just put the ticket in the car and I'll be right with you."

Once back, he told her about his vivid flashback, but also that he was sure the priory's gatehouse he'd seen hadn't been where they were standing. He pointed out the car park sign.

"I think it was just the name, not the place itself, because there's nothing here I recognise from my time with Jusuf."

"I'm not surprised. I asked at the information centre and they said there's hardly anything of the priory left, and most of that's stones now incorporated into other buildings around the town."

She then waved one of her leaflets at him. "You know how I am with maps, but I reckon, from this one," which she carefully avoided him seeing, "the road that runs past here at the lights is the one from Lostwithiel, the one Jusuf must have arrived by."

Colin's mouth went dry.

When they got to it, he stared back down towards the mini-roundabout. None of it looked familiar, although this time the lie of the land told him it should have been.

"It's just so much busier, cars and people and far too many buildings. It's hard to say," but then he looked across the road at what appeared to be a municipal building on the far side of a small square. "There's something familiar about that place, though, but it's only vague."

"Come on, then, let's carry on. Just say if anything strikes you," and Kate stepped out, leading the way down the hill. She kept looking back, but none of it struck a chord with Colin. When they arrived at the roundabout, it was the confluence of its roads that brought his eyes to narrow. Then he looked across at a church on the other side.

"Ah," he sighed, but somewhat uncertainly. "A tall, square entrance porch. And three west end windows under their own separate gables."

"You recognise it?"

"Hmm, well, yes and no. It looks remarkably like Saint Petroc's, but there's no spire. This one's got a squat square tower on its far side, so…well, no, not really." When Kate again glanced at her leaflet's map and said that it was indeed Saint Petroc's, Colin felt disappointment flood in and swamp his hopes.

"So it's not as Jusuf saw it?" she asked.

Colin turned his mouth down as he shook his head. "Although that road up the side looks right, the same bend and rise. I remember it being cobbled, though. But if that is Saint Petroc's, then that'd be the way to Mistress Trewin's smithy."

"Okay. Let's carry on that way, then. See what we see, eh?" and they were soon climbing its short incline.

Again, little seemed familiar to Colin, far too many properties, a lot fewer trees and bordering paddocks and fields, the road straighter, busier and largely of an even width. They walked for a good ten or fifteen minutes, until Colin called time.

"The feel of the land's deserted me," he told her. I don't recognise its lie anymore, and we've been going too long. Let's backtrack a bit." Then an idea came to him: "As I've never experienced Jusuf going any further up this road than the smithy, then when it feels right again that should be where it was."

He took it slower on the way back, reaching his senses out to feel the land beneath his feet, the contours of the surrounding terrain, the shade and shadow and light—then, before long, he stopped and looked around. "The feeling's back. Ah, of course."

"What? Is this it?"

"This junction; the lane round the back," and he slowly turned around, "and the rise of the land opposite; that other lane coming in over there, on the other side of the road…Chapel Lane," he read from its nameplate. Then he turned back to stare at their own side of the road, blankly at a patch of grass on the other side of the junction. Nipping between cars queueing to get out onto the main road, he was soon standing before it.

"Well?" Kate said as she joined him, staring minutely at his face.

Colin could almost see the smithy's barn before his eyes, where the grass of the verge beyond a low wall now grew. Its quarry flags lay beneath the pavement at his feet, the gable end of its attached cottage sticking out to the edge of the dirt road at his back, the forge off to his other side. Then the quietness of everything around it seeped in to fill his ears. He remembered his thirst as Rodrigo had led him out to call at the Tremethyk's on their way to the priory.

He turned once more and stared hard across the empty dirt road, intent only on a short wall of rough stones to one side of the lane's narrow entrance opposite.

"That must be the spring," he said, without looking aside at Rodrigo, and stepped out to cross the road to find out.

A deafening blare startled him, brought a loud screech to his ear as his sight bleached bright blue and pain shot down his arm.

21 MAGNA BRITANNIA

A shout of "Colin" screamed loudly in his ears as his gaze snapped back to the road. Slewed to a halt in front of him was a car, mere inches away.

"For Christ's sake, Colin; what the fuck are you doing?" and he recognised Kate's frightened voice as he stared into the startled face of the car's front seat passenger.

"Eh? What? Er…where did that come from?" he stammered, but couldn't quite hear Kate's reply, not against the deafening sound of the blood pounding in his ears.

"Shit!" he eventually heard her say as she dragged him further back. "Here, sit down on this wall," she said, and before he knew it he had a cigarette between his quivering lips, his shaking hands failing to light the Zippo they somehow held. In a daze, he watched the short queue of traffic he'd caused finally growl off down the road.

"Ow! My arm hurts," he said, once Kate had taken the Zippo from his fumbling hands and flicked it to a flame. She snatched the cigarette from between his lips and lit it for him.

"You're damned lucky that's all that hurts, you idiot. What were you thinking?" and she jabbed the cigarette back between his lips.

He felt at his shoulder and quietly moaned as he took a long, deep drag.

"I'm afraid," Kate said, "that was me. I grabbed your arm."

He could hear the tremor in her voice and lifted his bemused eyes to see anger in her own, but an anger tempered by fear-filled relief.

"Christ, Kate, but I don't know what came… No, that's not true. I do know what came over me—this place."

Her shoulders slumped as she let out a long breath, then she sat down beside him on the wall. "Do you want to tell me?"

He looked at her and drew his lips to a thin line, but then nodded. "Can we go somewhere a bit quieter, though?" and he remembered the spring that had caused all this. "Let's go across to the lane over there. It's a bit more away from the road than here."

"All right, but you're going to hold my hand, you hear? I'm not having you scaring the shit out of me again."

"Okay."

Together, hand in hand, she led him a few yards down the road to a pedestrian crossing and pressed its button. Her grip of his hand tightened as she held him back from the kerb. The lights changed, marked by the usual rapid beeping, and she walked him smartly across, back up the road and to the start of Chapel Lane.

To one side stood a modern retail unit selling tiles, but on the other ran a short verge backed by a stone wall, its nearest end doglegging around a small, neatly bordered pool. Colin wandered onto the grass, Kate still clutching his hand as she followed, and they stood before it. Where the wall ran behind the pool, two verdigris-stained taps jutted out just above the waterline, a date stone inset a few feet above them.

"It wasn't like this in Jusuf's time," he told Kate.

"Clearly not," she said in a steadier voice, and he saw what she meant: "1849" stared at him from the date stone.

"This was where I…where Jusuf told Rodrigo about his vision of Mistress Trewin, well, of you really." Colin slipped his hand from Kate's and knelt beside the pool, dipping his cupped hands in, as Jusuf had done.

"I wouldn't drink it, Colin. It says here," and he looked up to see her reading one of her leaflets, "that in eighteen-eighty-one it was the source of Enteric Fever, similar to Typhoid, and that thirteen of sixty cases proved fatal."

Colin opened his fingers, letting their scoop of water rain back down into the pool.

"Hey, but listen to this: it also says that there were two blacksmiths amongst the victims, who, 'through their hot work, drank large quantities of the water'." She stared aghast at him. "Blacksmiths whose…whose 'smithy once stood opposite'."

Colin got to his feet, wiping his hands on his jeans, and together they looked back at the empty grass verge directly across on the other side of the road. "Well, Kate, what do you reckon? Have we gone beyond circumstantial yet?"

"Hmm, well, technically, no," and she held up the leaflet, "but I have to say: it's looking a lot more convincing."

But then Colin thought of the deaths of the two blacksmiths and took Kate's hand in his, his gaze searching her eyes. "I don't think I said 'Thanks', so…so thanks for pulling me back," and the pain in his shoulder seemed suddenly small in comparison.

She wrapped her arms around him and hugged him tightly, her voice small and muffled against his chest: "You're an idiot, Colin. Do you know that? But I'd hate to be without you." Her body shook against his for a moment, then she rubbed her eyes against his arm. "What would I do without you?" and he tenderly stroked her back.

They called in at a café on their way back into the centre of Bodmin—together settling their nerves—then climbed the hill towards the car park. Just before the traffic lights, though, they followed a sign for the town's museum.

It took them across the small square to a strangely ancient-looking building. Its Romanesque windows struck Kate as being at odds with a high oriel window at one end and a narrow balcony at the other.

"It looks strangely Romano-Italianate," she expanded. "Like an abbey that's been mucked about with by Giotto."

"Right," Colin said, spotting the sign for the museum's entrance. "Looks like something Disney dreamt up, to me."

The building turned out to be the town's Public Rooms, the museum itself confined to its lower ground floor. The usual glass cabinets in its almost deserted rooms displayed an eclectic assortment of artefacts, mostly from considerably more recent times than Jusuf's. Something in a tall and wide display case, though, eventually drew Colin's eye. He stood before it, scanning the objects standing on their small Perspex shelves.

"Hey, now this is interesting," and he pointed out a leather mug, described on its label as "A Drinking Jack". "That's what Jusuf and Rodrigo were drinking from in the Salutation tavern, although theirs didn't have silver rims like this one. I think Jusuf's was more likely pewter."

For the next quarter of an hour or so they searched through the displays, finding nothing of further interest. That was until Kate drew Colin's attention to an old book, open at a page containing a drawing that had Colin closely bending over its cabinet.

"Wow. That's it, Kate. Saint Petroc's. The one Jusuf saw," and there in the small drawing rose its tall spire. "Struck by lightning in 1699," he read out to her, but she was already ahead of him.

"The resultant fire destroyed both the one-hundred-and-fifty-foot spire and its roof." She lifted her gaze and gave him a smile.

"Phew," Colin drew out to a long sigh, before grinning broadly. "So that answers that one. But," and his face dropped, "it's still only circumstantial."

"Keep looking."

They were about to move on when a man's voice interrupted them. "I couldn't help overhearing," and they turned to find a tall, elderly gent smiling welcomingly at them both. "I work here. Well, actually I'm one of the volunteers, helping with the cataloguing. You sounded as though you were after something in particular, and I wondered if I might be of assistance."

"Thank you," Kate said, smiling at him. "Yes, we're...we're doing a bit of research into my family tree."

"Ah, yes," the man said, as Colin narrowed his eyes at Kate, "that does seem to be becoming something of a popular pursuit these days. And your family were from Bodmin?"

"A long time ago, yes."

"Well, we do have a lot more in storage than we can put on display, some of it going back to the seventeenth century," and his words carried a hint of pride.

"How about the fifteenth?" Kate enquired. The man's eyes widened, his brows lofting.

"The...the fifteenth. Well, not a vast amount from so early, I'm afraid, most of which is already on display. Do you have a name? It may jog my memory, you see. I have been a volunteer here since seventy-one, when I retired, so you never know."

"We only have a surname, I'm afraid: Trewin, Mistress Trewin...wife to a blacksmith at a smithy on..." and she quickly checked one of her leaflets. "On Dennison Road, as it's currently called, opposite Cock's Well at the end of Chapel Lane. Fourteen-ninety-seven...or thereabouts."

The man pressed his lips together and stared between Kate and Colin.

"Well, we do have an early edition of Magna Britannia, Volume Three for Cornwall. Not a first edition of eighteen-fourteen, you understand, but it's still old enough to need rather, well, rather careful handling."

"I'm Kate McKinley," and she extended her hand as she added, "An assistant archivist and researcher at the John Rylands Library in Manchester," and with her other hand she rummaged in her handbag for her ID card.

"The Rylands? Oh, well," and he vigorously shook Kate's hand, "in which case, please, if you'd like to follow me. I'll take you through to my little den," and he grinned broadly at them both.

"I'm Colin, by the way."

"Oh, how do you do," and he briefly shook Colin's hand, too. "I'm Derek Foster, one-time borough surveyor of this fair town, but long since put out to grass," he addressed primarily at Kate and grinned again.

Part storeroom, part office, the room Derek took them to looked neat and tidy, as though used by more than one person. He offered Kate the only chair other than the one behind a small desk, leaving Colin standing like a spare part. Derek then leant to a long metal document cabinet and opened a drawer, taking a cloth bag out. He laid it on the desk and sat down before removing a leather-bound volume. Opening it at one of its bookmarks, he carefully placed it on a bookstand sitting to one side of the desktop, turning it to Kate.

"Here's the entry for Bodmin," he told her, his fingertip hovering above the thin paper. Colin moved in closer, beside Kate, and bent to see. He then had to lean in yet closer still, so small was the print.

"As you will know, Mrs McKinley, the Magna Britannia is a collation of both existing and previous primary and secondary sources, so," he then directed at Colin, "it is rather ad hoc. But one of the things it does is to present extracts from various accounts, to illustrate such things as the cost of living at the time, for example."

He turned the page over and again pointed. "Here we have some items from the ancient corporation-accounts during the reign of Henry the seventh."

Kate read one out as Colin followed her finger: "Paide and yeven in malmesey to the under-sheryff, 4d".

"Indeed," Derek said, "all quite interesting in their own right. But your mention of a blacksmith reminded me of one taken from the priory's accounts," and he ran his finger further down the column of text until it came to a halt. "Here we are, what the author describes as 'the following curious items', from which you'll probably see why it stuck in my mind. Rather unusual, wouldn't you say?"

Kate and Colin brought their heads together as they leant even nearer the text. There, running from beside Derek's fingertip, read the line: "Item. Paide and yevyn to the black moor smythe Joseph to his costs when the had hung anew the chapterhouse door, 16½d".

As close as their heads were, Kate and Colin turned to each other, she grinning broadly before she stole a quick kiss from his uncertain lips.

22 "WOW"

They sat together on a bench in the square outside the museum and Colin lit a cigarette. Its smoke curled up into the still afternoon air and seemed to take with it most of his cares—except one.

"You sure it's conclusive, Kate?"

"Yes, which is another way of saying ninety-nine point nine percent, where old documents are concerned."

"But…but the name was Joseph, not Jusuf."

"Spelling hadn't been standardised by then, Colin. Caxton had only recently died, so it was too soon for printing to have had its effect. People chose whatever letters and their arrangement suited their purpose."

"Like using a 'y' for a 'g'?"

"Exactly, as well as for an 'i'."

"Oh, yeah."

"And just imagine Brother Jowan telling his accounts scribe that the Blackamoor smith Jusuf had done the job for one and fourpence ha'penny. Quite understandably, he'd have likely heard Jusuf's name as the more familiar 'Joseph'. It is, after all, the anglicised version of his name."

"Is it? Oh, right," but being an engineer, Colin still wasn't entirely convinced, and it must have come out in his voice.

"Trust me, Colin. Trust my feel for these things, and don't worry about it," and so finally he didn't, which freed an exhilaration that promptly took him by surprise.

"Wow," he at last managed, then stared into the distance as he tried to come to terms with the impossible. "I still can't believe it, Kate. It's… It's like when I phoned up uni' to get the results of my finals. You remember? And they'd said I'd got a first."

"On holiday, yes, I remember, in that phone box just outside the west front of Wells Cathedral. And then you asked them 'Is that a pass, then?'," and she laughed as she shook her head at the memory. "You wandered around in a daze for the rest of the day, saying 'Wow' every now and again, exactly as you did just now."

He turned to face her, fixing her amused eyes in his gaze. "Wow!" he said again, and they both broke into laughter.

When they got to the car park, Kate wondered if Colin fancied calling in to have a look around Lostwithiel, or maybe Fowey, on the way back.

"It's a bit late, isn't it?" he said, looking at his watch. "It's getting on for three. Maybe another day, eh? I wouldn't mind taking a bit of time just to digest today's revelation, maybe with a little spliff or two."

"Which brings us," Kate said, once Colin had slipped in through the driver's door and reached across to unlock her own, "to what we do next about Jusuf," she concluded having swung it open. But she froze, staring off into the distance, her hand resting on the door, until Colin asked if she was all right.

"I think it's only just sunk in with me, Colin."

"What has?"

She got into the car and slowly turned to face him, wide-eyed. "That we're blithely talking about someone who…who really did exist; a real person; real flesh and blood and living here five hundred years ago."

"I know. Wow, eh?"

She nodded and echoed "Wow" herself as Colin started the car.

They drove out of Bodmin in silence, each lost in their own thoughts, Colin's going back over what he'd experienced through Jusuf—through the real flesh-and-blood man. He eventually got to remembering their arrival at the smithy, and then something struck him.

"What did Mistress Trewin mean when she asked Brother Hammett if Jusuf was a Turkoman? You remember, before she'd let them in at her door."

"Hmm? Oh, that. Yes, I do remember. Well, the Turkomans were slave traders who used to pillage these coasts, stealing Cornishmen off to work in the mines of the Ottoman Empire, and other labour elsewhere. It went on for hundreds of years."

"What? They came all the way from Turkey to Cornwall?"

"No, they weren't really Turks. They were Barbary Corsairs from the north and west African coasts. I think the 'Turk' part came from the Turkish Empire's early influence on their cultures."

"North Africa? You mean like Morocco, where Jusuf came from?"

"Yeah, black Africans taking white Europeans into slavery."

"I never knew that."

"Nothing's new in history, Colin, and evil's always been a two-way street. It's still part of the folklore down here, though. At its height, a couple of hundred years after Jusuf, some fishing villages were abandoned. It was just too risky living on the coast. Imagine what that did to their fishing industry."

"Blimey. So that's what old Derek meant by that entry of Jusuf's being 'Rather unusual'? A *blackamoor* blacksmith in Cornwall!"

"Exactly. But more especially, so far inland; in Bodmin. They were probably quite used to seeing black sailors in coastal places like Fowey, but far less so here."

"I wonder if that was something to do with why the old woman came over to touch Jusuf when he first arrived outside the Ship Inn."

Kate laughed. "I'd not picked up on that, but it sounds like something my gran once told me. She said that when she was a young woman in Plymouth, seeing a black man was regarded as lucky; like a black cat crossing your path, I suppose. I don't remember her saying anything about touching them, though."

"Jusuf was lucky himself, then."

"In what way?"

"Bumping into the brothers. He might have had a different reception had he not been with them."

"Yes, I must admit, I did wonder about that myself."

As they eventually got nearer the chalet, back along the coast road that was already starting to feel more familiar to Colin, his thoughts began to crystallise. "You know, Kate, there are a couple of things about all this that really bug me."

"Only a couple?"

He took a glance at her before the next bend coming up forced his eyes back to the road. "The biggest one for me is how the hell this could be happening. What mechanism's allowing me somehow to pass back in time and occupy a real person? Someone real from the real past, for Christ's sake."

"And for that *real* person to see into our own present."

"Yeah, there is that. And in some ways that's even more mind-blowing." He concentrated on taking the bend around the head of the cove they were presently above, then the turn for the track to the chalet appeared ahead. "There's some bloody earthshattering new laws of physics involved in this, Kate. I can't help thinking we ought to tell someone."

"You'd have to be able to demonstrate it, though, otherwise it'd be just a story, something you could easily have made up after doing the research. And anyway, what was the other thing bugging you?"

He drew the car to a halt in front of the chalet, beyond which the clouds he'd seen in the morning had grown to a white-topped wall of grey above the sea's dark horizon. Colin applied the handbrake and turned to face Kate.

"Why. We still haven't answered the 'Why'. Today we've discovered that the 'Effect' is certainly real, but we're still ignorant of the 'Cause'. Why *is* this happening? Is it just some random phenomenon, or is there a conscious purpose behind it, and if so, whose?"

"Well, Colin, there's only one way we can possibly find that out."

"Yeah, well, first off, I'm going to have at least one spliff for my own enjoyment, before I have one for the road—the road back to Jusuf that's now clearly beyond circumstantial."

23 A TENURE DUE A TENURE

As Colin hitched his leather bag higher onto his shoulder and wearily approached where the dirt road widened outside the smithy, his long day's walk demanded he quench his thirst before going in. He made a beeline for the spring opposite, absently noting a handcart standing in the late afternoon sunshine before the barn's door, its shafts tilted down against the quarry flags. Some of their neighbour's children were playing there, briefly halting their game of tag to wave across and call "Master Joseph". He waved back, smiling, although the children themselves seemed not to smile.

One of the smithy's buckets stood beside the spring, full of water and unattended, and at which Jusuf frowned before dipping both hands in to lift a drink to his lips. His narrowed gaze drifted across at the smithy again, at the half-open wicket door, through which one of the boys now slipped. Although dark within, he could just make out people milling about.

Jusuf scooped up another drink, its invigorating cool edge bringing him to close his eyes. When he reopened them, Rodrigo stood before him, his usually sunned face seemingly wan and drawn.

"I suspect you've ill-tidings to unfold, my friend," Jusuf said, wiping his sleeve across his mouth as he stood and once more stared across at the smithy. "It's not Mistress Trewin, is it?"

"Not exactly; her husband," which words captured Jusuf's gaze. "One of her neighbours from down the road returned this morning."

"From the rebel army?"

"They've only just brought him up to see the *senhora.* Although he's in a poor way, he insisted on speaking to her face-to-face. He…he saw her husband fall at the battle of Blackheath."

"Fall?" and Jusuf could barely bring himself to imagine Mistress Trewin's distress.

But Rodrigo surprised him when he said, "She's been remarkably strong; seems keen to see you."

"Me?"

"I said I'd take you to her as soon as you were back from Rame."

When Jusuf came to stand in the smithy's doorway, its barn seemed smaller, crowded as it was by its half dozen awkwardly disposed men and women. The subdued hubbub dwindled away the minute he stepped in, towering above them as he stared amongst their faces for that of his mistress.

"She's in her cottage," Rodrigo quietly told him, coming up beside and nodding towards the door through from the barn, the one beyond which he'd never dared venture. "She's with Old Meg from next door, the man himself still and a couple of his women neighbours who helped him up here."

Jusuf passed between the familiar but averted faces and approached the doorway. In the poor light within the cottage stood two women, either side of a man clearly uncomfortably seated on a wooden chair set before an unlit hearth. Their backs to Jusuf, they faced Mistress Trewin, herself sitting in a chair behind which hovered a grim-faced Meg. The old woman noticed Jusuf and beckoned him in before bending to whisper in the ear of the mistress.

Mistress Trewin immediately lifted her haunted gaze to him, recognition and a fleeting glint of something else distracting him from her resolute lips. She placed her hand on the man's then looked up at Jusuf once more. Those about her followed her gaze, each settling their own on Jusuf.

As though by prior arrangement, in turn they nodded first at her and then at him, before helping the injured man up and finally to hobble past Jusuf as he stepped aside.

"Thank 'e, Master Wilfred," the mistress called after the man. "I be grateful for thy time and kind effort. God speed your healing," but he only paused in the doorway and nodded before briefly turning his scarred face up at Jusuf. Then he hobbled out, leaving Jusuf and the mistress alone together.

"Please, come in and sit 'e down, Master Jusuf."

"Shall I close the door, Mistress?"

"No…no, best not. We can…we can talk privy enough."

He eased himself into the man's vacated chair, its wood creaking at his weight, and placed his shoulder bag down by his side. At last, he nerved himself to look her in the face, unsure what he saw there other than an emptiness about her eyes.

"Mistress," he slowly said, searching for his words, "my English be too poor still to speak true of what I…of what I feel at your loss. But—"

"Thank 'e, Master Jusuf," and she sniffed back a tear as she briefly leant forward and touched his hand. "'Tis good of 'e, but your concern can be of more use if you just let me tell you something of my past."

She smoothed her skirt at her knees and stared down at her hands, which she then folded upon them before looking aside at the cold hearth. The light coming in through the window opening at the end of the room behind Jusuf painted the beauty of her features pale against the dimly lit room behind, like a half-moon in the grey sky of a cold winter's eve.

"Once, Master Jusuf," she quietly said, her gaze still fixed upon the hearth, "the flush of love for my husband-to-be coursed hotly through my blood. The kind that can only spring forth from a maid of fourteen years. The kind that before long quickened my belly in our carefree pleasures, despite us not having plighted our troth. That left me foolish enough to hold a still warm heart so close to a man ill-chosen."

When Jusuf only frowned, now looking himself at the hearth, the mistress turned back to him, her gaze catching his eyes, drawing them to the wet glaze of her own.

"Maeloc, my husband, did right by me, though, Master Jusuf. He eventually stood at my right side before the door of Saint Petroc's, before its canon priest, and there we said us vows to each other in front of those gathered to witness."

"You had a…a child?"

"Nay, Master Jusuf. Within a two month, poor mite had slipped from my carrying, a three month afore due and me left sickly near unto the same fate. But Maeloc cared for me, I'll give him that. Worked harder then for his father and me than ever he did thereafter. Certainly not once I took to looking after this smithy's affairs when we came to dwell here. But though I remained a wife to him, my womb never quickened again, my love all the while waning at the prospect that lay before me. I grew up quickly then, Master Jusuf, saw my husband for what he truly were: lazy and a poor workman. As the proverb goes: 'Hot love be soon cold'."

Voices rose in the barn, one of the women who'd attended the man popping her head through the doorway to announce: "We need to get Master Wilfred home, Mistress Trewin. He be none too good all of a sudden, but better for having told 'e himself. We're truly sorrowful for your ill-tidings, mistress, that we are. 'Tis a shame an' all, but we want 'e to know us thoughts be with thee," and at a nod from Mistress Trewin, the woman was gone.

"I don't understand, Mistress," Jusuf presently said. "But why are you telling me all this?"

"Maeloc's death—if it truly be so—most cruelly straitens my prospects, Master Jusuf. And so I'm brought to lay my future in your good hands…your more than capably good craftsman's hands," and she briefly placed her own on his.

"You said 'If it truly be so', but Rodrigo told me your husband had been seen to fall."

"Fall, aye," then she looked about the dimly lit room and softly sighed. "Maeloc be a tenant blacksmith here, Master Jusuf. This smithy and its land be demesne of the priory, us tenure here held in consideration of moneys paid each quarter day. That contract, though, be in his name only."

A quiet knock at the open door interrupted, and Rodrigo called in if he may enter. He carried a mug of small ale for Jusuf and asked after Mistress Trewin's needs, but she demurred. Then she clearly realised and bade Jusuf forgive her her thoughtlessness.

"You must be parched after your long journey. Are you hungry?" but Jusuf shook his head.

"Later, Mistress," and he thanked Rodrigo as the man quietly slipped from the room. The ale did far more to quench Jusuf's thirst than had the spring water, and he felt a little sharper of mind when the mistress carried on.

"At my husband's death, that contract, and so my own right to dwell here, will come to an end."

"And so, too, my service to you," Jusuf voiced, a sadness washing over him: the thought of having to find a new position elsewhere, but also the predicament in which it would then leave his mistress. "But surely, with Master Wilfred's report, isn't the contract already broken?"

"Master Wilfred saw Maeloc's *fall*, not his…" but the wetness that had hung about her eyes at last trickled onto her cheeks. She checked herself, dabbing at her eyes with her sleeve. "Forgive me, Master Jusuf, but though my love for Maeloc long ago cooled, I will sorely miss him still."

They sat quietly for a while, Jusuf unable to take his gaze from Mistress Trewin's hands in her lap, hands she absently wrung together. Finally, she sniffed back her tears.

"Maeloc's friend Master Wilfred did not see my

husband's mortal remains. He's assured me he could not swear to his death, not in truth upon a Bible, nor in truth by his own conscience, knowing the hurt it would bring my position. Without mortal remains it would take three good men and true to swear witness upon the deed, for Maeloc then to be pronounced as having departed this life."

"So, you have a little time yet, then, Mistress, at least until others return from the battle."

"Or if none saw him die or are prepared to swear upon it, then until three years have passed. I'm told it's not uncommon for the defeated dead to be consigned to a common grave, their names never known, their deaths unattested."

"Three years," and Jusuf contemplated what this might mean. "Would it be possible," he eventually ventured, "for the time Rodrigo and I remain here—until next Spring in all likelihood—that my labours for the smithy could carry on paying what would be due each quarter day?"

For the first time, Mistress Trewin smiled, a small smile that lit Jusuf's heart far more so than her own features. "I would be beholden to you, Master Jusuf. Truly I would. For ever in your debt, for, you see, my sewing alone could never bring in enough coin."

Jusuf sat back and considered it further. Certainly, the mistress had been kind to take them both in in the first place, but he recognised something else that coloured his thoughts. Something that sat uneasily with the burden he'd long since taken on, and which only now, regrettably, he allowed himself to remember.

Then he wondered why Mistress Trewin had felt compelled to disclose the loss of her love for her husband, and the loss of the child she'd carried. It seemed somehow far more than simply an explanation for her restrained wifely grief.

Mistress Trewin averted her gaze whilst he thought some more, again staring into the hearth. This time, though, as he too stared that same way, it felt as though a warm fire blazed there. His face felt the heat of those imagined flames, and he spoke before he'd really concluded his reasoning, his voice sounding unlike his own.

"I will promise you my labours, Mistress Trewin, for as long as your husband's contract of tenure should last." He couldn't, though, quite bring himself to lay his final condition upon the tail end of his words: that his promise must end when the Nao Providência be free once more to carry him and his burden to Santander.

24 THE WEAVING OF STRANDS

When Jusuf came to leave Mistress Trewin's cottage and went back into the almost deserted barn, he found Rodrigo had prepared him some food. His bowl and a chunk of bread lay on one of the benches, not far from where Old Meg sat on a stool, his friend leaning against the bench behind her.

"How be she?" Meg quietly asked.

"Bearing up," he told her as he put his bag down to one side on the bench.

"She be a strong maid, that one," and the woman rose a little stiffly to her feet, then stared at him as he sat down to his meal. "But then, a maid's strength can only go so far, Master Jusuf. Only so far in this world of ours afore she be a-needing a man's name."

Jusuf stopped his spoon before his lips and slowly turned to look up at the old woman. Behind her back, Rodrigo smiled to himself. She curtly nodded and creaked her way towards the cottage door, freeing Jusuf at last from her stare.

He noisily slurped at the spoonful of hot potage as

Meg called out, "Am I all right a-coming in, Gwenna?" Then, as she closed the door behind her, they heard her say: "Just wondered if there be anything I could do for thee, afore I get off home".

Jusuf stared at Rodrigo. "What was all that about?" he said in Arabic.

"She doesn't miss a thing, our Old Meg, though I reckon I'm not that far behind her myself," and he seemed somewhat amused.

"Well, whatever she meant, I've something just as puzzling you might cast some light on," and as Jusuf ate, he went through, for Rodrigo's ears, what the mistress had told him.

Rodrigo's eyes steadily widened as his brows lofted. When Jusuf had finished, he whistled softly to himself, but then said nothing, only propped his elbow on the bench, raised its cupped hand to his chin and stared off into an unseen distance.

"So," Jusuf eventually had to say, "why tell me about her and her husband, and the babe she lost?"

"Hmm, well," and a twinkle appeared in Rodrigo's eyes, "that last one's plain enough to answer. If she's been made barren by her loss, then the mistress will have little chance of finding a new husband. No man is willingly going to choose to die without a blood heir to follow him on."

"Do you think that's what Meg meant when she said a woman could only go so far?"

"You may be slow sometimes, my friend, but you are at least making a fine name for yourself as a blacksmith; I'll give you that. I keep my eyes and ears open when I'm about, you know, especially in the taverns. Only yesterday there were some miners in the Garland Ox talking about coming to see you, something about improving their tools. And I know the priory are more than content with your work. Mistress Trewin was only saying the other day how she'd never seen Brother Jowan so pleased before, certainly not when paying out for work done them."

Jusuf could only stare at Rodrigo, his mouth gaping, the remains of the food in his bowl for the moment forgotten.

"You know, Jusuf, you could do far worse than settle here in Bodmyn. At least you'd be your own man, not servant to a master as you are in Ceuta."

"Here? In Cornwall? I don't think I could live the rest of my life in such a cold place, Rodrigo, and this is its summer. And anyway, that's the only reason I'm abroad: on my master's errand; in service to his orders."

"Cornwall's a long way from Ceuta, Jusuf. A very long way."

Jusuf thought hard about this novel idea, almost too afraid to believe it could really be within his own choosing. But he knew, deep down, he would have to deliver his burden to Santander, his chance of living here in Cornwall then lost for ever.

"You could always return to Bodmyn from Santander," Rodrigo was saying, but then brought himself up short. "Ah, but the Nao Providência would have to return straightaway to Ceuta, with whatever lading could be taken onboard before you'd be allowed ashore to do the deed. The captain would insist on covering some of his losses. So how, without our ship, would you get away promptly enough from Santander? For if you stayed with us and sailed on to Ceuta, you'd never get back here in time to meet the smithy's next quarter day payment."

Jusuf, though, had already decided, seeing no way to

weave all the strands together into a serviceable cloth. Certainly not one to clothe such an unthinkable hope.

"How long," he asked Rodrigo, "do you really reckon it will take the captain to have his petition to the King granted? Keeping in mind how Henry's thoughts must be consumed by his war with Scotland. And not helped, of course, by the unrest fomenting here in Cornwall."

Rodrigo sucked in air through his teeth as he poured ale into his mug from a jug by his elbow. He took a long quaff and stared hard at Jusuf. "Quite honestly, despite what the captain said, I'd be surprised if he got back before, well, before the end of next summer. I've already decided to make my own way back to Portugal if we hear nothing from him by then."

"More than a year, eh? But still less than the three Mistress Trewin's likely to have left of her tenure here—provided the payments are kept up."

"Which reminds me: I know you said your gift would remain potent for a long time, but long enough to last through to the end of next year?"

Jusuf laughed, but quietly, wary of disturbing the mistress and Old Meg with such an unseemly sound. "I was assured, my friend, that it would remain 'Efficacious for a thousand years'."

"A thousand, eh? Is that so? In which case, if by the time the Nao Providência is once more at our service, and the mistress has found another place to lay her head by then, you could still complete your master's quest and return with us to Ceuta as planned. Better late than never, I suppose. But you've time on your side, Jusuf, so there's no pressing need to make up your mind either way, not just yet."

Jusuf finished off his meal then reached across and upended his bag, spilling its contents onto the bench. "Well," he said, sorting through his things, "at least I've work to keep me occupied. This new bell headstock and frame I've got to forge should make a pretty penny or two for the smithy. It's going to need the finest of iron, though, properly wrought, and quenched just right."

"Well, of all the blacksmiths in Bodmyn, I'm sure you're the best for the task, my friend," but then the cottage door opened and Meg came through.

"I'll see 'e both anon," she said to them as she crossed the barn to the wicket door, where she then stopped. "I don't think the poor maid's thought to eat since Master Wilfred's tidings, so maybe thee'll conjure up something for her, eh? Then you might keep her company and her mind from her worst fears." Again, she held Jusuf in her gaze before nodding the once to them both and stepping out into the early evening light.

"I'll sort something out for her, Jusuf. You go and invite her through to join us," and Rodrigo pushed himself away from the bench. It brought Jusuf to be thankful that Rodrigo had taken to doing much of the cooking, in part payment for his portion of their lodging, for Jusuf doubted his own efforts would have sufficed.

"Right," he said, somewhat absently, trying hard to get his mind around all the day had brought. He'd a feeling something had eluded him, but something everyone else somehow seemed to know full well. He didn't ask, though, for a voice at the back of his mind seemed to whisper a hint at least of what it might indeed have been.

But then Rodrigo called from the forge, "Oh, and by the way, do you think you'd be all right looking after yourself and Mistress Trewin the week after next? You know, with all that's happened. Because there's somewhere I'd like to go that week."

"Er, well," but then Jusuf reckoned he could get by well enough, now he was more confident with the local speech, although he'd also miss Rodrigo's superior shipboard-style cooking. "Where were you thinking of going?"

"Well," Rodrigo called back, "you know I've been getting more carpentry work?"

"Reviving the skills you learnt as a young shipwright, eh?" Jusuf said as he wandered into the half-light of the forge.

"Indeed; before the sea called me away." Rodrigo smiled, stirring a pot on the hearth's charcoals. "But the thing is, some of the other carpenters have been talking about a church that's having new pews fitted. I thought I'd offer my labour for…well, for free."

"For free? I know you managed to keep your money safe from Captain Treffry's men, but that seems a bit—"

"I feel a need to give thanks properly, Jusuf."

"Thanks?"

"To God. For having bestowed salvation on us all from that storm," and Jusuf finally understood, standing quietly beside his friend as he waited. "Actually, I've already offered to carve a pew end."

"Carve?"

"Yes, something that… Well, something that came to me in a…in a dream: the Nao Providência within the teeth of the storm, its rigging torn down, and…and you, Jusuf, lifting the mast away from my chest."

At first, Jusuf could only stare at Rodrigo, smitten by his words, lost for his own. But then embarrassment brought its own reply: "It wasn't just me, though, Rodrigo. Others helped me—"

"Yes, but it was you who first came to my aid. You who led by your fine example. And the one I least expected—which shameful thought drives my need the more to give thanks to God. Thanks for salvation, and…and for a true if unexpected friend."

Jusuf didn't know what to say, but then Rodrigo went on: "And what more befitting way, eh, Jusuf? With God's good grace, I may leave something that will last the ravages of time, just as we survived the ravages of that storm. Then, my friend, my gratitude can speak out to the many who'll come its way long after I've left this life."

The pan began to boil over and Rodrigo swore as he lifted it away from the heat, Jusuf unable to hold down his rising mirth.

"Maybe I couldn't do any worse while you're away," he told Rodrigo as the man hastily set the pan down on the stone floor. "So yes, of course I'll cope, and you can feel free to get yourself off to… Where did you say this church was?"

"Saint Winnow. It seems we must have passed it on the way up the Foy estuary, for it sits on its eastern bank, not far south of Lostwithiel." Then they both looked down at the pan.

"If you think you can rescue that," Jusuf said, "I'll go and ask the mistress if she'd like to come through and eat," and he smiled at his good friend's beleaguered look. Then he laughed and slapped him on the arm. "Let's just hope she's really hungry, eh? Or she'll just have to make do with the fine bread you bought," and at that, Jusuf left him and went through the barn towards the cottage door.

As he drew near, he again heard that whisper at the back of his mind, the one that had tried to warn him earlier of where his heart was going. But he still wouldn't heed it, even when that heart leapt in his chest as he rapped on Mistress Trewin's door, and as he listened out for her sweetest of voices.

25 FINALLY BROUGHT HOME

Saint Winnow had proved stubbornly absent from Colin's road atlas, neither in its index nor anywhere along the River Fowey or its estuary on the relevant map page. The only clue seemed to be the thin red vein of a minor road that led to an unnamed end on the east bank of the estuary, south of Lostwithiel.

They'd set off there early in the morning, eventually turning off the main road not far before Lostwithiel, south down a narrow Cornish lane signposted for Lerryn and Couch's Mill. Both these, too, appeared to have been overlooked by the atlas.

Now onto minor roads, little could be seen over the high hedgebanks, just the occasional glimpse into fields and beyond, to low rounded hills in the west. Colin began to doubt they'd plumped for the right junction as the lane narrowed yet further still, snaking its way towards the morning's grey, cloud-smudged southern sky.

After a couple of forced U-turns, they at long last and with some relief came upon a junction almost invisibly signposted for "ST WINNOW". It was some time, though, before this even narrower lane took them down through dense woods and out to their first sighting of a square church tower, rising some way beyond low farm buildings off to one side. The lane soon came to an abrupt but wide end, facing the waters of the estuary.

Parked to one side of what was clearly a turning circle stood a lone car, facing a gravel track opposite that led off towards the church. Colin pulled in beside the car, and he and Kate got out.

The silence seemed almost deafening, the view across the estuary sublime, the sweep and swoop of house martins almost magical in the warm and still air. Colin, though, felt rain in it and so pulled his and Kate's jackets out of the boot. As they slipped them on, Colin asked Kate if she felt as nervous as he did. She nodded and bit her lip before grinning uncertainly.

"If it's still here, Colin, still recognisable from Rodrigo's description, then…then it'll be as near as damn it conclusive," and she widened her eyes in wary excitement.

The churchyard at the end of the track surprised Colin by its size, its wide drift of weathered and angled headstones surrounding a typically late medieval church building. It stood on a gently elevated position beside the estuary. Colin felt a few spots of rain as they followed a path between the graves to the church's south porch, through whose heavy inner door they slipped into a musty but bright interior.

The place seemed deserted, devoid not just of anyone else but of any sound other than the soft tread of their feet on the stone-flagged floor. Despite the overcast sky without, the stained-glass of the tall, narrow windows lent a joyous clarity to the air within, even with its close and clammy feel. Here, the colours of saints and of miracles cut sharply through the scent of age-old damp stonework and dry, dusty timber.

As though an imposition on its tranquillity, Colin and Kate stepped as quietly as they could into the central aisle. There, they stood between the nave's glossy, rum-brown pews.

"Do a side each?" Colin whispered, and Kate nodded. He'd only looked disappointedly at his first couple of pew ends, though, before Kate's echoing gasp startled him.

"It's here," she tried to whisper, her excitement, though, echoing about the church, and Colin hurried to her side.

"Shit," he hardly breathed, his mouth then hanging open. They both crouched down for a closer look.

"Wow," Kate said, clearly in expectation of what Colin was about to say.

"Wow," he dutifully whispered, reaching a tentative finger out to feel the relief of the carving. "Just think, Kate, I'm touching what Rodrigo touched all that time ago. What my true friend carved with his own hands. Christ, but that's a weird thought. And look, there they are: Jusuf and Rodrigo. Although…it's a bit hard to see exactly what they're doing; but isn't that a bit of the mast poking up above the ship's rail between them?"

"It could be," Kate said, peering even closer, "but it is well-worn, and a bit of the wood's flaked off, but I'd say the one on the left definitely looks African, and the one below him European. And it's even got a couple of the sails they didn't manage to furl up in time."

"And that must be the captain on the quarterdeck,

there. See?" and he ran his finger over the figure's face. "But what's he looking at? Hey, there in the clouds, do you see? There's a monkey!"

"I think it's meant to be the face of the storm, Colin, blowing down on the ship. See? All these lines coming from its mouth."

"Oh. Right," but then Colin screwed his face up. "He wasn't a very good carver, though, was he, our Rodrigo? Not much of an artist. I mean, it all looks a bit, well, a bit…"

"Primitive?" Kate suggested. "But just look at the power of it: the angry swirling of the clouds, the terror in their faces, the turbulent sea tossing beneath the ship, the horror and fear he's managed to capture."

"Yeah; yeah, I see what you mean."

"And can't you sense Rodrigo's relief? Don't you feel it? The joy of having come through it all alive, of being here, safe and sound, able to carve the whole thing as a statement of thanks to both God and his close friend, Jusuf. What was it he said? 'So my gratitude can speak out to the many who'll come its way long after I've left this life'. Well, there you are, Colin; I reckon he achieved that in bucket-loads, far better than a lot of the more polished stuff you'll see. That's got real emotion to it. It really has." But to Colin, that now wonderful work of art had become blurred, its image swimming through a sheen of tears that had welled in his eyes.

Before he knew it, he was standing in the south porch, staring out through gentle rain. The gravestones glistened along their shoulders, the grass more vibrantly green between, the trees beyond the graveyard's wall a touch more pastel in their rain-veiled stands.

"You all right?" Kate's soft voice said at his back, and her arms slipped around his waist.

He nodded, not trusting himself to speak.

They stood there for a while, watching the rain wet the world outside, feeling the air lighten as the sky grew steadily brighter. Then the shower eased off and the heavy scents of summer rose about them as the air warmed. A hint of blue sky appeared above the trees, a slash of hope for a drier day to come.

Colin drew in a ragged breath and shivered. "It's silly, really," he quietly said, squeezing his crossed arms against Kate's own about his waist.

"No, it's not, Colin. It's understandable. Rodrigo's become just as close a friend to you as to Jusuf; he's bound to have. You've been Jusuf, after all, closer to him than to anyone else, really, so it's hardly surprising."

"It's just that… Well, this has been the first real physical contact with either of them; something we've both handled, that Rodrigo actually made. And maybe even Jusuf got down here to see it. You never know. And he'd have certainly run his hand over it, as I just did. I'm sure he would have. It sort of took me by surprise, that's all."

They eventually left Saint Winnow for Lostwithiel, both in silence at first as they retraced their route to the main road. Colin, though, had been thinking hard, trying to square a circle that had been a consistent worry since that first day he'd pushed a joss stick into Kate's holder, back in the hot summer of seventy-six. For all his science training, for all his degree had equipped him to reason rationally, he now knew that that demanding discipline fell far short of the whole truth.

By the time they'd parked up in a Pay and Display on the outskirts of Lostwithiel's town centre, Colin had at last come to terms with the gaping hole riven through his touchstone of a rigorous scientific approach. Wasn't this, after all, what science demanded? he thought to himself as they searched out the old riverside quay. To be tested by observation, and always open to being found wanting.

They soon found the quayside. Colin then unerringly led Kate through the streets of Lostwithiel, the familiarity he continuously experienced no longer unnerving him. The awe the beautiful parish church instilled turned out to be—he here joyfully acknowledged—a mix of his own and what he remembered of Jusuf's. This truly warmed his heart, enough to bring an irrepressible smile to his lips long before they finally stood outside The Globe Inn.

"So, this is where the brothers took them for breakfast?" Kate said as Colin stared up at the remarkably recognisable building.

Inside, it turned out to be a little less familiar, cluttered as it was with its centuries of history and all its more modern changes. But it still had a feel Colin readily recognised, as though the stones themselves carried the memory. Once they'd bought drinks and ordered something to eat, the quiet pub meant they easily found an out-of-the-way corner table.

Kate took a sip of her gin and tonic. "You know you said the pew end was the only physical contact you've had with them, well, there is Jusuf's burden, remember—our joss stick holder." Having taken a drink of his St Austell's Tribute pale ale, Colin opened the eyes he'd close and looked at her across the small table between them.

"But that's still only conjecture, Kate. We've no proof that that's what it is. And I'm beginning to wonder if we're wrong. It seems Jusuf's dead set on getting his burden to… Where was it, again?"

"*Castilla y León*, which I'm pretty sure was the bulk of what's now Spain; two once separate kingdoms united through marriage; the usual historical manoeuvrings."

"Indeed, set on getting his burden there to use somehow against the Christian infidels, the ones who'd nicked his own people's country."

"Amongst which infidels he ended up living, albeit the ones here in Cornwall, one of whom he seems to have got the hots for," and Kate grinned.

"Eh?"

"Mistress Trewin?" and she shook her head at his perplexed look. "Surely you've twigged that one?"

"What? Jusuf and…Gwenna, wasn't it?"

"Bloody 'ell, Colin. You can be as slow as Jusuf sometimes; do you know that? Yeah, Gwenna."

"Well, yeah; she is beautiful. I know Jusuf sees that. He couldn't not, now could he? I mean, you've got the same blood as her, so she's bound to be stunning," at which Kate's pixie look rapidly bloomed across her quickly down-tipped face, her dainty ears suffusing coral-pink.

"Well, be that as it may," she managed, avoiding his grinning eyes, "but from what you've described, I'd say it's pretty mutual."

"But he's no chance…has he?"

"What? Because he's a black man?" and she gave him a snooty laugh. "There wasn't the same cultural racism then, Colin. *Everyone* beyond your own village was foreign in those days, and so not to be trusted, regardless of their colour. No less so than the English if you were Cornish."

"I was actually referring to his religion."

"Oh. That. Right. Well, yes and no." She took a longer sip of her drink. "Depends if they wanted to get married or not. But even then, they could just plight their troth to each other, which in Canon Law was enough to make them wed, whether it was in a church before a priest or not. It *was* usual, though, to have it witnessed, I must admit, to avoid later dispute…and to ensure the community's approval."

"Which wouldn't have been a problem for Jusuf, given how valued he was as a blacksmith."

"Maybe, but then, the smithy was owned by the priory, remember? Where much of his work came from. So they'd probably have frowned on such simple handfasting. On the other hand, if it meant their retaining a brilliant blacksmith, well, they could always have turned a blind eye, I suppose. Business was business, even back then."

"Right," Colin mused, staring absently across the bar's lounge for a moment before returning his gaze to Kate. "But coming back to Jusuf's burden: I'd say he ended up taking it to Santander, that it didn't end up staying here at all. He was obviously dead set on finishing off his task, which would then make our joss stick holder something else, and a far safer something else, thank God. Although that would leave unanswered what the damned thing really is."

He pushed himself back into his seat and sighed. "This is all doing my head in. Do you know that, Kate? And I can't help thinking it's Jusuf who's driving it all, that he had a purpose in mind. That he wanted us to do something for him. But I'm blowed if I can think what."

"Maybe that's yet to come, Colin. After all, until

the fat lady sings, and all that."

"What? Oh, yeah. Or until Jusuf shows me what the hell he wants from me."

"And lets you know before his dope runs out. Don't forget that. After all, when we're back in Manchester, *you* can always go to Jimmy Wrigley's and buy some more."

26 FINGERS CROSSED

"So, did you manage to get hold of Louise?" Colin asked Kate when she eventually came back into the chalet.

"Finally, yes. There were two young teenage girls jammed in the phone box, obviously giggling away to boys on the other end, but I got through to her in the end, before she'd left work."

"And?"

"There isn't any tea going, is there?"

"I'll make us one."

Colin went into the galley as Kate sat down on the sofa and told him: "She assured me that nothing of the sort happened in Castille and Leon anywhere around that date. Nothing to threaten the country, anyway. In fourteen-ninety-nine there was a Moorish uprising in the recently conquered Granada that was soon put down, but that was far away in the south. The other end of the country from Santander. Otherwise, Spain has remained a pretty stable country all the way through to the present."

"And she's the Rylands' expert for that period?"

"If she says 'Nothing happened', then nothing happened."

"Well, I know the Moors never returned to Spain—even I know that—so whatever Jusuf's burden was meant to do clearly couldn't have worked. But I was hoping there'd have been at least a record of his attempt."

"Maybe his burden didn't quite remain 'Efficacious for a thousand years', eh? Maybe not even one."

Colin left the tea to brew and went back in to join Kate, sitting down beside her. "Or maybe it did but stayed here in Cornwall—unused."

"Maybe."

"And then found its way to you in Manchester," and they both stared at the joss stick holder, still sitting innocently on the table opposite.

"We need to know more, Colin."

"All right. After tea this evening, then; speaking of which…" and he got up to pour their brews.

After they'd eaten that evening, washed up and put away, Colin settled down beside Kate in their deckchairs in the garden, to roll a spliff.

The day had indeed turned out to be dry and sunny, and pleasantly warm after the morning rain in Saint Winnow. Now at its waning, its dark-blue sky to the west had taken to it a fiery red blaze. Shafts of golden light speared through a vestige of cloud along the horizon as the sun sank behind the dark mass of land that rose beyond Portwrinkle. Overhead, the brightest stars already pricked through the inky blue sky, leaving Colin feeling it couldn't get much better.

"Still a fair bit left," he told Kate as he applied the flame of his Zippo to the lump of dope, softening it so it could be crumbled into the waiting line of tobacco. Before long, he rested back in his chair and stared up at the expansive but rapidly darkening heavens.

For a while he waited, watching the sky darken to velvet black, the perfect cloth from which the myriad stars could blaze. He lit the spliff and took a long toke, staring out at the seemingly unending ocean, one that rightly took the name of the greatest of great Greek gods. Atlas held all that majesty upon his shoulders, and it took Colin's breath away.

Arching across it all, pointing at far off South America, swept what Colin knew to be the spiral arms of their own great galaxy: the Milky Way. So vast and open did the sky seem that he could almost see a depth to it, almost felt dizzy at the panoply of stars that studded their own small view of this, their vast and truly awe inspiring universe.

A short streak of white trailed briefly high up above his gaze and he gasped "Wow, a shooting star" before crossing his fingers and making a wish.

"Aw, I missed it," Kate said, putting her cup of coffee down on the grass and staring up. "You'd better—"

"I already have," and Colin smiled, hoping it would presently come true.

When he'd finished his smoke, they went back in to the warmly-lit welcome of the chalet. There, they sat either side of the table, the joss stick holder between them. Colin removed a stick from its pack, finding it only a little more difficult with his fingers still crossed.

Before long, he was hanging up his leather apron on its hook and wiping sweat from his bare arms and chest with a towel. He glanced around the forge, satisfied he'd left everything safe, then picked up his shirt from where he'd left it and went through to the cottage.

The small table against the wall beside the door was already set for their meal, Gwenna at the trough under the unshuttered window opening, straining vegetables from a pan. Even with the fire set for the hearth's oven, the cottage still felt refreshingly cooler than the stiflingly close forge.

Gwenna glanced over her shoulder. "I won't be long, then 'e can get here to wash thee self off. There be an already hot kettle above the fire, and you can take your time. The food won't spoil."

Jusuf became entranced by her shadowed shape, slight against the opening: her narrow waist and broad back, her fluid but strong arms, the awry tangle of hair at the nape of her neck that had escaped her kerchief.

"I'm glad you be a-cooking while Rodrigo's away, Gwenna. I don't think we'd have lasted long on my fare," but the distraction of his words didn't work, and still he gazed at her industrious figure.

"It's helped keep me busy, Jusuf, and you've been so busy yourself, what with your work for the Saint Germanus bell, so it's only fair. Especially as I've not had much sewing in. Here," and she stepped aside from the trough, half turning to face him, pan in one hand, colander in the other.

She froze, but against the glare of the daylight behind her, Jusuf couldn't quite read her face to say why.

"Er," she managed to get out, then, "I'll…I'll just put this to keep warm, then I…then I need to check the meat," and she hurried past him to the hearth.

Jusuf soon scrubbed up, drying himself off before slipping his shirt back on and tucking it into his breeches. Gwenna was by then no longer in the room, although he heard her coming back through the barn. She carried in a full bucket of water and placed it down by the hearth, all the while keeping her eyes averted.

"Can I help," Jusuf offered, but she said not, only that he'd to sit at the table and she'd bring him his dish. They finally sat facing one another, Gwenna hurriedly saying her own form of grace, to include Allah, before they both tucked in.

After a while, keeping her gaze to her food, she quietly said, "Has thee heard the tidings yet: about my husband's cousin?"

Jusuf said he hadn't.

"Seems he were hanged as a traitor a few days after Blackheath, along with that lawyer and some peer of the realm who'd joined them along the way, their heads then gibbeted on pikestaffs on London Bridge."

Jusuf stopped eating and stared across at her.

It drew her gaze from her dish. "Oh, sorry, Jusuf. I didn't mean to spoil your eating."

"No, that's all right. It was just that it made me wonder if…"

Gwenna slipped her hand onto his, pale against his bark-brown skin. "I know Rodrigo being down in Saint Winnow," she said, "means we don't get to hear his tavern-talk, but I still see what I need to in the eyes of some of the returned men I pass in the street. I see what I know they saw, but what they're kindly keeping close to their chests for the sake of my tenancy, for which I'm grateful. Although I must admit, I do sometimes think, just for a moment, that the noises you make are Maeloc's, your hammering and your working the bellows. But I'm already finding my peace, Jusuf, so thee need not tread so softly."

All the while, her hand had remained warm upon

the back of his, her voice softer when she then said, "Your labours here, Jusuf, are bringing new memories to replace old, and for that alone I'm grateful." Her hand slipped from his, back across the table and into her lap. "But I cannot deny my fears, Jusuf. The prospect… Well, the prospect of having to leave this smithy fills my heart with dread."

For the first time since those fateful tidings had come upon Master Wilfred's lips, Jusuf felt able to ask, "Have you not got family who'll take you in?" Gwenna stared at him, her mind clearly elsewhere, then she hurriedly ate another mouthful before taking a large drink of the fresh spring water and swallowing hard.

"Father was taken by the sweating sickness a year afore I wed. Mother nearly went herself but for God's good grace; an ague I was for some reason spared."

She began to lift another spoonful to her lips but paused, gazing deep into Jusuf's eyes. "Not long after Maeloc and me moved here, my mother met a trader from Falmouth whose wife had recently died. It wasn't long before she'd moved in with him down there, with him and all his brood."

"But, wouldn't they have room for you?"

"It's eight years now, Jusuf, and I've seen neither hide nor hair of her. I don't even know if she be alive still," and Gwenna finally took a mouthful from her waiting spoon.

"Your husband's family?"

She laughed, bitterly, and shook her head. "They blame me for stealing away their only son, of tricking him into marriage. So, what of them, eh? Now their son's run away from a regretted marriage. And by it, met his end. And those I know well enough don't have the room, Jusuf. Meg's only got the one, though she's offered to share her pallet, bless her. But it wouldn't be fair, nor likely last our friendship long. I'm afeared, Jusuf, that for such as me, only the…only the streets or…or worse now stare me in the…"

She lowered her head, her shoulders rounded as silent sobs trembled through them. "I've tried hard not to…" she attempted, but her downcast words were swept away by her tears.

Jusuf quickly went to kneel at her side, slowly slipping an arm around her shoulders, tentatively offering comfort. She sniffed and slanted a wary look into his eyes, hers glistening and seeming so large in their nearness.

She choked back her tears and took in a deep breath. "I've tried hard, Jusuf, I really have, not to make you feel trapped. You're too kind and gentle for that, too honest and trusting, which is what… Which is what has so stolen my heart," and she buried her face in his shirt, shuddering in his surprised embrace. And before long, the breath of her sobs spread a deep but damp warmth against his chest.

When her distress continued unabated, he gently slipped his hand to her cheek, then under her chin and angled her face up to his own, her silken lips to his, their breaths then mingling as one. Their kiss, though, quickly pressed beyond uncertainty, urgent in its hurried heat and hunger. Gwenna's chair then tumbled unheeded to the floor as Jusuf stood, lifting her into his arms as he pressed her close to his heart.

27 NOTHING THAT RINGS ANY BELLS

A hollow echo reverberated through Colin's mind as he found himself standing at the chalet's table. The look on Gwenna's face seemed somehow more familiar, then it was Kate's face; her eyes narrowed, intent, lips slightly parted. She slipped around the table without a word and embraced Colin close to her heart, then drew him down to the sofa.

The evening steadily grew older about them until they eventually stilled in each other's arms, entwined as one. Kate must have felt the cooler night air for presently she stirred, pressing herself yet closer. She trailed her finger down his back, his soft sigh following in its wake.

"Well," she barely breathed, her voice tickling his chest, "that was quite a surprise."

Colin kissed the top of her head, then remembered Gwenna's face, before her cottage had given way to the chalet, and he wondered. He must have tensed, for Kate angled her head to look him in the eyes.

"Something wrong?" she said.

"No, nothing."

She tilted her head away and studied him more closely.

"You know how I made a wish on that shooting star?" to which she nodded. "Well, it didn't come true." Kate shivered and slowly untangled her limbs from his. She kissed him on his forehead and got up in search of her clothes.

"So, what did you wish for?"

"To find out if that really is Jusuf's burden," and he nodded towards the joss stick holder.

"And you didn't?"

He shook his head. "But I reckon *your* wish came true," and he smiled up at her.

"Mine?"

"You thought Jusuf and Gwenna had the hots for each other. Well, I can tell you now: they did."

"What? Come on, then, Colin. Tell me all," and as he did so he finally got dressed. By then Kate was sitting at the table, scribbling away on her pad.

When Colin had finished, she sat back and stared at him, where he sat on the sofa.

"Are you thinking what I'm thinking?" she said in growing wonder. "That out of the blue I somehow picked up on…"

"It does seem a bit odd, and I definitely felt I'd been pushed out of Jusuf's mind somehow. Sort of…excluded at the crucial moment, which only seems right, I suppose."

"But… But that would mean there's a connection between me and Gwenna, not just you and Jusuf."

"What did I say the other day, down on the beach? You as the fishing line. But maybe it's more than that."

"More?"

"Maybe you're the…the anchor."

"Now you really are stretching the analogy."

"But think about it. You're somehow of the same line as Gwenna, the same blood, whereas I'm certainly not of Jusuf's. And you wondering if there really was something developing between them does seem to have guided my phantasm—straight to the defining moment."

"Shit. But do you think so? Really? Damn, but I can't remember what it was that was in my mind before your other visits."

"Well, it doesn't really matter now. But if I'm right, I reckon it will next time. Before I stick another lit joss stick into that holder," and again he nodded towards it, "we'd better make sure you have just the right question in mind, nice and clear and targeted."

"Nice and clear and targeted," Kate repeated, like a mantra. "But which question? And if it's not how Jusuf and Gwenna's entanglement's getting on, then how do I stop my natural curiosity from spoiling whatever we do decide we want to know?"

"Ah. Maybe this isn't going to be quite as easy as I thought."

Kate stared blankly at him for a moment, her skin still glowing. "The weather report for tomorrow's not ideal for going on the beach," she finally said. "How do you fancy a walk?"

"Yeah. I think we need a break from the fifteenth century, and it might just give us a fresh focus on what we want out of the next phantasm."

"Give *me* a focus," Kate said, more to herself, "but how can I stop wondering how Gwenna and Jusuf are making out?" then she smiled, a hint of the pixie once more about her gleaming eyes.

"Shall we go to bed?" she said and grinned, and Colin was more than happy to be led there.

The following morning, Colin drove them the few miles east along the clifftop road to where it turned sharply inland. On the inside of the bend lay a triangular verge on which a couple of cars had already been parked, and where Kate suggested they leave their own. From a junction opposite, a narrow open lane carried on towards the peninsula, down which Kate led Colin as he hitched their rucksack onto his shoulder.

"I thought we'd go along the coast path from Rame Head to Cawsand and Kingsand," Kate said, "have some lunch there and then make our way back here on the road we used the other day; you remember? Coming back from Millbrook."

Colin did, recognising the sharp bend they'd parked by as the one that had so suddenly revealed this dramatic view of Whitsand Bay. He also remembered Kate mentioning that the Lizard Point was sometimes visible and turned that way. Gwenna's cousin-in-law, the fateful leader of the rebellion, had come from there, but the view this time proved even hazier.

The lane slowly slanted them away from the coast, then past a large farm and to a junction, where they followed a signpost for Rame Head and its coastguard station. Presently, when the tree-arched lane climbed more steeply around a bend, a church slowly came into view beyond. Somehow, it all looked familiar, but when a lychgate and a narrow spire-topped tower appeared, Colin came to an abrupt halt. A shiver ran down his spine.

Kate backtracked and stood beside him, intent on his face.

"You recognise it?" she quietly asked.

The small, low church stood stark against an open and expansive cloud-studded sky, beyond where the trees bordering the lane finished. The way it seemed to squat into the brow of the rise, aloof but somehow enticing, held Colin from answering at first. It wasn't so much the rough dark grey slate of its walls, nor the unfussy climb of its short tower and spire that stirred his memory, but more its setting. He felt as though he'd once before laboured up this incline, a leather bag upon his shoulder, and once before been caught by its unexpected and unassuming appearance.

He slowly turned his half-seeing gaze upon Kate and realised his mouth felt slack.

"This is Saint Germanus, isn't it, Kate?" and she nodded.

"But you never saw this in any of your phantasms, not that you told me about, anyway."

Colin narrowed his eyes, his brow puckering, his thoughts going over all he could recall from each time he'd spent in Jusuf's mind. Finally, he concluded he'd never been here before, and certainly not with Jusuf.

"So you must have had some kind of access to his memories, then," Kate suggested. "It must've still been on his mind when he neared the smithy that day Wilfred brought Gwenna the bad news."

He nodded, already delving into what else he may have unknowingly carried back, but nothing came to him.

"Let's go in," he said, his voice seeming to come from a long way off. "If it's open."

"It will be. Churches are never locked, Colin. Not remote ones out in the countryside like this. After all, they are meant to be a refuge at any time of day for those in need."

The short sloping path beyond the lychgate up to the

entrance porch ran a good eighteen inches below the level of the surrounding graveyard. The church itself likewise stood below that same level, behind a narrow dry moat of sorts that ran around the base of the ancient slate walls. Colin stopped at the entrance to the porch and turned to stare at the forest of raised gravestones.

"I suppose getting on for a millennium of stacked remains is going to do that to a churchyard," he mused. But Kate had slipped inside the porch, the sound of a latch and then a door opening drawing him to follow her in.

The interior seemed no more familiar than any other church. It had a musty smell he'd now come to associate with great age and its silence with a long tradition of reverence. Naturally enough, the bench ends first attracted his interest. Most were plain or simply adorned, just the odd few blessed with more interesting designs. None, though, rivalled Rodrigo's.

Kate, he noticed, seemed more intent on him than their surroundings. He finally smiled at her and lofted his brows.

"Nothing?" she asked into the deserted stillness.

He shrugged as he shook his head, then caught a glimpse of an archway, partially hidden beneath a low organ loft at the west end of the nave. Beyond it he could see uneven stone flags in what looked like a small room. Then he realised it must have been the base of the tower, and that earlier shiver returned to his spine.

As he passed beneath the organ and through the archway, Kate behind him, the dimly lit space he entered struck him as even smaller than he'd thought. A free-hanging bell rope caught his eye and he looked up, following its rise to a hole in a high wooden ceiling. Before he knew it, he'd grasped the soft cladding of the rope's end, feeling the resistance of what it was attached to, out of sight in the belfry above.

"Probably best not ringing it," Kate said as she placed her hand on his at the rope, and Colin nodded, staring back up at the ceiling.

Although only lit by the meagre light of a louvered slit opening half way up the wall opposite the archway, he could see a trapdoor in one corner. From it descended an aluminium ladder, bolted to the wall behind him.

Colin cocked an ear, then poked his head back through the archway, to check the entrance door. "Nip back to the porch and watch out for anyone, Kate. I'm just going to see if I can get a quick look into the belfry."

She looked up the length of the ladder. "You sure?"

"Yep. Cough loudly if you see anyone coming. Okay?" to which she nodded uncertainly as Colin put their rucksack down on the floor. He grinned reassuringly and waited until she'd gone to stand by the door, which she then cracked open. He was quickly up the ladder, its creaking seeming loud enough to raise the proverbial dead.

He stopped at the top and listened. All remained quiet. The hatch had no handle or latch, and so he reached up and firmly pushed at it. It lifted easily, a light draught slipping through to cool his face. He climbed a little higher and swung the hatch fully open, poking his head through the opening.

Then Kate coughed loudly and he heard the door close, her footsteps hurrying back as he hastily closed the hatch above him. When he stepped off the bottom of the ladder, the door's latch rattled and voices drifted into the church.

"Grockles?" Colin whispered, shouldering the rucksack again, to which Kate grinned back as she nodded. Then, having said "Hello" to two middle-aged women who'd not yet got further than a table of pamphlets near the entrance, Colin and Kate wandered out into the churchyard.

"Well?" Kate said.

"I only got a quick look, and it was all poorly lit, but nothing rang any bells."

"There's unlikely to be much left from Jusuf's time, I wouldn't have thought. However well made his stuff might have been, it has been five hundred…" then Kate sighed and slowly shook her head as Colin broke into laughter.

"Ha, ha," she laboured. "Funny man, eh?"

He gave out a couple more short laughs and clapped his hands as he set off back down the path to the lychgate and the lane.

"Come on, then," he called back. "Let's get on with this walk of yours. I can feel a thirst working up for some of the local ale."

Soon side by side, they carried on up the lane beside the churchyard's high retaining wall, the spire beyond silently pointing at the heavens. The narrowed lane took them onto the back of the headland, here exposed beneath a broad and open sky.

At its end would be Rame Head, where Kate had planned they'd join the coastal path for Kingsand and Cawsand. But for the time being, with little to see but cloud-dotted sky beyond the low hedges, nothing rested in Colin's mind but the prospect of an ale or two when they eventually got there. And maybe an oggy—as Kate had told him pasties were called down here—to soak it all up.

28 A THIN LINE

Presently, they came to a roughly surfaced car park at the end of the lane, beyond it a small, squat white building festooned with aerials—clearly the coastguard station. A long window on its far side faced out to sea, to a view that took Colin's breath away.

Against the broad spread of ocean before them rose a steep-sided hill at the near head of the peninsular—the woman's breast Colin had seen at his first sight of Rame Head. Upon its narrow summit stood proud a small, simple and clearly ancient stone building.

"Rame Head Chapel," Kate told him. "Originally the head was an Iron Age hillfort—you can see the remains of the ditch and rampart across the narrow part."

Colin looked down the slope of an open field below the station, down to the saddle of land below, not at all sure he could.

"The chapel's not as old as that, of course; not even as old as Saint Germanus."

It turned out to be little more than a hollow rough-slate building, earthen-floored but complete with a solid ridged roof. They clambered down onto the concrete base of an old World War Two gun emplacement on its seaward side. The view from there proved even more spectacular, nothing but ocean on all three sides. A good few miles straight out to sea rose the lonely finger of the Eddystone lighthouse, defiant and protective upon its remote pedestal of rock.

The headland marked the very start of Whitsand Bay, its long sweep stretching away into the heat haze towards the west, like a broad and welcoming smile. To the east, the coastline curved gently away, ultimately hiding Cawsand, Kingsand and finally Plymouth itself.

The sense of being so exposed—of being thrust out into the lonely sea's embrace—kept them there for a while. Despite the sun feeling hot when it came out, in the shade of the slow moving clouds the ocean breeze felt chill on Colin's bare arms. It eventually urged them back the way they'd climbed, down into the field below and onto the coastal path.

Here, the bordering hedges held a close heat that chased away the memory of the ocean breeze. It held to it a bejewelled haze of butterflies, each gem fluttering joyfully from the warmth of the ground and magically ahead of Colin and Kate's approaching feet. Glimpsed through gaps in the hedge or laid open where the rise and fall of the path lifted them above it, the gorse-shrouded land fell away to hidden cliffs far below.

Eventually, they came to what Colin thought was another romantically ruined chapel. It turned out to be a folly at what Kate then said was Penlee Point. Beyond it, where the coast curved away from the ocean, the path dipped into the cool shade of woodland, and here the world of their walk abruptly changed. Now cool, still and enchanting, the cathedral of trees steadily took them lower and nearer the village of Cawsand. Occasionally, they'd briefly glimpse its gaily rendered houses through gaps in the steeply sloping canopy.

Their woodland path became a track, then a narrow lane, before finally channelling them out into Cawsand's small village square. About it, a higgledy-piggledy rise of pastel rendered properties clung to the steep confines of the narrow valley. On the far side more buildings stepped up the side of a short promontory that hemmed Cawsand in to its narrow cove.

A tumble of Jusuf's memories crashed in on Colin's mind, not of Cawsand itself but of its similarity to parts of Fowey. It shocked him that he'd almost forgotten about his phantasms, so enthralling, enchanting and wholly engrossing had been their walk. Then he saw a sign for pasties and suggested they eat.

Hot greaseproof paper bags in hand, Kate led Colin from the store and across the square, then down an alley to the small cove's busy beach. To one side of a short and low concrete promenade stood a couple of benches, up against a grey stone wall bathed in the heat of the midday sun. They found space to squeeze in and tucked in to their meals, forced to silence by the wonderful taste.

Colin stared absently at a half dozen tarpaulin covered boats and dinghies pressed up against the edge of the promenade in front of them. Then his gaze wandered over people enjoying the beach, and out amongst the clutter of bright white boats and yachts anchored in the small bay. By the time he'd finished eating, the question of what Kate needed to ask of his next phantasm had likewise slipped in and quietly dropped anchor in his mind.

"Time for a drink, then?" he said as Kate finished her oggy, wary of any talk of phantasms being overheard in the press of grockles, and Kate nodded.

"We'll walk through to Kingsand," she said. "There's a nice pub on the seafront there."

Colin had no idea when Cawsand gave way to Kingsand, the whole place seeming to be all one and the same. From there, though, it became clear the two conjoined villages were on the same small bay, although each clearly had its own short stretch of beach.

Mere yards from Kingsand's own, the Devonport Inn looked straight out to sea from within its eclectic, brightly rendered row of ancient properties. Colin and Kate sat outside with their drinks, on a rickety wooden high-backed bench, and let their eyes follow the inn's own contented gaze.

"This place is magical," Colin said, having wiped the foam of his first drink of beer from his mouth. "It's just wonderful. Who needs to go abroad, eh?" and he relaxed into the slow-paced, seagull-whirling warmth of this still foreign land.

Before he could raise the issue of what question they needed to pose of his next phantasm, their morning's walk began to make some unexpected sense. A sense that was other than its simple pleasures of sights and sounds and scents, other than the invigoration of its healthy exercise. It seemed to Colin that it had contained a lesson, one he needed to heed.

"It's odd, isn't it?" he finally said to Kate. "How so much of the world comes in pairs; you know, from little things like the two wings of a butterfly to the big ones like good and evil; with everything conceivable in between, like our left and right hands, men and women, and the land and the sea. We're even in one of a Siamese twin of villages, for heaven's sake."

Kate at first only stared at Colin, her glass paused at her lips, then her eyes narrowed a touch.

"And how sometimes," Colin went on, "we walk a fine line between the two, like our walk along the coast this morning: the land of Cornwall on one side, the Atlantic Ocean on the other. And how, within the here-and-now, we've touched so intimately upon an Iron Age hillfort, a late medieval church, an Early English chapel, an eighteenth century folly, and an historically recent wartime gun emplacement. You know, Kate," he now said quite quietly, "we unknowingly walk a fine line between the past and the present."

When Colin looked at Kate again, her glass still hovered before her lips, but lips that were lightly parted. She blinked and they silently snapped shut.

"Colin," she carefully said, putting her glass down, "you didn't by any chance have a sneaky spliff before we left this morning, did you? You're not going to get on to Yin and Yang, and Cheech and Chong, are you?"

He grinned at her, a little sheepishly. "Until just now I was going to suggest our most important question of my next phantasm would have to have been what that damned joss stick holder's all about. But our walk today has taught me that there's something even more important."

"Which is?"

"Which is, my dearest love, why Jusuf has gone to all the trouble of breaching that normally inviolable line between the past and the present: 'What, in God's name, does he want with us?'," and at that, he raised his glass to his lips and sank half his pint of beer.

"Well, it was probably more likely in Allah's name, but be that as it may, there's also…" but then she shrugged, her gaze stolen away by the view across Cawsand Bay. "Yeah. Yeah, you're probably right," she finally said without looking at him.

"You don't agree?"

"No, no I do; you are right. I can see that. But then it's…well, it is only a feeling you had, that he wanted us to do something for him. We've nothing concrete to support that idea. But if that's what you want, then it's fine by me. How the hell I'm going to formulate it in my own mind so it's 'Targeted', though, I've no idea."

"Well, if I go back there again this evening, after we've eaten, that'll give us the rest of the day to come up with some ideas."

Kate nodded. "Okay."

After they'd leisurely drunk up, they spent a couple of hours wandering the byways of both ancient villages, sampling ice-cream and window shopping in the various craft shops. Finally, they made their long way back up the road to where they'd parked the car. Before Colin unlocked its doors, though, he stared out across Whitsand Bay, to a grey line of land now visible along the furthest horizon.

"Is that the Lizard?" he asked Kate and pointed.

"Er…yeah, that's it."

"The most southerly point of mainland Britain," Colin said whilst wondering what it had really been that had driven Michael An Gof, the blacksmith, to leave his parish of Saint Keverne and march to his death at Blackheath. And again, Colin felt that thin line between the here-and-now and the past once more blur, if only a little, and if only for the briefest of moments.

29 DECEIT

The forge had become Jusuf's favourite place to be, now the summer had given way to autumn, the only one other than his bed where he really felt warm. Outside, the rain lashed down, having already turned the road into a river.

He grabbed a horseshoe in his tongs from its bed of whitely-glowing charcoal and turned it over, judging its orange glow as being no more than that of a quarter-hour-to-sunset sun. Another minute or so and he swiftly rested it, the yellow-white of an hour after dawn, against the anvil's horn, striking it repeatedly with his hammer. Then it was straight back into the charcoal until its colour once again looked right.

Thrusting a long-handled spike sharply through one of its cleat holes, Jusuf carried it quickly through to a stallion hitched to the post in the barn, the beast still contentedly eating from its nosebag.

"Here we are, my beauty," he soothed as he ran his free hand down the horse's off-hind fetlock and caught the lifted hoof. He offered up the shoe, now clearly a perfect fit, before resting the horse's pastern against his leather-aproned thigh and pressing the hot iron home. A fizzle of horn blew out swirls of blue smoke that drifted about Jusuf's head as he squinted through it all at his work. Then he drew the cooling shoe away and dropped it to an abrupt hiss in a nearby bucket of water.

He groaned as he straightened and looked out through the open doors at the rain, shivering at the sight, hoping Rodrigo hadn't got drenched. When he lifted the shoe from the water, he found it had cooled enough and so reached into his apron pocket for some cleats.

Before long, the new shoe had been nailed snuggly to the stallion's hoof, deft strokes of a file smoothing off the points left protruding from its wall. A quick brush of neatsfoot oil brought the horn to a glossy finish and removed the parings that had got into the frog, the job well and truly done.

"Master Trefowlin?" he called towards the door through to Mistress Trewin's cottage as he wiped his hands on a rag. "Your lordship's stallion be ready."

The horse finally put its weight on its new shoe, lifted its tail to one side and defecated onto the stone floor, steam rising from the dull-green pile of dung. Just then, the cottage door opened and a portly man squeezed through into the barn, Gwenna behind him.

"Thank 'e for the oatcake an' ale," the man said over his shoulder, but his gaze was already upon his master's horse. An expert eye appraised the hoof, which was lifted for inspection, and he nodded approvingly.

"His lordship were well pleased with her ladyship's mare, 'specially after all this sucking mud we've had." he said, lowering the hoof and straightening to face Jusuf. "Feather in your cap he's sent you his prize stallion, Master Joseph. I think you'll be seeing more of his mounts. Oh, and his lordship instructed me to settle up a bit more than we agreed, as a mark of his gratitude, which I've already done wi' Mistress Trewin."

Jusuf smiled and nodded his thanks, then removed the horse's nosebag and unhitched it. Once Master Trefowlin had fastened his coat tightly about himself Jusuf handed him the lead rope. The man then pulled a wide-brimmed hat down over his head and grinned at Jusuf.

"Good to find a blacksmith who handles horses so well," and he leant a little closer, "without need of a stick or switch, eh?" He winked before curtly nodding and lashing tight the neck of his coat.

As he led the stallion out into the rain, Gwenna came beside Jusuf. "Ah, a bit more goodness for our vegetables," she said, and Jusuf turned to see her take up a shovel.

"No, Gwenna, I'll do that. There be quite a pile, and you ought to be staying in the dry," but she pushed him out of the way and bent to the still steaming dung.

"I be no weakling, Jusuf, and I certainly ain't ailing. So out of the way wi' thee," and she scraped up the stallion's gift for the garden.

Jusuf caught himself and stood back, watching as she brushed the excess onto the shovel and carried it two-handed to the back door. As it closed behind her, Rodrigo's voice startled him.

"Lover's tiff?"

When Jusuf turned his narrowed stare to him, he found Rodrigo standing just inside the barn's doorway, a broad grin across his face, but the eyes within looked clouded.

"Eh?" Jusuf could only find to say.

"Come on, my friend. I'm not blind, you know. Ever since I got back from Saint Winnow you've both been—"

The back door opened and Mistress Trewin hurried in, shaking water from her skirts.

"Ah, Master Rodrigo. You ought to be out of that coat and getting yourself dry," she called. "You'll catch your death like that," and he looked down at the puddle about his feet. "I'll go get you something hot," she said before replacing the shovel and vanishing through into her cottage.

Rodrigo stamped his feet on a dry patch of floor before coming in fully and taking off his coat. He hung it up to dry on one of the coat hooks and took up a brush, quickly sweeping both the stain of horse muck and the mud from his boots out into the road.

As he placed the brush back against the wall, he quietly said, "It's your own business, of course, but it seems to me you've been a bit more out of sorts these past two weeks." By now he'd turned Jusuf a concerned look.

Jusuf stared at him for a moment, seeing a valued friend he'd hardly treated as such, not when it came to the really important things—like trust. He shivered in the cold damp air gusting in from the rain and drew in a long breath as he glanced at the cottage door.

"You'd best come through to the forge," he said and led the way into its gloom.

He drew two chairs up to the hearth, offering one to Rodrigo, then sat heavily in his own. His friend held his hands out to the heat, rubbing them together as they warmed. They quietly sat like this for a while as Jusuf tried to sort through his thoughts, then Gwenna came in with a bowl of hot pottage.

"Here we be, Master Rodrigo. Get yourself around this. Do you want some, too," she aimed at Jusuf, but he shook his head and thanked her for the offer. "Then I'll get back to me sewing," she said, a small frown sent Jusuf's way. When he imperceptibly nodded, she wiped her hands on her apron and nodded back herself, a glance at Rodrigo before she quietly withdrew. The sound of the cottage door softly closing soon came to their ears.

Jusuf gave Rodrigo time to eat, time he spent fruitlessly choosing his words. Eventually, his now unaccustomed Arabic slipped unguardedly from his mouth of its own accord.

"Mistress Trewin is with child."

Rodrigo froze, spoon in hand, eyes wide and upon Jusuf. Then the man swallowed with difficulty before his mouth dropped open.

"Yes, it is mine, my friend," Jusuf answered to the unspoken question.

"But," was all Rodrigo could summon.

"Clearly Gwenna's womb was not made barren, after all," and Jusuf sighed, "so the blame has to be laid at the feet of her husband's weak seed. I did wonder: him being an only child; like father, like son, eh?" and Jusuf leant forward towards the heat and rubbed his face with his large black hands.

"When…"

"This is her second missed bleed," Jusuf said, lifting his hands away to speak, and he could see Rodrigo counting on his fingers.

"April then?"

"Unless my own seed proves weak, not that it has before."

"Due when the captain could turn up at any time."

Jusuf shot Rodrigo a pained look. "I cannot abandon her, my friend. I cannot. If I survive this damned cold land's winter, then I must be here for her. I must provide for them both."

"But what of Santander? Of your burden-of-a-gift to *Castilla y León*? Your master in Ceuta?"

Jusuf sat up, his jaw set firm as he searched Rodrigo's eyes. "Which brings me to a great favour I need ask of you; a favour I fear you will deny me when you hear of my deceit."

"Deceit?"

After taking in a deep breath and slowly releasing it, Jusuf turned his gaze to the crackling and now amber charcoal, the lash of rain on the roof of the forge bringing a shiver to his back. His chair creaked as he shifted uneasily.

"When I set out from Ceuta with you, you were just one of the Christian infidels, one of the enemies of Allah. You and the captain believed I carried a weapon to strike only at the heart of *Castilla y León*, at the heart of a troublesome neighbour not just of the Saracen world but also of Portugal. But my burden, Rodrigo, would have struck far wider than that…far, far wider."

The suspicion that had taken a hold of Rodrigo's face hurt Jusuf in a way he'd once never believed a Christian's look could ever have done. It made him feel dirty, unworthy of the man's friendship.

"What is your burden, Jusuf al-Haddad? Really. What did we aid you in bringing to our Christian lands?"

Jusuf drew his lips to a thin line and stared through Rodrigo.

"Plague, Rodrigo. Plague."

"Plague?"

"Of the sort never before seen here in these northern lands, not even in my own land of *al-Maghrib.* It was brought at great cost over hundreds of leagues out of a country far south of my own, far down where people are few and far between, isolated in their villages within the great forests there. It is a heinous affliction, an unstoppable curse that draws the organs of the body as a suppurating mass through every bodily orifice, that soon erupts through ones it creates itself."

"And you've seen this for yourself?" Rodrigo's face now showed true horror.

"I said it had been brought north at great cost, a cost I have seen with my own eyes. A cost I risked myself when I was set to oversee its preserving and imprisoning within its glass phial."

"I now see you're a man of far wider knowledge than would be expected of a simple blacksmith, and clearly well-versed in the arts of subterfuge." Rodrigo got up and went to stand in the opening through to the barn, as though distancing himself. Eventually, he stared back at Jusuf.

"Unstoppable, you said. So it would have crossed the mountains into Portugal?" Jusuf nodded, unable to speak the words. "And so where would it have ended, eh, Jusuf? At the northern shores of the Eastern Sea, perhaps?"

"At my successful return, or at the first tidings of the plague itself, my master's master, and all rulers along the northern coasts of our lands, would have barred their ports to trade. No ship would have been allowed in until the following spring, by which time the cold northern winter would have destroyed what was left of the plague. Leaving the way clear for an invasion by the combined forces of Allah; may his providence forgive me my sins."

"Would? You keep saying 'Would have'," but at Jusuf's silence, Rodrigo came and stood before him, his head turned away slightly as he clearly came to a realisation. "You've already decided, haven't you, Jusuf?" he said in a softer tone, "not to strike with your lethal weapon." He bent and placed his hands on the arms of Jusuf's chair and stared him in the face. "Otherwise, you wouldn't be telling me this now. So, has it taken a Christian woman's charms to bring you to this?"

Jusuf looked up into Rodrigo's eyes. "Not just one woman, nor one man," and he grasped Rodrigo's arm, the man flinching, "but all those I have come to know here. All those Christians who have accepted this Blackamoor so readily into their midst. You and they it has been who have shown me that we are no different, that good and bad reside here in no greater part than amongst us Arabs and Moors."

"And your plague would have travelled this far, would it? All the way to Cornwall?"

"To the borders of Christendom."

Rodrigo snatched his arm from Jusuf's grip and clapped his hand to his head as he turned away, staring at the darkened roof above him. Then he turned sharply back to Jusuf. "Where is your plague-burden now, Jusuf? Where is this work of the Devil? Not still up in the loft's rafters above our pallets, I hope."

"It's been far away and safe for a while, Rodrigo. Where no one can stumble upon it."

"Thank sweet Jesu for that. And don't tell me

where, Jusuf. I don't want to know. Take that sinful knowledge with you to your grave."

"A grave I now know must be here in Cornwall's soil, one way or another; whichever way you choose to grant me that favour I mentioned."

"Ah, yes. That. Well, go on, then. Tell me what need you have of me that will keep Christendom safe." and Rodrigo stepped back a pace, a wary look still in his eyes.

"If you no longer trust me, my friend," Jusuf told him, spreading his arms wide to lay open his breast, "then your favour to me must be to strike me down right now, and so consign the Devil amongst you to its long and lonely imprisonment; to kill me for the sake of your beloved Christ and all his followers."

Rodrigo remained silent, his gaze pinned to Jusuf's breast, his hand already at his belt, upon its dagger's hilt. His words came hesitantly and quietly then, as though roused from deep within a dream: "Aye, it would truly be just for all His faithful followers—all but Mistress Trewin and her unborn babe," and he turned his back on Jusuf, turned his back and slowly shook his head, his hand no longer at his knife.

His shoulders lifted as he clearly took in a deep breath, then he asked, "So, Jusuf al-Haddad, bringer of great evil to our lands, what is the nature of the favour you have been brought to ask of me? A favour I would have given before without the slightest thought, whatever you would have asked, but which I now may need some time to consider."

30 ARMAGEDDON

"My plague-burden, as you called it, is of immeasurable value," Jusuf said when Rodrigo had seated himself once more in his chair. "A wealth greater than all the amassed riches of all the Muslim worlds. The greatest weapon of war, needing only a single thrust, its fatal wound then likely seen as no more than an act of your own God's retribution. A natural calamity, and so without blame of man nor nation."

Rodrigo ominously kept his own counsel as he stared into the embers of the forge's hearth.

"It's not only its potency, though, Rodrigo, but its rarity. Uncommon even in its own lands, to have it for use in Moorish hands so far from there renders it rarer still than hen's teeth."

At last, Rodrigo stirred and turned a jaundiced eye upon Jusuf. "So your master's master is unlikely just to shrug off its loss and console himself with ordering more siege engines be built."

"Far from it. They'll come looking for me once the Nao Providência returns to Cueta without me, and once no tidings of plague reach the ears of their spies. They'll search me out to recover their crowning weapon, so it can be aimed once again at the heart of Christendom—unless…"

Rodrigo only lofted his brows.

"Unless such prospect be made impossible in their eyes."

"Impossible?"

"For its whereabouts to have gone with me beyond all earthly knowing. But, seeing your heed of Mistress Trewin and her unborn babe has stayed your actual hand in this, it now only leaves its fatal blow to be played out in a story told."

"A story told?"

"Convince them I was swiftly taken by some ague of this country's cold winter, and with it thereby the whereabouts of my burden. There would then be no profit in sending their agents here to Cornwall, for it could never be found without me."

"So," Rodrigo drew out, clearly thinking the idea through, "this is your favour of me: that I deliver either—your death actual or death feigned." When Jusuf only nodded, Rodrigo sat for some time, staring into the dying embers of the charcoal as the rain thundered down more heavily on the roof of the forge.

Eventually, he slowly nodded, his eyes searching out Jusuf's. "I do not forget the debt I owe you for my life, Jusuf al-Haddad. I thought it would be for ever writ upon my heart, but now, by granting you your own, that debt will have been settled, and I will owe you nothing more."

A simple curt nod from Jusuf sealed their deal, although bitter regret filled his heart.

"Very well," Rodrigo said, "then you'd better have

died somewhere other than Bodmyn, just in case they don't believe me. I'll say we were on our way to seek work in Falmouth when you succumbed to the wet and cold and soon died in Truro, buried in a pauper's grave."

"When we do part company, then, you'd best take my gold ring. My master will know it. It'll add weight to your claim." Jusuf raised the distinctive ring to his gaze, wondering how difficult it might be to remove. Its loss would be a great regret, he knew, for it was the only memento left him of another woman for whom he'd sacrificed all.

Then he caught sight of Gwenna, sitting patiently on the far side of the hearth, leaving him perplexed he'd not seen her enter. He stared at her, wondering if his thoughts of sacrifice had somehow conjured her before nothing more than his own mind's eye.

"Well?" she said. "What happened?" but Jusuf felt a single tear trace a chill path down his cheek, his heart now leaden at Rodrigo's friendship lost. At first, his words wouldn't come, not until alarm flooded Kate's face.

"I'm… I'm sorry," he almost wept and shot unsteadily to his feet. Grabbing his cigarettes, he turned for the door but then stopped. "I just need a moment to myself, Kate. Don't worry; I'll be all right," and he stumbled out into the late summer evening air.

Colin fumbled a cigarette from its packet but failed to find his lighter. A familiar rasp came from behind him and he turned to find his lit Zippo in Kate's outstretched hand.

"Do you still want to be left alone?" she said, once he'd lit up.

He shook his head and Kate slowly embraced him, squeezing some reassurance into his chilled bones. And there they remained whilst Colin's untouched cigarette burned down between his fingers, until Kate's warmth steeled his heart enough for him to summon the words he needed to tell his tale.

They retreated to the warmth of the chalet once Colin had finished. Kate's pad still lay untouched on the table, beside the joss stick holder, clearly forgotten.

"Shit," was all she found to say.

They both sat down, facing each other across the table, the holder menacingly between them.

After a stunned silence, Kate nodded at the thing. "But there's no trace of glass about it."

"No," Colin agreed, lowering his gaze and once again peering minutely through its many holes. "Not now. But was there?" He then breathed a sigh of relief. "It can't be Jusuf's plague-burden. If it was, then it's no longer as it started out, for there's definitely no glass left, and so its plague must have escaped, which we know can't be true."

He sat back and stared at Kate. "I mean, does it really look like their equivalent of a nuclear bomb? Because that's in effect what his burden was. Bigger even, if it genuinely could have wiped out the whole of Christendom back then."

"Far more now, Colin. Just think about it. Think of the free and fast movement people have about the world today, flying here and there on holiday and business; the vast amount of trade there is compared with back then. And Jusuf's description of it makes it sound a lot like those outbreaks they had in Africa, back in seventy-six."

"Oh yeah. What was it called?"

Kate couldn't remember, but thought it'd something to do with the name of the river near the village where it started. "If I recall," she said, "because they couldn't treat it, there was some talk of it spreading unstoppably to the rest of the world, even from its remote corner of Africa. I know Cornwall's not exactly an international hub, but imagine if it got out here. It wouldn't take long for the millions of grockles who holiday here to carry it to places like London. Then it'd be just a few short hops to becoming a worldwide epidemic."

"Well," Colin said, "at least this holder isn't his burden. I'm pretty sure of that now. But it must mean it's still out there somewhere, still hidden in Cornwall. Oh, and we still don't know what Jusuf needs us to do, but it's got to be about keeping his burden safe. It just has to be."

"Ah, right," Kate said, lowering her gaze. "Sorry about this, but there was something else I couldn't help asking just before you stuck the joss stick in. Something I clearly got answered, though."

Colin could only gawp at her.

"It was just this issue of me and Gwenna being linked, you know, through our bloodline." Colin was mystified. "Her being barren bugged me. It would have meant I couldn't have been a direct descendent, only through a relative, which doesn't seem nearly direct enough for what's been happening."

"Right. I see what you mean. Yeah, fair point, but now we know—she wasn't barren at all. More to the point, though, it's what finally decided Jusuf to stay here, and with him his blasted burden."

"A plague that'll stay active for a thousand years, Colin. Remember? A thousand years."

"But still safe in its hiding place."

"Or will it be?"

"Eh?"

"If that was true then why the phantasms, and why your conviction that Jusuf had something he needed us to do?"

"And something I reckon he's not yet aware of, himself."

"Uh?"

"He's still no idea we're spying on him; thinks his vision of you came from their past, not their future, just like his grandad's 'Songs of Our Forebears'. Something's yet to happen, Kate, I'm sure of it. Something that'll make the penny drop for Jusuf, and that something is what we need to find out next. I just need you to be as convinced of it as I am the next time I light a joss stick," and he stared down at the holder again.

"Ebola," he said. "That was its name; I remember now." But he felt happier that the thing before him wasn't a fifteenth-century Ebola equivalent of Nuclear Armageddon. He knew full well, though, that such a deadly thing still lay hidden somewhere not a million miles away, hidden but somehow not safe at all.

31 MOULD

Jusuf was in something of a daze, following his discourse with Brother Cagan at Saint Petroc's. He was trying to remember all the man had told him as he approached the doorway out from the nave of the church into its porch. Huddling closer into his coat, in preparation for the midwinter cold without, he didn't at first recognise the robed figure also going that way, arms laden with rolls of parchment.

"Ah, well met, Jusuf al-Haddad," Dom Francisco's confident tones cut to Jusuf before being swallowed by the large space of the nave. The Dom's intelligent eyes held Jusuf in their gaze for a moment, across the top of the parchments. "If I could prevail upon you?" he said as he stood before the closed door.

"Of course, Dom Francisco," and Jusuf opened it for him.

"Here measuring up for some work or other?" the Dom asked, jerking his arms to stop some of his load from slipping.

Jusuf stared at him for a moment. "Oh, no. Some

other business with Brother Cagan, Dom Francisco."

"Oh yes," and the Dom's eyes briefly narrowed before he stepped through into the porch. Jusuf followed him. "If you wouldn't mind again?" and the Dom nodded at a side door within the porch.

Jusuf swung this door open for him too, revealing a tight curve of steeply rising steps within.

"There's another at the top if I could press you into sparing me the time," and Dom Francisco nodded up the staircase.

It proved a bit of a squeeze for Jusuf's large frame, and somewhat dizzying as he carefully trod up the triangular treads, pushing open a small door at the top. It opened into an airy and bright cell, a narrow window-opening in the far wall and a square mullioned one to his left. The still day's low winter sun slanted through this and into his eyes. The air in here had even more of that sharp edge to it that so reminded Jusuf of his childhood winters in the Rif mountains.

Dom Francisco had hurried to a large sloping desk in the centre of the room, onto which he spilled his burden. One of the parchments rolled off, falling at Jusuf's feet. He bent and retrieved it, returning the yellowed document to its fellows.

"Thank you, Jusuf al-Haddad." The Dom then sat on the desk's bench and began sorting through the pile.

Jusuf was about to take his leave when Dom Francisco said, "An accommodating man, our Brother Cagan. I did expect a little reluctance, I must admit, but he seemed quite keen to share his wealth of knowledge with me." There seemed a delight in the Dom's eyes, a warm smile playing about his mouth. Jusuf found himself relaxing a little in the man's reassuring presence.

He stepped nearer the mullion window and stared out at the sharp outlines of the rooftops of Bodmyn below. The creak of a wagon came to his hearing, the top of its load slowly passing beyond the churchyard wall bordering the road to Liskeard. A cry of greeting cut through the thin air from somewhere further towards the town, a reply lost to the distance.

"I trust the brother proved just as helpful to your good self, Jusuf al-Haddad?"

"The brother? Oh, yes. Indeed, Dom Francisco. Most helpful, but it's still all new to me."

"New?"

"Hmm? Oh, I mean this business of…" Jusuf turned and stared into the Dom's eyes, seeing a welcome there. "I am to take baptism, Dom Francisco, into your Christian Church."

"Well, well; that is good to hear."

"But there are many things I'm required to accept; things I need to think hard about."

"Indeed. That I can well imagine. But I'm pleased to hear you are seeking sanctuary in our Lord's teachings, Jusuf. Or… Or is there a more earthly imperative, I wonder. A cause pursuant to a certain smithy's mistress, perhaps?"

Jusuf shot him a guarded glance.

"Sit here with me, Jusuf al-Haddad," and the Dom patted the bench beside him as he shuffled up to make room.

When Jusuf had sat down, Dom Francisco turned his placid face to him and placed his hand on top of Jusuf's. "I know I should not speak this aloud, but our Christian Lord has ever had a place in your Muslim faith. Islam has always held the Prophet Īsā ibn Maryām in high esteem, Jusuf, as I'm sure you already know. Our Lord Jesu is rightly recognised as the Muslim prophet who came before your own and final Muhammad; that our Lord's holy teachings did pave the way for his own."

"It is so, Dom Francisco. You know your Quran well," and Jusuf's respect for the Dom strengthened, but more so at the ease with which he spoke his words rather than their bare meaning.

"Your conversion to our Christian faith need not be seen as a betrayal of your Islam one, my friend, but a settling of your spiritual eyes upon its earlier teachings. After all, it was from the holy words of Īsā ibn Maryām, our Lord Jesus Christ, that your own prophet's wisdom came. And so, through a Christian faith, may you still honour Allah."

Jusuf's mouth hung loose, a clarity and an appeasement of his closely felt guilt cascading through his previously troubled mind like a mountain stream. Before he could express his gratitude for the Dom's thoughtful words, the man patted Jusuf's hand, removed his own and leant away a little.

"But my understanding, from no more than a passing interest, of course, is that the mistress be still wed."

"Ah, yes, indeed so, Dom Francisco," Jusuf said, lowering his voice, "but there are some who were with her husband at Blackheath who have recently come forward with accounts born of freshly revived memories. It seems there are three who now have clear recall of his passing from this world."

"How…how fortunate, *Senhor* Jusuf. Clearly a sign of God's own benevolence; of His bestowing His gift of Grace upon your forthcoming betrothal. And I assume these previously forgetful fellows are at last willing to offer such witness?" to which Jusuf nodded, briefly hiding his face from Dom Francisco's knowing smile.

"Well," the Dom wondered, "perhaps it's the proximity of the venerable Saint Petroc's bones that has brought you such beneficence." When Jusuf only stared blankly at him, Dom Francisco grinned and tapped the parchments before him, drawing Jusuf's attention.

"I came all this way from *Mosteiro de Santa Maria de Alcobaça* to study the renowned Bodmyn Gospels, scripted here in this very priory. To feast my eyes, Jusuf, upon its now five-hundred-year-old recounting. Although, I suspect I have seen intimations of a Breton hand in parts. But be that as it may, my journey has proven wonderfully… Well, *illuminating*," and he let out a single laugh at his own jest.

"But Saint Petroc's bones, Dom Francisco?"

"Hmm? Oh, yes. Now where was I? Of course, the patron saint of this and I believe a few other churches hereabouts. Did you know the venerable saint's remains were stolen from this very church? Well, not this new one, but the one that was here before it."

Jusuf shook his head.

"Apparently, a canon by the name of Martyn was bribed by a house in Brittany—the abbey of Saint Méem's of Mevenus at Laon—to steal the relic away into their hands. That was long ago, though: in the year of our Lord one thousand, one hundred and seventy seven."

"But you said…"

"The loss was eventually noticed, Jusuf, finally getting to the ear of the then King Henry. Irate, he threatened—as only a wrathful king can—the abbot of Mevenus, who soon relented and had the relics returned. They were sent back here in an ivory cask, in way of appeasement, although missing a rib—I wouldn't, though, go so far as to say in way of apology, as this letter from the shameless abbot to Prior Roger makes abundantly clear."

He tapped the sheet of parchment in question, drawing it once more to Jusuf's notice. This time, at the disturbance, its wax seal slid from the sheet and dropped over the edge of the desk, hanging by its cut tongue of parchment.

Jusuf stared at the seal, his brows furrowing, then at Dom Francisco.

"Is something wrong, *Senhor* Jusuf?"

"Wrong?"

"You seem distracted."

Jusuf lifted the heavy seal in his hand, gently rubbing a thumb over its surface. "I've not seen a seal since landing on these shores, Dom Francisco, but this one looks different from the ones common in my own land. Is it fashioned from something other than beeswax?"

"Ah, I see. No, *Senhor* Jusuf, bar some minor differences in elements they are the same. It's just that this one is so very old."

"But I have seen a couple reputed to be just as old before and they've never looked anything like this, not at all as dull and chalky."

Dom Francisco laughed, but not unkindly. "You have much to learn of these cold and wet northern lands, my friend. Much to learn. Here, things are subject to all manner of spoiling rarely seen in our fairer lands. Here, they seldom dry out fully, and so are apt to become invaded by all manner of moulds."

"But I was led to believe sealing wax remained unchanged by the passage of time, like…like *glass*."

"In the hot, dry south, yes, but not here, Jusuf.

Here, it's made brittle by such moulds as this. Like so," and he took the seal from Jusuf and easily broke a small piece from its edge.

Jusuf drew in a sharp breath, his eyes wide and staring at the crumbs in Dom Francisco's outstretched palm.

"It seems important to you," Dom Francisco noted, but Jusuf hardly heard, so furiously were his thoughts now tumbling through his mind.

32 DOWN THROUGH THE UNFOLDING YEARS

Having mentioned the work awaiting him at the smithy, Jusuf left Dom Francisco to his studies and returned to the porch. Cold air caught in his throat as he stepped out and along the path beside the church. Although his mind lay elsewhere, something he passed lying on the grass caught his eye. He stopped and bent to pick up a fallen branch, deadwood from the churchyard's trees, its black and sodden bark encrusted with a velvet-like bloom of greys and yellows and whites.

"Mould," he said to himself and shook his head. "Only three hundred years of it eating into that document's seal and Dom Francisco could already so easily crumble it between his fingers."

He thought back to the glass phial in which the plague had been trapped, at the length of its neck he'd seen filled with sealing wax. "About twice the thickness of the abbot's seal," he reckoned.

Jusuf did a quick calculation. "Some six hundred

years. Six hundred!" and he let the branch slip from his fingers, wiping its stain from his hand on his breeches.

As he went down the steps from the churchyard and into the road for the smithy, he stopped and watched a small group of children at play. One, a girl of some four or five years, had a look of Gwenna about her. She'd been pushing a younger boy but then turned and stared at Jusuf. A smile blossomed on her face, and Jusuf smiled back.

Will my own child be such as this? he thought. She was like a ray of sunshine, now so entranced by his own unusual size and colour. Would he and Gwenna likewise have a girl child? For some reason he believed they would, that the now clear swelling of Gwenna's belly held such as this mite, still smiling at him from across the road.

He waved as he set off, and the child waved back. Then she fell to her knees as the boy finally got his own back with a determined push. As a scuffle broke out and a woman came storming out of a doorway, Jusuf saw in his mind's eye his own daughter: full-grown, belly distended, another girl within. With Allah's… No, soon to be with this Christian God's blessing, his line would one day dwell hereabouts, when the phial's seal would at last let in a Cornish summer's warm and damp air.

By the time Jusuf could see the smithy ahead his mood had soured. It must have shown on his face, for unusually few greeted him in passing, though fewer still he noticed in his distraction.

Despite the cold, he stopped by the spring opposite the smithy. There seemed to be something nudging at his mind that needed both peace and time to be heard. And here, the thin sun warming his face and making his thoughts more fluid, he frowned down into the glistening water.

"I cannot go back and fashion any better the phial's seal," he told himself. "Its wax is the finest there is, but here in this northern land it will fail; I know that now. If only I could warn my daughter's offspring, and those they beget in times to come, until, in some distant day, one could make good the rotting wax."

But how? he thought, then asked the bubbling spring, "How can they be made to hear my warning whilst ensuring its secret's kept? To hear the warning of their long dead forebear... *Forbear*?" Sharply, he drew in a breath as the childhood memory of his grandfather's song drifted hauntingly through his mind.

Jusuf's mood had risen greatly by the time he rushed in through the smithy's wicket door and abruptly came up against Rodrigo, clearly on his way out.

"Ah, you're back," Rodrigo said. "Master Hammett was here earlier, wondering when you'd have his—"

"Never mind that, Rodrigo. I've something I need to think through," and he was about to push past when Rodrigo asked him how his visit to Saint Petroc's had gone.

"Oh, well enough, although I think my talk with Dom Francisco proved far more helpful."

"The Dom was there?"

"I bumped into him on my way out, but I really do need to—"

"Ah. Before you do, Jusuf, that brings me to something I should have brought myself to tell you earlier."

"What?"

Rodrigo drew Jusuf through into the forge and pulled out their chairs, placing them beside the damped-down hearth. "I want you to sit down," he said.

"Why?" and Jusuf warily removed his coat.

"Just sit down, will you?" and so Jusuf did, looking up at Rodrigo in the half-light of the forge as he stood behind his chair, hands steadied on the top rail of its back. As Jusuf laid his coat across his lap, his once good friend cleared his throat.

"The other day, I too met Dom Francisco. He mentioned he was returning to *Santa Maria de Alcobaça* at the end of March and wondered if I'd like to avail myself of an offer of free passage."

"Passage? The end of March? But that'll be well before you expect the captain back…and before Gwenna has her birthing. Why so urgent?"

"Because, with you now being dead and your plague-burden lost, there's no longer any need to sail to Santander. And your master would expect such tidings of calamity be brought him directly."

"Directly?"

"The Dom's ship will be landing at Foy, so I can leave word for the captain at the Ship Inn of what we've agreed has happened and where I've gone. Then no one will be sent here looking for us when he does get back, thus avoiding their chance discovery that you're still very much alive…and becoming something of a Bodmyn figure."

"A Bodmyn figure?"

"I'll be able to find onward passage to Ceuta from Nazaré, and at a pinch the captain can make his own way there without me, for just that one voyage. Although, how many of his crew he'll find I've no idea. I imagine he'll be doing the rounds of Foy's taverns, looking for willing muster."

"*If*, Rodrigo. If he does get the Nao Providência back," Jusuf quietly reminded him, his high spirits having long since plunged.

The closeness there'd been between them may not have returned since Jusuf's revelation about his burden, but there was still something there that Jusuf would sadly miss. But he could rightly see that the sooner they carried out their subterfuge, the surer would be the profit for himself and thereby for Gwenna and their child.

"Very well," Jusuf finally allowed, hardening his features.

Rodrigo gazed at him for a moment, as though he'd words to say that were somehow the wrong shape to spill from his mouth, but then he looked down at his feet. "I'd… I'd best be off. I've things to do. And the end of March is still some way off." His outline briefly filled the opening into the barn before the forge finally fell eerily silent.

Jusuf stared at Rodrigo's empty chair, thinking back to the last time they'd sat here together: the day Jusuf had destroyed their friendship. His gaze then wandered over the hearth and into the gloom beyond; the gloom where he'd seen his last vision of…of *Kate*.

How had I known her name? he asked himself yet again.

Then the insight he'd had at the spring brought him the answer, rushing in once more like waves crashing onto a rocky shore. And now he understood, understood his grandfather's Songs of Our Forebears, and finally knew what he had to do. But would he still have enough *kief* left for it to work? Enough to carry his guidance down through the unfolding years.

33 OF UNIONS: FOUND AGAIN AND FORGED ANEW

The morning turned out wet and surprisingly cool. Rain laced against the bedroom window and lashed across the tin roof above Colin as he groggily poked his head out from beneath the bedcovers. Otherwise, everything seemed still and quiet within the chalet.

"Kate?" he called out.

"You awake at last? You want a cuppa?" she said, her voice raised and coming from the other side of the thin partition wall behind his head.

"That'd be lovely. It's raining!"

"It's supposed to clear by lunchtime, according to Radio Cornwall."

"Are their weather reports the same vintage as the music they play?"

"Ha. Ha," and the floor creaked as Kate clearly walked across the living room. "They probably just looked out of the window: I can see blue sky coming in."

"What do you want to do today, then?" Colin called as he prised himself from the bed, his back aching where a mattress spring must have poked it during the night.

He opened the narrow bedroom door and found Kate, still leaning over the small table and peering through the rain-lashed window. "And don't say go swimming in the sea."

She turned to him. "Hmm, that's nice," and she gave his nakedness a salacious smirk.

"I don't think I'll be rising to any expectations you might have, my lovely, not in this cold."

"It's not *that* cold, certainly not enough to make you such a…*shrinking* violet," and she giggled.

"Hey. Do you mind?"

"It's only the damp air that's making it feel chill. And anyway, the sea's the best place to be in the rain: you can't get any wetter."

"You know, I reckon you really mean that."

"We often went swimming in the rain. It gives a great sense of impunity."

"Impunity, eh? I'm sure it does," and Colin wandered past, out of Kate's reach, and in to sort out some clothes from the small bedroom's chest of drawers.

As he dressed, the enormity of the previous evening's phantasm rushed in on him. He froze, one leg through his underpants, and stared blindly through the chalet's wall. Then he heard the kettle being filled and it snapped him back to the here-and-now.

"We've got to find out where Jusuf's plague-burden is," he said to Kate as he finally stood, now fully dressed, in the galley doorway behind her. Kate finished spooning tea leaves into the pot, then turned to him, a serious face of her own.

"Seeing we're not going swimming, you up to doing another phantasm this morning?"

"What? Dope before the sun's over the yardarm? You are becoming bohemian."

"It's the end of our first week, Colin: Friday, if you've lost track of time. We can't afford to waste what we have left. And anyway, we'll have to get some shopping done pretty soon; we're down to our last quarter pint of milk, for one thing. If you do it this morning, it should be dry by the time we've got some more supplies in. Then we can get off somewhere to enjoy a walk maybe, or for a drink. Somewhere where we'll be able to think through what more you might have learnt by then."

"Okay, but I need that tea first. Nothing worse than going to the fifteenth century without your first brew of the day."

A little later, and nicely stoned, Colin once more pushed a lit joss stick into the holder, a vaguely familiar metal object replacing the feel of the stick between his fingers. Those fingers, now large and dark-skinned, held a small and shallow bowl by its three legs. As Jusuf inspected its chamfered rim, though, he couldn't help but bring to mind the previous day—when they'd finally said goodbye to Rodrigo.

For now, though, he cast the memory out, returning his mind to the distraction of finishing off forging his own answer to his grandfather's *sebsi*; the pipe Jusuf had learnt as a child had been so central to those Songs of Our Forebears. It had taken him a long time to think of what to use in place of his own *sebsi*, something more appropriate to this land devoid of *kief*. But he knew full well, for his idea to work, that it all depended on there one day being imbibers of the storyteller's herb amongst his bloodline to come.

"May God grant England its timely salvation of

good *kief* from *al-Maghrib*," he quietly prayed as he placed the bowl down on the bench and crossed himself. Then he noticed the groove around his finger, where his ring had been.

"You'd better not forget to take this with you," he remembered saying to Rodrigo as the man had stood before him, his bulging bag at his feet. The bright light of a promising spring day, framed by the barn doorway behind Rodrigo, had unfortunately made his features hard to read. But his rounded shoulders had given Jusuf some kernel of hope. He'd then slipped his arm around his newlywed wife's burgeoning waist. His hand had rested upon their soon-to-be-born child as, in the palm of his other, he'd offered Rodrigo the broken ring.

"Couldn't you get it off any other way?" Rodrigo had asked after Jusuf had tipped it into his hand.

"I didn't try. You wouldn't have bothered keeping it whole if you'd been removing it from my corpse, so it would have looked a bit suspicious otherwise."

"True."

"And anyway, it's hardly likely I'll ever see it again."

"No. No, I don't suppose it is."

Gwenna slipped her arm around Jusuf's waist, a single squeeze bringing him much needed comfort.

"Before I go, though..." Rodrigo began but then lowered his gaze to Jusuf's feet. "I think it only right to tell you that I've finally come to see that you had...had no other choice." He snapped his gaze back to Jusuf's face then glanced at Gwenna. "I think what I'm trying to say is that at last I understand." He took a step nearer Jusuf. "I'm sure I'd have done the same, had the tables been turned. I honestly don't want to part company with any bad feeling between us. Not leave such a sour taste as my parting gift, not after all we've both been through, my…*my friend*," He'd then reached out his hand to Jusuf.

Those final two simple words seared painfully raw through Jusuf's mind, rawer still at the memory of the embrace they'd all three then fallen to, each clinging tightly to the other. Jusuf choked back a wetness about his eyes and reached out to his work once more, still waiting there on the bench.

Absently, he turned it around, hoping the hurt of his loss would somehow hide behind his new creation's pleasing form. He would need a clear head soon, he reminded himself, hardly promised by dwelling on such regret.

But he couldn't help remembering Rodrigo's departure, the words he'd cast their way as he'd walked out of the smithy for the very last time: "Maybe one day, my friends, I will darken your door once more; come and see you and your babe," then he'd waved behind him as he's stridden off down the road.

Jusuf and Gwenna had silently lingered outside the smithy, gazing after his diminishing figure, seeing him briefly glance back the once before vanishing into the distance.

Reaching across the bench, Jusuf took down a small pot from a shelf above, its muslin cover speared by a splint of wood. This he placed beside the shallow, three-legged bowl. From beneath a clean rag at the back of the bench he then slipped out a taller, round bowl, about the size of a large apple. Its curved sides were peppered with holes, it broad opening, like its partner's, boasting a chamfered rim. This he set down on the other side of the small pot, from which he removed the muslin cover.

Clearing his mind of everything else, he scraped out a blob of the pot's greasy yellow flux with the end of the splint. Slowly and carefully, applying it repeatedly to the chamfered rim of each bowl, he gave them both an even layer that glistened in the spring light coming in through the open barn doors.

After a while, and one last close peer at his handiwork, Jusuf finally stuck the splint back into the pot of flux, covered its opening with the muslin and placed it back on the shelf. Stepping back, he held his breath as he stared at the two metal pieces. Beseeching his new god, he willed each to submit to this: the greatest demand he'd ever had on his smithying skills.

He carried them both into the forge, placing them down beside the hotly glowing hearth. Beside it lay a small hammer, and on a chair before it a large leather funnel—what the English here called a tun-dish—and a fold of cotton cloth. From the cloth Jusuf removed his last saved lump of *kief*.

About the size of the end of his thumb, he carefully placed it at the centre of the shallow bowl, then upended the taller one and slowly lowered it, until their rims perfectly mated. A few taps with the hammer and a shiny yellow line oozed out from around the join. Jusuf stepped back and once again held his breath, until letting out a long and heavy sigh.

"May Allah and my new Christian God take me back to my childhood years with open ears," he intoned, staring up through the dark-hidden roof of the forge, "that I may truly remember my grandfather's time-honoured song." And with that, he reached for the arm of the bellows and began pumping air into the hearth's close-pressed charcoal, gently humming as he watched it grow brighter and whiter.

Snatches of words and some of a tune crept into his mind, the wavering voice of his aged grandfather seeming to guide his own faltering song. He tried hard not to force the memory, to let it take a hold in its own good time, to lay himself open to being filled with the ghost of his forebear.

On he pumped and the charcoal burned ever brighter, sending up flickering sparks into the gloom beyond its eventually blinding glow. What his childhood ears had once heard as a wailing dirge on an old man's quivering lips now steadily settled to a harmony, to a weaving of tone and shape and finally words that formed a long skein of his bloodline's path through time. A skein that stretched out from those who'd long gone before him to the ones yet to be born into its far off future.

Half-blinded by the glare of the hot coals, Jusuf let go of the bellows and groped beside the hearth for his tongs, finally grasping them in a hand that no longer seemed his own. But then the tongs were about the conjoined pieces, carefully lifting them as one by their lower half before gently settling them into their nest of bright-white fire.

Jusuf again took to the arm of the bellows as the legs of his creation slowly glowed red, then brilliant white as their bloody colour rose into the body of metal above. So fixed was he on the particulars of what colour had reached where, and how evenly the fizzling union ran, that for a moment he almost overlooked the leather tun-dish.

Quickly, he snatched it up, barely breaking from his

pumping as his voice carried aloft a plaintive song that quickly engulfed him, that soon rose higher and sweeter and more compelling. The metal glowed white-hot throughout, the *kief* within hissing and spitting and bubbling. Its smoke issued in long blue tendrils through the host of holes, rising like escaping snakes.

Now was the time, Jusuf knew. Now!

He swung the tun-dish above his creation, as near as he dared to its sizzling sound and now billowing smoke. Then he fixed his lips about the funnel's spout. Tensing at the prospect but gathering his resolve, he drew in a long, deep lungful of hot choking smoke, holding it for as long as he could bear.

In an almighty rush, like the crashing of some celestial choir, his mind soared high above him, drawing with it his very own Songs of Our Forebears. And higher and higher they went, each deep draught of smoke searing out into his flying words. Its refrain possessed him, sweetened his voice yet more and lifted his song, reaching ahead through the rushing blackness of time. Onwards he sang, ever onwards, towards the distant pull of a familiar and welcoming bright white light: the light of his and all this world's last hope of their many bloodlines' future salvation.

34 AN OVERSIGHT

"Your story must have a beginning, a middle and an end, Jusuf," the voice of his grandfather spoke to him from the billowing skein that carried them so swiftly on. "A beginning to draw your listener in when their mind may be anywhere but upon your tale."

"A beginning?" Jusuf sang in his mind. "A beginning?" and he felt his grandfather's hand upon his arm, steadying, reassuring, marking out a new rhythm for his song: the rhythm of the sea.

"I will start at the beginning of my journey, Grandfather," Jusuf decided, "for the first step of any journey always holds most promise, sets intrigue within the mind."

"Good. Then spin your thread, Jusuf, my boy; spin it so it may be woven into this very cloth, and by it read in times to come. Make it start, then, upon the sea, Ceuta behind you and intrigue along its tempting course ahead."

Jusuf did. He spun his thread, spun it from his last view from Bab el-Zakat of Ceuta's Monte Anyera, then of his sight of the lands of his people that had been lost to the thieving Christian infidels. This he then wove into his and his grandfather's cloth, wove it as a bright thread through an otherwise dull fabric.

Then he spun a thread of storm, a dark thread of terror and mortal fear, and this too he wove into his tale, its pattern one of merciful escape and the fateful saving of an enemy's life. And on he spun and wove, until his design depicted Foy and their loss of the Nao Providência to the pirate *Capitão* Treffry, to the need to hide his plague-burden and then on yet further still to… To his first vision in the Ship Inn, unknowing he was her forebear, of—of Kate.

Kate who, after his painful black loss of Rodrigo's friendship, many more woven threads brought him to see again, there across the hearth in his forge. Threads that revealed he'd seen her before: glimpses from the corner of his eye, like when he'd heard those cracks of thunder so close above the Salutation Inn.

But already that part of the cloth had swept on by, and with it his and Gwenna's first kiss and the shock and joy of learning she wasn't barren, then Saint Petroc's bones and the crumbling abbot's seal, and on and on. Until here he was: sending his own Songs of Our Forebears to the very one he now knew could do no other than hear. The one he saw, sitting across a small table from him in a simple wooden building. A hovel that boasted rain-lashed glass in its window openings.

Glass in such a humble dwelling—it could only be his distant future, a future to which he had to speak.

"And here I come to the end of my story," he calmly told Kate. "The story of your forebear: not what I want of you, but who I truly am," and the fabric of that story billowed out silently behind him.

"In your deepest darkness, let a simple candle's light guide your way," but Kate's eyes only narrowed, briefly, before she let out a yelp and shot to her feet.

She soon knelt beside him, where he writhed on the floor, his mind aflame within a suffocating tapestry that swirled all about him. Then he groaned, loudly, sat up and puked down his tee-shirt, the chalet spinning violently about his head.

"Oh, God," he groaned and was sick again.

"Shit, Colin. What's wrong?"

He couldn't answer, not until he'd writhed onto his stomach and gripped the threadbare carpet tightly in both fists, but even then he could only manage "Bad trip" before heaving once more.

Kate tended to Colin as best she could, as his writhing and mewling and groaning would allow. She cleaned him up then brought him orange juice to drink. By the time the morning had worn on towards noon and the rain given way to sunlight, Colin found himself sitting groggily on the sofa.

He felt wretched.

The room had stopped spinning, but it still swayed alarmingly whenever he moved his head. The bright sunshine flooding the view through the window opposite eventually tempted him to open his eyes, but its glare sent sharp slivers of pain through them. Only once Kate had chivvied him into eating a little dry toast did he begin to feel a bit better.

He looked at his watch, closed his eyes and groaned. "I don't think," he at first slurred, but then gathered his meagre reserves. "I don't think we're going to get that shopping done, Kate."

"Don't worry about it, Colin. We can just about get by on what we have in until tomorrow."

"I'm sorry."

"It's all right. I'm more worried about you."

"I... I do feel a bit better. That toast helped."

Colin drew in a long breath, relieved his mind stayed still, even a strange calmness settling within it.

"There wouldn't be any more toast, would there?" he said, opening his eyes to find Kate looking much relieved.

"I'll get you some. Then, when you feel up to it, maybe you could tell me what the hell happened, eh?"

He carefully nodded.

This time Colin's slow unfolding of his phantasm allowed Kate to write it all down without interruption. Only when he came to Jusuf's long, deep and repeated tokes on the funnel's spout did she need to speak, and this time to prompt him on.

"It was just a weird trip," was all he could find to say.

"Yeah, but what kind of trip?"

"A bad trip."

"I know that; you said before. But what happened during it?"

"Just weird stuff," and when Kate only lofted her eyebrows, he gave her a beseeching look. "Not much of it made any sense. Like I said: weird. Stuff about cloth."

"Cloth?"

"Weaving cloth. Well, I suppose it was some sort of analogy, you know, for Jusuf's... Yeah, for his *story*; that I do remember. His Songs of Our Forebears."

"But what about the whereabouts of his plague-burden?"

"Dunno. Don't remember anything about that. He just seemed to be going back through what we already know happened to him."

"What, like making sure he left threads through his story's fabric that we could follow to home in on the significant bits?"

Colin stared at Kate. "Yeah. Just like that. Of course. Now it makes a bit more sense, but there's a lot of it that's still just a jumble. I can only assume Jusuf was far more tolerant of dope than me. I mean, the amount he smoked just blew me away."

"So you don't remember telling me something before you slipped from your chair?"

"Telling you something?"

"Sounded gibberish to me… Well, maybe a bit Arabic, I suppose, or maybe a fifteenth century version."

"I remember he'd been talking with his grandfather, so maybe it was fifteenth century Berber?"

"I don't know. Come to that, I've never heard twentieth century Berber, either, not that I know of."

"Well, Kate, I was so stoned it can't have been me speaking. I was just too far gone for that. So, it had to be Jusuf himself, Jusuf seeing through the clear water beneath the tide's inrushing surf."

Kate gawped at him. "You're obviously still stoned, Colin."

"No. It makes sense: for him to have spoken to you through me, he must have been *seeing* you; seeing you like I've been seeing Gwenna. Seeing his distant future descendant."

"In which case, if he knew who I was by then, he must have been telling me where he'd hidden his burden. He must have been. So we could go and fix its damned crap seal."

Colin closed his eyes and leant his head back against the sofa and groaned. "Oh, shit," he drew out. "The most important thing we needed to hear, the whole point of all the phantasms he set in motion, and he told you the answer to the entire mystery in Berber! What an idiot; a real effing idiot."

He shook his head in despair.

"Because, Kate, what I do distinctly remember is that he used the last of his dope in making *that*," and he nodded towards the joss stick holder on the table under the window. "Whatever he said to you, he knew it was the last time we'd ever be in contact. The very last chance he would have to tell us how to save the world. And he blew it!"

35 THE POWER OF SUGGESTION

Despair and despondency drove deep into Colin's weakened state. Kate didn't press him further, clearly giving him time to recover, and the afternoon steadily wore on to their evening meal, largely conducted in silence. He'd eaten with a bit more enjoyment than he'd expected, feeling surprisingly restored once they'd cleared away and sat down on the sofa.

It must have shown, for after a while Kate asked, "You feel more up to discussing this morning?"

Colin stared at her for a moment, then nodded "Okay".

"You sure?"

"Yep. Feel strangely as fit as a fiddle now."

She looked at him for a moment, clearly thinking. "Which is what's got me to wondering."

"Wondering?"

"Hmm. You only had the one spliff before the phantasm, so… So how come you suffered so badly?"

"Because of the amount Jusuf smoked; a lethal amount."

"Yeah, but it didn't actually get into your body. The one that stayed here. And your mind couldn't really have been exposed to it, and even if it somehow had, then it was no more than a couple of seconds' worth."

"It felt longer. And it felt like I'd physically smoked that much."

Kate clamped her lips together and squinted at him. "Exactly. It felt like it; only *felt* like it. But you couldn't have done. Could you? Not really. And you've recovered so quickly."

"Well, when you put it like that, no, I don't suppose I could have. Not physically."

"So your bummer of a high must've been psychosomatic."

"Just suggestion?"

"Hmm."

From Colin's close perspective it proved hard to agree, but the facts did seem to point that way. "So what you suggesting?"

"Well, if you weren't really experiencing a bad trip, then surely your memory of what happened shouldn't have been affected, just displaced somehow. Overshadowed by what you thought was happening to you."

"Go on."

"If I were to read aloud the notes I made, sort of get you to relive it without any dope in your system at all, then maybe, in the cold light of day, you could unearth those memories."

It sounded a bit risky to Colin, the thought of going through another bad trip too much even to consider. But then there was a lot riding on it. That he couldn't deny, and so he finally found himself nodding.

Kate had a perfect narrator's voice, well-paced and with enough feeling to it to bring everything back surprisingly strongly, so much so he became nervous as she neared describing Jusuf taking up the funnel.

But he needn't have worried: the memories of what had happened after Jusuf's massive tokes just came back to him as nothing more than that. They still seemed inexplicable, but the detail was there, all of which Kate carefully wrote down. And finally, they came to Jusuf's words to her, words that sat in Colin's mind more as meaning than spoken thoughts. He considered how best to convey them, and at last spoke.

Kate wrote them down, then looked up, her face a picture of confusion. "There must be more," she urged. "There must be. This," and she stabbed the pad with her pen, "tells us nothing."

"Read it back to me, Kate," and she did.

"'And here I come to the end of my story. The story of your forebear', which is pretty straightforward, but then we get: 'Not what I want of you, but who I truly am'. I mean, surely that's exactly what he did want: us to do something. Something damned important, like make his bottle of plague safe, for Pete's sake."

"Well, maybe—"

"And the coup de grace turns out to be a riddle: 'In your deepest darkness, let a simple candle's light guide your way'. Why set a riddle when he could just have told me straight out? Eh, Colin? Why the man-of-mystery? Why not 'It's under the middle front row seat in the High Street Odeon cinema in Truro'?"

She threw her pen down on her pad and crossed her arms. "You must have forgotten what he said after this," she levelled at him, "or slipped from your chair before he finished."

A sense of guilt welled up in Colin's chest, the

thought he might have been to blame for their failure, that somehow he'd not lasted the course. Lamely, he quietly told her he was sure there'd been nothing more, that Jusuf had seemed relieved to have spoken those words as his final ones to her. But the doubt still left him feeling uncomfortable.

Kate took a deep breath, raggedly expelled, then softened her features a little. "I'm sorry, Colin. I didn't mean to… Well, to accuse you of anything. But you've got to admit, Jusuf's words are hardly helpful."

Colin took up Kate's pad. "Not what he wanted but who he was," he paraphrased. "It sounds to me like he was worried we wouldn't believe his message, not without understanding who he was and what he'd been through. You know, the context. Maybe he wasn't sure we'd have already been following his story, that we might not have come across it before he spoke to you. It's as though he's saying: know who I am through what happened to me, then you'll know the importance of what you need to do."

"Then why not just say so, then tell us where he'd hidden the damned thing."

"Well, he was stoned. I mean, *really* stoned." But then Colin rubbed his chin thoughtfully, going back in his mind through all he knew of Jusuf, all the insights he'd had from his intimate company, mind within mind. He looked across at Kate, her expression one of confusion at the nascent grin he felt sure his own now held.

"Jusuf was a straightforward man, Kate. A skilled blacksmith, yes, but although not brilliantly well-educated, far from stupid. A kind and gentle man who tried to take what he found at face value. No complications. Like me, an engineer, a clever one, mind, and so I reckon what we should do is just take what he said at face value: 'In your deepest darkness, let a simple candle's light guide your way'."

"Well, we're in our 'Deepest darkness' now, Colin. A darkness of despair, and a darkness that's stopping us seeing what we should do next—and more to the point: *where*."

"Have we got any candles?"

"Candles? Well, yes, there should be some. Before the chalet got mains electricity it had gas mantles. The Calor gas bottles tended to have a bit of a habit of running out without warning, so there were always some to hand."

"Do you think you could find one?"

"I imagine they're still somewhere in the shed. Why?"

"Because, once we've brought 'Deepest darkness' to this room, by turning off the electric lights, I think we're going to need a 'Candle's light to guide our way'."

By the time Kate had found an old box of household candles in the shed, dusk was fast slipping into nighttime. She came in and dropped it and her torch on the table as Colin came through with a couple of mugs of tea.

"Oh great, you found some," he said. "Just need a saucer, then," and he went back into the galley to get one. "And then wait until the night's at its darkest," he called back.

"Well, that's going to be about one in the morning," Kate said, as Colin stuck the candle to the saucer and placed it on the table, beside the joss stick holder. As they began their wait, Kate asked what he was up to.

"I don't quite know yet. We need to wait and see."

"You know, Colin, I think you and Jusuf really did

come out of the same mould; a damned infuriating engineer's mould."

He grinned at her at first, but then said, "His final words told us to know who he was, right?" Kate nodded. "Well, he was a blacksmith."

"So?"

"So what do blacksmiths do?"

"Shoe horses?"

"Work metal," and he nodded towards the joss stick holder. "Metalwork like that."

Kate peered at the thing. "But what about it?"

"I don't know, not yet, but I suspect we might find out as soon as it's dark enough," and they continued their wait. Kate half-heartedly tried to read her book. Eventually, Colin got up and lit the candle from his trusty Zippo, then drew the curtains. "Time for deepest darkness, I reckon," and he switched off the light.

They both sat at the table, peering at the candlelit holder. It looked no different, not to Colin's eye, yellower, dimmer, perhaps a more noticeable lustre, but otherwise unremarkable.

"Well?" Kate said.

"Hmm," and Colin moved the candle around the holder, looking for any telltale marks or indentations, or maybe some pattern or other that only the candlelight could reveal. He found nothing. Nothing more than what they now knew to be centuries of wear-and-tear.

"All right," he said, raising his brows, "maybe I've been barking up the wrong—"

"Colin!" Kate almost spat. "Move the candle back a bit…to where you had it just then." Slowly, he did so. "There. Hold it there. Do you see it?"

"What?" and he peered harder at the holder whilst

trying to keep the candle still.

"There," and Colin realised she was pointing at the wall, the bit between the bottom of the curtains and the table top. "See it?"

He did. A pattern of sprinkled dots of faint candlelight wavered there in the holder's shadow, in sympathy with his unsteady hold of the candle. Then he understood.

Without saying a word, he looked around in desperation and spotted Kate's notepad. He put the candle down on the table, much to Kate's protestations, and picked the pad up off the sofa, propping it against the bottom of the curtains.

Clearer now, the candle at last steady and the wallpaper's confusing pattern hidden behind the pad, Colin could make out a couple of strange words that dimly glowed from the paper. Like an electronic calculator's matrix display, they said "inscrybd stone".

"What the hell does that mean?" he asked, but Kate had got up and was searching for something in the gloom. She came back with a scrap of paper, on which she wrote down the ghostly words.

"There must be more," she said, and so Colin slowly rotated the holder by its feet. More words seemed magically to form, this time "hedestocc", which ran above "insyde bellfrye". When he again rotated the holder, only "Myke save" appeared from the candlelight's projection through the holder's newly aligned peppering of holes.

At last, after yet another turn, the answer they'd been so desperately hoping to find dimly stared back at them. An answer that shocked them both to silence, until together they sighed "Wow", and turned to each other with the widest of wide eyes.

36 AN INITIAL DISCOVERY

"Christ, Kate, my head must have been only feet from it!"

"And I wasn't much further away at the bottom of the ladder."

They stared at the pad, across which "St. Germanus" dimly but clearly glowed, "Rame" below it. With shaky fingers, Colin again rotated the joss stick holder; "inscrybd stone" reappeared.

"That's it, then; the full message," he said.

"Put the light back on, Colin," and he did, snuffing out the candle before standing behind Kate. He peered over her shoulder and watched as she wrote each word out again using their modern spelling, finally rearranging them to read: "St. Germanus Rame, inscribed stone, headstock inside belfry. Make safe".

"When you think about it, Colin, Jusuf couldn't have chosen better."

"What? Choosing Saint Germanus?"

"Yeah. Where's most likely to last down through the centuries? A church. And which is least likely to be changed? A small remote one that's about as far away from being important enough to warrant alterations as you can get; unlike Bodmin's Saint Petroc's. Don't forget, that was almost completely rebuilt only twenty years before Jusuf arrived."

"And," Colin furthered, "somewhere to which he had legitimate access. Somewhere he could make as much noise as he needed in hiding his burden, given he was there fitting their bell's new headstock."

"Well, Bingo, Colin; there we have it. Found. We just need to work out how we're going to get at it, to make it safe for the next five hundred years."

Colin pointed out what Kate had said about rural churches never being locked, and that the belfry's hatch hadn't even had a catch. As for whatever stone it was hidden behind, he reckoned it wouldn't take much to scrape out what little mortar he remembered the church walls having. Kate then asked if he'd thought of a secure way of resealing the bottle.

"Araldite."

"Araldite?"

"Yeah. You know, two-part epoxy resin."

"I know what Araldite is, Colin. It's just I would never would have thought of using it for this."

"It's the easiest and safest way I can think of. Easy to apply, takes less than an hour to cure, doesn't shrink or expand in the process, and last for yonks."

"Would that 'Yonks' be five hundred years, though?"

"Er, well, I reckon so. I can't think of anything better, not that we'll be able to do in the middle of the night by torchlight, stuck up a church tower."

Kate stared at Colin, her face immobile. Then she swallowed hard.

"You all right, Kate?"

She slowly shook her head. "No. Not really."

"You've gone white."

"I never, not in a million years, ever saw myself breaking into a church in the dead of night, never mind hacking into one of its walls."

"We won't be breaking in; it won't be locked."

"You know what I mean."

Colin sat down at the table. "It'll be okay. In the dead of night around there it'll be as dead as a grave."

"I assume you're trying to be funny," but Colin stared blankly at her, which brought her to ask, "Why don't we just explain it all to the vicar, then ask for his permission to look for it?"

"You were the one to tell me we'd no concrete evidence. He just wouldn't believe us, Kate."

"But we've got the joss stick holder's message now."

"Which has no provenance at all. So, if we're not convincing enough, all we'll end up doing is revealing our hand, then we'd be stuffed. And imagine it: 'My friend, here, has had a few dope-induced phantasms that have revealed the end of the world is nigh, so we just wondered if—"

"Okay, Colin. I get the idea."

"So, we're on our own, in which case…I can feel a list coming on."

As he started writing on the pad, he happened to notice how more ashen Kate now looked.

"Don't worry, chuck," Colin assured her. "It'll be fine. I'm sure it will. I'll just finish off this list, then anything we haven't already got we can pick up tomorrow when we go shopping. We should then be able to get it done tomorrow night."

Kate was dead set against this, arguing that

weekends were the busiest time for visitors around there. "Let's leave it till Monday night. It'll be a lot quieter."

"Well...all right, then, Monday night it is," and he went back to compiling his list.

When Monday night eventually came, they drove to the coastguard station car park at pub throwing-out time, parking in a dark corner as though two lovers in search of seclusion. Come midnight, the windows by then convincingly steamed-up, they quietly got out and locked the car.

Aided a little by the distant amber stain of Plymouth's streetlights lighting the clouds inland, they quietly walked back the half mile along the lane towards Saint Germanus. Colin hitched their rucksack more comfortably onto his shoulder, confident it held everything they'd likely need. But the nearer they got to the church, the more he began to worry about things unforeseen.

"I wish you'd worn something darker, Kate," he whispered. "I can see that jacket quite clearly."

"I packed for coming on holiday, not cat-burgling. This is the darkest I've got."

For once, Colin was thankful for the seclusion of the Cornish hedgebanks, even though they weren't that high here. However, it did mean that if anyone came along the lane itself towards them, there'd be nowhere to hide. Then he noticed he could just make out the church spire ahead, black against the faintly amber-lit clouds.

"In here," Kate quietly said, stumbling up a short grass verge to what looked like a gap in the hedgebank.

"Where you going?"

"I'm sure there's a back way into the churchyard here."

"You never mentioned it. I thought we were going in by the lychgate at the front," and Colin stumbled after her.

"Only just remembered, but it'll mean we're off the lane a bit sooner. Ah, yes, here we are," and Colin could hear what sounded like a wrought iron latch being lifted.

Beyond the gate, the starlight only just revealed a churchyard that slanted away towards the low dark mass of the church, the tower at its western end still clearly outlined against the clouds. On each side of an overgrown path rose gravestones, mourning-black against the ghostly-grey grass between, each seeming silently to watch Colin and Kate pass by.

Once within the utter darkness beside the wall of the south aisle, they had to feel their way towards the tower, careful not to fall into the deep ditch that ran around the building. After what seemed like an eternity of groping in the darkness they found themselves beside the entrance porch on the north side. Its pitch-black interior gaped forbiddingly at them, into which they each took a step, stunned to a stop by the utter darkness within.

"Hang on," Colin whispered, slipping the rucksack off. He drew a torch from one of its side pockets and promptly startled them both with its intense but narrow beam. He clicked it off.

"Sorry," he whispered, his heart beating ten-to-the-dozen as he blindly peered out into the churchyard, listening intently.

He felt Kate beside him. "I thought you said the insulation tape would stop it being so bright."

"Well, it always works in films. Maybe I didn't make the slit quite narrow enough."

"Stick your hand over the lens, then, and try again."

The glow still proved worryingly bright, but not as intense, tinted pink by the fleshy filter of Colin's hand. It let Kate quickly find the door latch, though, and to Colin's immense relief, the door opened—emitting a loud and protracted creak.

"Shit," Kate whispered. "I don't suppose you brought any oil."

"Just get in, will you?" and after a moment, he was ever so slowly and hence a little less noisily closing the door behind them.

Inside Saint Germanus, beyond the torch's pool of restricted light, it looked blacker than he imagined outer space to be, except for its barely amber-lit stained-glass windows. They seemed to hover about them, spectre-like in the still, musty air. Then he jumped when Kate prodded him, to prompt him to show a bit more light.

"You're covering the torch too much," she told him. "Come on. Let's get this over with."

Wary of the slit opening in the far wall of the base of the tower, Colin kept the torch's light low, illuminating the uneven stone flags at their feet.

"Here," he said. "Take the torch and I'll go up and open the hatch."

As before, it lifted easily, clicking loudly as it swung back against a stop. It held in place.

"Colin?" Kate hissed. "How am I going to get up with a torch in my hand?"

"Ah. Er, well, hang on a sec'," and he climbed back down. "You go on up ahead whilst I light your way," and he took the torch from her. "Once you're in the belfry, I can feel my own way up in the dark."

She didn't move.

"Go on, then," but she only looked down at her feet.

"What's wrong?"

Kate cast him the glint of a sheepish look. "I'm… I'm not that good with ladders. Sorry."

"But… But why didn't you say so before?" She didn't answer. "Look, I tell you what, seeing I can't do everything on my own and so need you with me, what if I climb up behind you, so you can't fall?"

"In the pitch-black?"

"No. Look," and Colin placed the torch on the ground, facing close into a corner, shedding enough light to see the ladder by. "I'll get you up safely then come back down for the torch. You okay with that?"

She slowly nodded.

Kate's progress proved slow and stiff, but eventually she climbed up into the belfry, the sound of her feeling for a place away from the hole in which to wait coming loudly to Colin's ears as he retrieved the torch. Once safely back with her, he took the torch from his pocket and turned it on. He quickly covered it with his hand, though, at the sight of narrow louvered slit-openings, one in each of the tower's four walls.

"Shit. I never thought about those. We're going to have to be really careful with the light, Kate, being so high up here." He gave the torch into Kate's care, then took his first proper look at the sizeable bell, suspended at waist height within its square frame at the centre of the floor. "Right. Just the one," and he reached into the rucksack and took out a woollen sock.

"What's that for?" Kate whispered, but Colin was

already on his stomach, reaching under the bell with both hands, despite its rim being barely a foot off the floor. He carefully grasped the bell's tongue, over which he slid the sock with a bit of difficulty.

"There we are; safe from us accidentally ringing out our presence."

"Wow. You've thought of everything, Colin…except that another torch might have come in handy," which comment he deigned to ignore. "So," Kate said, "which bit's the headstock?"

Colin got to his feet and leant over the bell. "This is it," he said, running his hand along a thick metal beam from whose cranked centre the bell hung. At one end was a large metal wheel, from which the bell rope vanished through a hole in the floor.

"Bring the light over here, Kate, if you would," and he peered at the rough slate wall a foot or so beyond the wheel. "Can you see any marks?" and when she said she couldn't, he lightly dusted the wall of cobwebs with his hand, revealing nothing.

"Let's have a look at the other side, then," and there they found a few slightly larger stones. "Bring the light a bit nearer, Kate."

Colin's mind froze as a shiver ran up his back, for cut into one of them, beneath a wispy layer of cobwebs, he could definitely make out the letter "J". Beside it, after running his hand over the stone, an "H" appeared.

At first he felt numb, unable to grasp that he had before him that very solid evidence that had for so long eluded them. An indisputable testament to Jusuf's hand in history. Colin nearly whooped in excitement but managed to rein it in, hard pressed to keep his reaction to a broad grin he cast Kate's way. It was a grin, though, that teetered on the edge of unrestrained jubilance.

"We've… We've found it, Kate," he finally managed to say, his voice quavering as he fought to keep it in check. "The inscribed stone. *Jusuf's* inscribed stone," and his grin now ached across his face.

Kate pushed in nearer, staring at the letters. "JH: Jusuf al-Haddad," but her own wide grin only looked menacing in the low angle of the torchlight. "All we have to do now, Colin, is get behind it," she said, and his near delirium fizzled out as his grin wavered and finally collapsed.

"Right," he said, rather flatly, and at last pulled himself together.

He'd soon removed an old wooden-handled screwdriver from the rucksack, placing the broad blade of its long shaft into the gap around the stone. Then he stopped, abruptly, leaving the screwdriver sticking out, and bent to pull some newspapers from the bag.

"Here, I nearly forgot. Help me lay these out beneath it. We have to be really tidy, and I want to use the debris as packing once we're finished; to make it look undisturbed."

There didn't seem to be much mortar when Colin came to scrape the screwdriver blade back and forth. What little did come out clattered noisily onto the newspaper. When he worked the blade along the top of the stone, though, it jammed. As he tried to prise it loose, an odd thing happened: the stone angled out a touch, as though hinged along its bottom edge.

They stared at each other in the gloom.

"Well," Kate whispered, "as you've already pointed out, he *was* a born engineer."

Colin returned his attention to the stone, gently prising at it with the screwdriver, his free hand against its face. It came loose, its weight lighter than expected, leaning out against Colin's palm.

"Here, take the screwdriver," he said, then used both hands to ease the stone further out. Only a couple of inches thick, it came free, its tenon-cut lower face lifting out of a mortice groove in the stone below.

He lowered it to the newspaper, and as he straightened, their eyes met, each like a rabbit's caught in headlights. Neither he nor Kate dared move.

"*You* look," she said and handed him the torch.

"Me?"

She nodded.

"Okay, if you insist," and Colin drew in a long breath before slowly turning back to where the stone had been. He leant nearer and peered in, hoping above hope that his would prove to be the first eyes ever to have done so since Jusuf had sealed it shut all those centuries before.

37 LOATHSOME CONTENTS

"Well?" Kate demanded, but Colin didn't quite know what to say. "Come on, Colin. Put me out of my misery. Is it there or isn't it?"

"Something is, but what exactly is anyone's guess. Looks like a five-inch-high wickerwork washing basket to me. You know, like a miniature version of the plastic one we have in our bedroom for dirty clothes," then Kate's head came beside his own.

"Ooh, you're right, it does. A pretty dirty one, mind."

"Not what I expected."

"No. What did you expect?"

"Well, a small glass bottle, for one thing." Colin found his mind reeling at seeing something of Jusuf's that so clearly vindicated his phantasms—well, almost. "It's got to be inside."

"Stands to reason."

"What does?"

"Glass is fragile, even thick glass, so they'd never have sent it so far without some packaging around it."

"Yeah. Obvious, really. Fifteenth century polystyrene, eh? In which case, I suppose we'd best get it out and look inside."

"Yeah," but they both just stared at the thing, as though mesmerised.

"Go on then, Colin."

"How durable's wickerwork?"

"I haven't the foggiest, but there's only one way to find out."

"Shit. But what if it just falls apart? We don't want whatever's in it coming loose and dropping to the floor."

Kate took off her jacket and held it below the hole. "Right, off you go, then, and for Christ's sake, be careful."

Having put the torch down, Colin ever so slowly reached in with both hands, his fingers shaking the more as they inched nearer, then he stopped.

"What if the seal's already leaked and contaminated the basket?" but Kate said nothing, although he was sure, out of the corner of his eye, he caught her shrug. "Oh well, in for a penny, I suppose," and he delicately touched his fingertips to each side of the miniature basket.

It felt hard and resilient—reassuring. He finally let out the breath he hadn't known he'd been holding and steadied his hands against the stone on which the basket stood.

"Right," he said. "As I draw it out and lower it to the floor, you keep your jacket right beneath it at all times. Okay? So this thing ends up standing on it." Kate nodded, mumbling something about always being able to buy a new one. Another deep breath and Colin gritted his teeth as he took a firmer hold of the basket. It didn't budge, not until he'd applied a little more force when it then snapped free, tottering from his fingers' grasp and against the restraint of his thumbs.

"Shit," he drew out, long and heartfelt, before grasping the basket a little more firmly and drawing it into the open. Together, they lowered the coat and the basket to the newspaper, and when the basket finally stood safe and secure, both knelt back and expelled long sighs of almost tangible relief.

Colin stared at the thing, at its curved and coarsely woven walls, at its deep round lid thickly layered with centuries of dust and muck and debris, in addition to a dead spider and two wriggling woodlice.

He lifted his gaze to Kate, drawing her own to his. She swallowed hard, and then, in a small voice unlike her own, suggested, "Best have that look inside, then."

The lid proved remarkably cooperative, easing away without complaint or resistance. As Colin laid it aside, they both leant over and looked inside the basket. It appeared to be full of grey matted hair.

"Urgh," Kate said, screwing her face up. "It looks disgusting; like a dead rat," and she leant away, as though it smelt putrid.

Colin smiled and gently ran his finger over its spongy surface.

"Men!" she dismissed.

"It's all right, Kate. It's just packing. Probably goat's hair, or something like that." He delicately dug the nails of his finger and thumb in and teased a pinch free. "See?"

"Thank God for that."

Some minutes of removing more, pinch by painstaking pinch, and Colin felt something hard beneath his nail. The thudding of his blood in his ears may have sounded loud by then, but it became deafening when he lightly dusted away some of the loose hair and revealed a circle of thin glass. It enclosed a pale chalky substance he immediately recognised.

Definitely in for a pound now, he told himself, and set to, teasing out more of the hair from around the bottle's neck, each layer exposing yet more of its pale and chalky seal. "Come on," he kept saying. "Come on and turn red, you bastard."

His nail had just felt what must have been the shoulder of the bottle when, to his immense relief, the pale colour at last gave way to a bright but narrow red ring.

"Jesus Almighty," he stretched out on a long expelled breath, his muscles at last relaxing. "It's still safe." He arched back and stared up at the dark-hidden spire above them, offering a silent prayer to a god he was beginning to think might actually exist.

He then checked his watch. "Bloody 'ell, it's half one. Look, Kate, I'm gently going to test if it'll slide out. Try and save us some time, eh?"

"As long as you're really careful, Colin."

He nodded, then lightly gripped the rim of the bottle, holding the basket steady with his other hand. As gently as he could, he tried to ease the thing out but it refused to budge. A touch more force and it jerked free, slipping mercurially from its hirsute cocoon. Disbelieving it hadn't broken, he nervously held it up between Kate and himself in the light of the torch.

"What in God's name's that?" Kate whispered, staring at the small bottle's ochre coloured contents.

"I think it's some sort of mould, crammed with what looks like really tiny grains of discoloured rice."

"Urgh. That's not rice, Colin."

He carefully rolled the bottle between his finger and thumb.

"They're…they're pupae of some sort," she reckoned.

"Pupae?"

"Maggots, Colin. Tiny maggots."

"But there must be hundreds of them. Hundreds of really tiny maggots sitting in some kind of evil-looking mould." He gently laid the bottle on Kate's jacket, thankful to be no longer holding it.

"They can't still be alive, though. Surely," Kate gasped. "Not after five hundred years."

"Well, Jusuf believed they'd been well enough preserved. Any anyway, we just can't risk it."

Kate peered at the bottle, disgust written plainly across her face. "Well, I don't suppose it'd be wise to find out, one way or the other."

"No," Colin barely breathed, and shivered at the thought. "But what are they maggots of?"

"Who knows? Tsetse flies? Mosquitoes? Fleas?"

"Don't fleas have eggs?"

"Well, whatever they are, let's damn well make sure no one ever gets to finds out, eh?"

"Right. In which case, pass me the rucksack, will you?" out of which he dug half a dozen packets of Araldite Rapid.

"You got enough there, Colin?"

"I didn't know how big the bottle was going to be, did I?" by which time he'd begun removing an assortment of containers: a yogurt pot, a porcelain eggcup, a plastic tube he said had been full of drawing pins, a small plastic bottle with its top cut off—but then he stopped and returned to the tube.

He measured it against the plague bottle, satisfied it would do. Before long he'd mixed together some of the first packet of Araldite's two tubes on a margarine tub lid and scraped the viscous liquid into the transparent tube. While it slowly oozed down into the bottom, he mixed some more, this time liberally and evenly coating the length of the bottle's neck and the exposed pale wax of its seal.

"Ten minutes should do it, Kate. It should have gone off enough by then that when I slide the bottle in it won't eventually sink through what's already nicely settled at the bottom of the tube."

"Will that be it, then?" Kate said, clearly anxious yet fascinated.

"Afraid not. To be absolutely certain it's well and truly sealed for all time, I'm going to fill the tube completely. We'll need to hang around, though, turning it to make sure the bottle doesn't end up touching the sides when the Araldite's finally gone off and set solid. Then, even if the damp were to get in, which I very much doubt it would, nothing could ever crawl out."

Kate noticeably shivered. "How long before we can put it all back, then?"

"Another hour should do it."

It took the rest of the first packet and some of the next before Colin had the plastic tube filled with Araldite. For a good half hour he kept turning it, to keep the bottle from touching the sides or the bottom. At last, the epoxy resin felt firm if a little tacky to the touch when he cautiously tapped it with his fingertip. A wide grin of satisfaction at last spread across his face.

"Phew. Done, Kate. That's it. And if I say it myself, that's just about perfect," and he turned the tube before Kate's eyes to demonstrate. "See? No bubbles and the bottle's dead centre; Jusuf's plague sealed away for another five hundred years. And not before time," he noted, staring closely through the yellow-tinged but now barely transparent epoxy at the remnant red ring of wax. A thin ring that had been all that had kept out the hot and humid air of that Cornish summer.

"Come on then," Kate quietly said, relief clearly flushing her features, the very image of what he himself felt had flooded his own. "Let's get it hidden away again, before someone notices we're up here."

Colin soon emptied the basket of its goat hair, slipped the solidly encased plague phial in and reused the hair to cushion it. With the lid back on, the basket looked no different from when they'd found it, bar the missing woodlice. Once back in place within the wall and the stone replaced, as Kate tidied up, Colin worked the old mortar back into the gap as best he could. Finally, he took out a soft paintbrush from the rucksack and used it lightly to sweep dust and cobwebs back over the stone.

For a moment they both stood back and admired their handiwork, content that to the casual observer it now all appeared much as when they'd first set eyes upon it. Colin let out a long breath, feeling Kate take his hand in hers. They turned to each other and smiled, wearily but happily. Then Kate switched off the torch, and in the darkness they softly kissed.

Colin, though, eventually noticed pre-dawn light seeping in through the louvered slits in the tower's walls, reminding him of how much time had passed and that they'd yet to get away unnoticed.

38 HOMEBOUND

They stopped at the door to the porch and listened for movement without. Nothing but the early stirrings of seagulls and the gentle murmur of the sea came to Colin's ears. He turned the torch off, slowly lifted the latch and cracked open the door.

The churchyard lay black beneath the new morning's barely pale-blue tinged sky, a canopy marred only by flecks of high blood-red cloud. The door protested in jarring creaks as he slowly eased it open, enough for them to slip through.

Their footsteps in the porch came loud to Colin's heightened senses, the dew-laden air cool and sharp against his face. As they came around the base of the tower, he saw there was an easy path they could have taken in the dark of their arrival. How did we stray off it? he wondered as the crunch of the path's gravel beneath their feet left its wake washing through the tiredly slanting gravestones.

They met not a soul on the short dash back to the car park, their little Fiat its only occupant. Quickly in and the engine started, Colin kept the revs down to thwart its raspy exhaust. He coasted where possible, down the lane and alongside Saint Germanus' churchyard wall, the tower they'd come to know so well now a shadowed grey against the fast-lightening sky.

They passed only one other car along the coastal road, coming the other way, its windows still misted with dew, a hand wiping a sightline across its windscreen. Then they were outside the chalet, its tin roof glistening in the quickening light of the sun's promised emergence from beyond Rame Head.

Neither Kate nor Colin moved when the engine fell silent. They both stared numbly at the stillness of the dawn world outside the car.

"I'm completely knackered, Colin. Drained," and Kate blew out her cheeks before releasing the breath they held in a long, resigned and quiet whistle.

"I could murder a cuppa, though," Colin enthused, feeling a strange euphoria warming his chest. "How about you, Kate?" and he turned to her.

She nodded, her gaze still blindly fixed on the chalet.

Colin leant over and kissed her gently on her cheek, its coolness chilling his lips. "Well done, lass. Tha's did well, tha knows," to which she couldn't help but grin.

"I think we both did, Colin, so let's get that cup of tea, eh? Then pray we never have to do anything like that again," and she shivered.

Colin unpacked the rucksack whilst Kate brewed up. He put everything on the table, beside the joss stick holder at which he then found himself smiling.

"You've led us a merry dance, Jusuf," he told it, "but I reckon we've done you proud." But then, in amongst the clutter on the table, he noticed a lone woollen sock. He stared at it for a moment, then his heart sank before he rummaged frantically in the rucksack for its partner.

"Bugger," he softly said, then more loudly, "Kate?"

"Yes?" and she came in from the galley.

"You haven't by any chance got my other sock in your pocket, have you?"

Her mouth dropped open as she stared at the one hanging limply from Colin's hand. "I thought *you'd* removed it."

They both slumped down on the sofa, speechless.

"I'm not going back for it, Colin," Kate said. "I don't think my nerves could take it."

Slowly, Colin began laughing.

"What are they going to think, though, if we leave it there?" she worried.

"Ha, maybe that they've got a disgruntled neighbour who's pig-sick of being woken early on a Sunday morning."

"It's not funny, Colin," but before long, she too fell to laughing.

"I'm pretty sure," Colin assured her, "they'll not notice anything else amiss. We left it looking pretty much as we'd found it, and I can't imagine they get up into the belfry that often to know any different."

"I hope so, and I hope it wasn't one of your good socks," then the kettle began boiling and Kate rushed back to make the tea.

"Good ones?" he called.

"Hmm, well," he heard her say to herself, dismissively.

"Maybe," he offered, "we ought to go back in a few days' time as grockles. You know, have a bit of a mooch around."

"What," Kate said, sticking her head through from

the galley, "and return to the scene of the crime? That'd be a bit hackneyed, wouldn't it?"

"Hmm. I see what you mean."

For the remainder of that week in Cornwall they heard no mention of any strange finds in Saint Germanus' belfry. Kate even bought the local newspapers and comprehensively trawled through them. Colin eventually consigned it to the back of his mind, assuming the sock would actually have made little real difference to a bell in full swing.

Although the weather hadn't been as good that second week, they still managed the odd day on the beach, and certainly plenty of invigorating walks in order to earn the refreshing drinks to which they inevitably led. Throughout it all, Colin's thoughts never once turned to rolling any more spliffs, what little remained of the dope left untouched. Jusuf had used all his up, so there seemed little point.

The joss stick holder itself kept his interest, though, and occasionally he'd marvelled at the way Jusuf had aligned the holes just right to pass through the light of his message. He'd even speculated to Kate how he reckoned Jusuf had done it, using clay through which he must have pushed long thin sticks.

But it had all largely been put behind them by the time their little Fiat burbled its contented way through the suburbs of Manchester, come the evening of that last Friday of their holiday. Their house seemed palatial compared with the confines they'd become accustomed to over the previous two weeks. Two weeks that had seemed like a lifetime.

Having unpacked the car, Colin finally sat on the sofa in the lounge and drank his cooling tea. Kate came in from wiping down the kitchen and unpacking her bags, and sat with him.

"Well," she eventually said, "I feel we've been away for ages, and a lot's happened."

"Sure has. I feel I've spent a lifetime with Jusuf. I must say, though, I do feel pretty refreshed, and…and with a sense of accomplishment I never anticipated."

"That's true. Same here. Though I could've done without the cat-burgling. But I think we did well, all told." Kate downed the last of her tea. "Anyway, I don't know about you but I'm knackered after that long journey. I'm going to go up a bit early, maybe get to finish off my Thackeray. You coming up?"

"I'll just have a last fag and a wind-down, then I'll be right up with you. In fact, I think I'll toast our success and finally say goodbye to Jusuf and the others with a last spliff. You going to join me?" but Kate said she'd skip on this one.

"Probably the last we'll get from what's left, Kate," but she still couldn't be tempted.

It wasn't long before Colin went up and found Kate still with her book propped up before her on the duvet. Beside her, on the bedside table, stood the joss stick holder. It reminded Colin of their nights in her student accommodation, back in nineteen-seventy-six, which brought a warm smile to his face.

"Have you seen the joss sticks?" he asked, to which she told him she'd put them in the cupboard downstairs. "Be right back," and he nipped down, soon returning with a lit one in his hand.

"Thought it only fitting we mark our farewell to your ancestors not only with a spliff but also a token joss stick."

"Yes, that seems appropriate," she agreed, "now it's all behind us at last."

Colin went around to her side, strangely fond memories of his times occupying Jusuf's mind pleasantly drifting around in his own. There, he slipped the joss stick, with seeming impunity, securely into the holder.

39 A THOUSAND YEARS

Colin was about to say something suitably final when the imposing porch of Saint Petroc's church appeared before his startled gaze, bright under a warm summer's morning sky. People in their fifteenth-century Sunday best were spilling from its doorway, Gwenna in amongst them, ushering out a small girl of about four years of age.

Behind her came Jusuf, deep in conversation with a man Colin vaguely remembered having seen before about Bodmyn. They laughed, easily, the man patting as high as he could reach on Jusuf's shoulders before bidding him a farewell.

Now together, Jusuf and Gwenna and the young girl broke apart from the rest of the worshippers, who were intent on the churchyard's gate, and wandered onto the grass.

"Off you go, Kayna," Jusuf encouraged the girl "and pick yourself a handful of buttercups and daisies," and he pointed at the dense swathes that laced the churchyard's open grass. Like a loosed sprite, she almost flew across the gay carpet of white and yellow flowers, before dropping to her knees and single-mindedly setting to, plucking up one after another into the tight grasp of her small hand.

When Colin turned back to Jusuf and Gwenna, Jusuf had wrapped his arm about his wife, she leaning her head against his chest, their eyes only for the girl. Then Jusuf said, "I wonder if it will be another girl," and Colin noticed him stroke Gwenna's belly as she smiled back at him. After a while he called, "That be more than enough, Kayna," and waved her over.

As the mite approached, hands hidden beneath her bunch of blooms, Colin realised how much of Gwenna he could see in her features: the slightly pointed ears, the wide set eyes, the taper of her chin, and a trusting wonder in the gaze she directed up at Jusuf.

"This be enough, da?" she beamed as she held out her offering, one or two slipping from her grasp. Jusuf slid his arm out from around Gwenna and squatted to Kayna's level, picking up the rogue flowers.

"They be more than enough, my little ray of sunshine," and his wide white grin opened up across his dark-skinned face.

Colin then noticed Kayna's own skin, a beautiful dusky complexion that couldn't as yet be likened in her own world to coffee. Her father carefully pushed the stems of the two dropped flowers back in amongst those in her hands, then reached into his pocket.

"I have a gift for thee. Would 'e like that, Kayna?" and the girl nodded, vigorously, dropping another couple of flowers.

Sitting on the palm of the huge hand he shot before her eyes was the brightly polished joss stick holder, and Colin's eyes lit up, like her own.

"For me?" she squealed, jiggling on the spot, hugging her momentarily forgotten blooms to her chest. Gwenna now stood beside her, clearly infused with the same excitement her daughter so freely spilled about her.

"This be just for thee, my treasure," Jusuf smiled, "but your ma and me will look after it for you, until thee be old enough to take good care of it thee self." He teased the flowers from her grasp and lay them at his feet, so he could help her take the weight of the holder in her hands. She drew it tight against her chest as she stared down in wonder.

"What be it?" she asked, her wide eyes now intent on her father's. Colin watched Jusuf smile again, a brief glance sent Gwenna's way.

"A flower cushion," he told his daughter, "like the one your ma uses for her sewing pins. The one that keeps trailing sawdust everywhere," and this time he gave Gwenna a grin.

"I keep patching it, Joseph," she said, "although maybe I do really need a new one."

"You know better than me that you need not carry on with your needlework, Gwenna. The smithy be earning more than enough now, enough to think of buying our own."

"Which be why I daren't think of giving up; not yet, anyway."

"A flower cushion?" Kayna persisted, and Jusuf ruffled her long, dark silken hair.

"Put it down on the grass and I'll show 'e," which she did. Leaning over, he picked out a buttercup by its stem and carefully threaded it into one of the holes, adjusting it to just the right length before ruffling its head to settle its petals.

"There thee go. Easy, eh?" he encouraged, unnecessarily as it soon turned out. Before long most of the flower cushion's metal had vanished beneath a haze of yellow and white that quickly became a thick cloud.

Jusuf stood, smiling across at Gwenna. Colin could clearly see in both their eyes that deep love he knew had so steadily grown stronger between them.

Then Kayna piped up, "And this be mine now?" the possibility that she may have been wrong somehow painfully clear in her expectant look.

"It be so, my little faerie. All yours," Jusuf assured her. "And when thee be older, when thee be a fine young woman like your ma, then thee can look after it all by thee self."

She beamed down at the flower cushion, well hidden beneath its burden of blooms.

"And one day, when you have your own daughter, you can pass it on to her—so it will be in our family for a thousand years."

"A thousand years?" she quietly queried, uncertainly, but Jusuf had already turned his gaze towards the churchyard's gate, his eyes narrowed. Gwenna and Colin followed his gaze, a lone figure standing there at the top of the steps down to the road. The man somehow looked familiar, gazing at them from across the daisy- and buttercup-strewn grass.

On his way past Colin, Jusuf's nearness raised a ripple of goose bumps across his skin. But then Jusuf and the man were before each other, stilled for a moment before they embraced, patting each other's backs for a long while.

Colin caught Gwenna's broad smile before Kayna turned a puzzled look at her and asked, "What be a 'Thousand Years', ma?"

"What's that, Kayna?" and Gwenna looked down at her daughter.

"Da said 'A thousand'—"

"Oh. That. Well, that, my dearest one, be your da's Berber way of saying *forever*," and she bent and gathered up both Kayna and her now inseparable flower cushion. Colin watched Gwenna's diminishing back as she rushed over to join Jusuf and Rodrigo, her daughter in her arms.

Colin was left gazing at the three embracing figures, the young one scurrying around their feet, until Rodrigo passed what looked like a broken ring into Jusuf's hand, before bending down to the girl. He then picked her up and swung her around him, her delighted squeals cutting joyfully to Colin as he gazed on, still gaping wide-eyed and slack-jawed at Gwenna's words.

"Shit," he said to Kate.

"What?" she asked, looking up from her book.

"*Forever*? I wonder how long Araldite really does last."

"What are you talking about, Colin?"

He told her what had just happened, recounting what he now somehow knew was certainly his last if somewhat brief visit to Jusuf. Kate's first reaction was to look at the joss stick holder and suggest they pick some of their own lawn's daisies, but then the full implication of what Colin had told her clearly sank in.

"Forever? You mean… You mean Jusuf's 'Thousand years' was purely figurative? That what he really meant was…*forever*? But—"

"I think, Kate, I'm going to have to go see Jimmy Wrigley again at some point; see if he's still got some of that Moroccan."

"But you said Jusuf had used up all his *kief*. So why

would you need to—"

"After which, I suppose, I'm going to have to put some serious thought into my own Songs of Our Forebears."

"Ah. Right. I'm with you. But I tell you what, why not a… Why not a *Book* of Our Forebears?"

"Eh? A book?"

"Yeah. Maybe one you really ought to call…I don't know; 'The Forebear's Candle' maybe. Then your own message can be hidden in full view behind a veil of fiction."

"The Forebear's Candle? Ah, I see what you mean. Yeah, excellent. Why not? You know I'm tone deaf, so I'd never be able to sing a song of our forebears. A great idea, Kate. And we've already got all the notes for such a book."

"But you're going to need more than just another score of dope, the flower cushion and a guiding book, Colin."

"Eh? Ah, right. I see what you mean," and he looked questioningly at her.

Kate put her book down beside the flower cushion, its smoking joss stick now an incongruity, and gave him that pixie grin of hers. The one guaranteed to melt his heart. Then, with a twinkle in her eye, she opened her arms invitingly and offered him a welcoming smile.

ABOUT THE AUTHOR

Clive Johnson was born in the mid-1950's in Bradford, in what was then the West Riding of the English county of Yorkshire. Mid-way through the 1970s, he found himself lured away by the bright lights of Manchester to attend Salford University.

In addition to getting a degree in electronics, he also had the good fortune of meeting Maureen Medley—subsequently his partner and recent Editor. Manchester retained its lure and has thereafter been his hometown.

Torn between the arts—a natural and easy artist—and the sciences—struggled with maths, youthful rationality favoured science as a living, leaving art as a pastime pleasure. Consequently, after graduation, twenty years were spent implementing technologies for mainframe computer design and manufacture, and being a Group IT Manager for an international print company.

The catalyst of a corporate takeover led to a change of career, and the opportunity to return to the arts. The unearthing of a late seventies manuscript—during loft improvements—resurrected an interest in storytelling, and one thing led to another. A naïve and inexpert seed finally received benefit of mature loam and from it his first novel—Leiyatel's Embrace—soon blossomed.

Find my website at http://www.flyingferrets.com

Connect with Me:

Follow me on Twitter:
http://twitter.com/Clive_SJohnson
Follow me on Facebook:
https://www.facebook.com/profile.php?id=100003080526007

04-05

37042168R00160

Printed in Great Britain
by Amazon